I WILL FOLLOW YOU

BRYAN BLEARS

Cover produced by Danielle Greaves.

ISBN: 9798394115172

For permissions, please visit:
www.bryanblears.co.uk

To Lauren, who helped me heal.

The strength of the vampire is that
nobody will believe in him.

Richard Matheson

Prologue

The night air was cold and still as it hung quietly above the Thames, the city lights obscurely reflected in the river's inky surface. Rebecca Doherty opened her eyes just a moment too late. She was falling. At that moment, if anyone had come to their window to take in the view, they would have seen the shape of her half-naked body plummeting towards the hard concrete below.

Seconds later, Rebecca hit the ground with a sickening thud, and the quiet of the early morning was interrupted by a loud scream from a passer-by. Looming overhead stood the Pan Peninsula building, a block of luxury apartments which looked out across the river. On the fifteenth floor of the building, a light came on, and the owner of the apartment stuck his head out to inspect the scene below.

Though he couldn't see the ground from this angle, he knew all too well what must have happened: the sickening crunch of bones onto hard concrete, the blood of his former girlfriend seeping out onto the pavement beneath him. Elliot Gardner edged away from the balcony, which was now open to the freezing night air.

'Jesus Christ,' he said, taking a fragile step back into the room where his girlfriend, Rebecca, had been sleeping, safe and sound, just a few minutes earlier.

Last week, Elliot's agent had called to congratulate him on yet another hard-won magazine cover – easily his greatest achievement to date, she'd told him – and he'd celebrated by buying himself a new sports car and a Rolex. He'd been standing on top of the world; everything he ever wanted, ever dreamed of, lay right at his fingertips. Now, as Rebecca lay lifeless at the foot of this luxurious building he called home, he could only think that all of that future – the future he had so meticulously planned out – had gone quite literally out of the window.

How had things reached this point? More importantly, how had he, a meticulous planner and careful cultivator of his own success, failed to see that something like this was eventually bound to happen?

'Come on, Elliot,' he said to himself. 'Get a grip. You've got about eight minutes to deal with this situation. Remember: everything, no matter what, is about appearances.'

He poured himself a glass of water from the Brita jug on the bedside table and tried to compose himself. How he could make this situation appear favourable, given the circumstances, was no easy task. The clock was ticking. For the first time in years, Elliot's mind was drawing a blank. To flee the scene would be suicide, and to ring up his lawyer at this time of night would be the action of an obviously guilty man.

'There has to be something you can do. Think, man, think!'

There were lots of people who, in ordinary

circumstances, might have come to his aid. There was the radio executive who still owed him a favour from last year, the powerful property developer who lived in East London just fifteen minutes away. Names flew through his head of all the wealthy and powerful connections he had made in the past seven or eight years of business. But these were no ordinary circumstances, and people would ask questions. Difficult questions.

No, there was only one thing to do. Drawing in a deep breath, he picked up the phone as calmly as he could and dialled the emergency services.

'Police, fire or ambulance please?'

'I need an ambulance,' he said, excruciatingly mindful of the tone of his own voice. 'My girlfriend's just...jumped from the window of our building. I live on the fifteenth floor. For God's sakes, please send help straight away!'

'What's the address please?' asked the operator. Elliot was already running through mental checklists in his head, aware that anything he said from now on *could* and *would* be taken in evidence.

'It's Apartment 268, Pan Peninsula Square. Please hurry. If there's any chance she might be alive...'

'Police and ambulance are on the way, sir. Can you tell me your name, please?'

'Yes, it's Elliot.'

'Okay, I'm going to need you to hang on for a few minutes. Can you do that for me, Elliot?'

'I...I think so,' he replied. He could already hear the sirens in the distance, could already, I suppose, feel the handcuffs locking around his wrists, bringing to an end this chapter of his first-class, jet-setting around the world, extravagant and luxurious five-star life.

First on the scene, Police Constable Claire Gasforth surveyed the area. It was the middle of the night, and only the building's lonely concierge had come out to speak to her about what had happened. He couldn't tell her much, but the scene spoke its own truth, naked and grisly, on the street in front of her.

The girl lay in a twisted mess, just a couple of meters away from the building. She was dressed in only her underwear; an attractive blonde girl, who appeared to be in her early twenties. Judging from the body, the fall had broken the victim's neck, causing fatal, catastrophic trauma. The bronze glow of the girl's skin was already fading in the cold, and her lips, once full and beautiful, no doubt, were turning grey. Claire swore under her breath. Working from instinct, she did what she could to secure the scene, covering up the poor girl until the investigators arrived.

While she waited downstairs, the boyfriend of the girl, Elliot Gardner, came down to speak to her.

'You're the one who called it in?' she asked. Elliot, it seemed, was one of the young, wealthy owners of an apartment here – a property which must have cost well over a couple of million pounds. He was dressed in a blue shirt with grey, pressed trousers: a fact which she considered noteworthy later, given that Elliot claimed to be asleep no more than ten minutes earlier.

'Yes,' Elliot said, 'that's me. I... woke up to a strange noise in my apartment. Then I noticed that the balcony window was open, and I looked outside, and...'

'Okay, slow down,' she said, never quite knowing how to deal with such a delicate situation straight off the bat. 'Are you her boyfriend?'

'Yes. Rebecca was, *is*, my girlfriend. Rebecca

5

Doherty.'

'And you say you were asleep? Was anybody else with you in the apartment?'

'No,' Elliot said, looking around. There were no crowds of hungry, swarming journalists lying in wait for him at this time of night, but still, he couldn't help but feel that he was being watched by a thousand prying eyes. 'Can I see Becky? Please, I need to see her.'

'We'll be able to arrange that in due course, Mister…'

'Gardner. G A R D N E R.'

'Mister Gardner. But right now, we need to ascertain exactly what happened tonight. You'll have to accompany me to the station, where you'll be questioned. Do you understand?'

'Yes. But I've already told you everything I know,' Elliot said. He looked as cool as a cucumber, given the circumstances. It was a detail she would remember later, at the trial, when she'd recall how difficult it was to believe that Elliot's girlfriend had just fallen to her death, given the calm exterior he was projecting.

Claire looked around with slight relief; her backup had finally arrived on the scene.

'I understand,' she said, 'but you'll still need to provide a statement, and after that, we'll be able to discuss suitable bail options.'

'Bail options? Am I… under arrest?'

'I'm afraid so, until we have more information,' she replied. 'The fact is, Mister Gardner, that you are the only person right now who can account for Rebecca's whereabouts tonight. So the most important thing you can do is to stay calm, and tell us everything that happened. You can do that, can't you, Elliot?'

'Yes, absolutely,' Elliot said. 'I want to know what happened just as much as you do. For her family's sake. I can't imagine how badly this will affect them.'

She looked him up and down. There was something about his demeanour which seemed, well... dramatic, like a TV soap. The grief-stricken words he said were like those from a well-written script, but his demeanour told a completely different story. 'Were you and Rebecca close?' she asked.

'Yes, very,' he replied. 'I... I thought she was happy. I was...I was going to marry her, in a couple of weeks. I never thought she'd do something like this, not in a million years.'

Everybody deals differently with loss. Some people break down and cry, others get angry, while some shut down completely, unable to function in the face of such severe emotional pain. Elliot, by contrast, seemed almost completely emotionless down at the police station, where Detective Inspector Neil Braithwaite, well-experienced in cases such as this one, questioned him about Rebecca's death.

'So, were you and Rebecca sleeping in the same room?' Neil asked him.

'No...not tonight. I was in the living room,' Elliot said, shuffling uncomfortably in his chair. 'Rebecca and I had a little too much to drink last night. We argued. It wasn't a serious argument really, just silly stuff, nothing major, but we slept in separate beds.'

'And when you woke, you said you heard a noise?'

'Yes. I don't know what it was, but something didn't feel right, so I went to check on Becky in the bedroom.'

Neil paused, collecting his thoughts. 'And you found

the bedroom door open?' he asked.

'Yes.'

'Did Rebecca ever have mental health problems? Anxiety, or depression, any longstanding issues which you might have been aware of?'

'No. Not that I knew of. There wasn't anything like that at all.'

'Mister Gardner, you realise how this looks, don't you?' Neil said. Fifteen years of experience told him that people did not wake up in the middle of the night and throw themselves from a fifteen story window without warning.

'Of course I do,' Elliot said. 'But all I can do is tell you what *actually* happened.'

'It looks as though you threw her from that balcony,' Neil continued. 'Is that what happened?'

'No. And I think that I'll need to speak to my lawyer before answering any more of your questions. Has he arrived yet?'

'I'll go and check,' Neil sighed, exiting the room. Pauline Emery, Neil's superior, had been watching the interview through the two-way mirror. She pulled him to one side as he walked towards reception.

'Well? What do you think?'

'I think that's about all we'll get out of him for now. Has his solicitor arrived yet?'

'Waiting downstairs,' Pauline nodded. 'And it's not just anyone, either. Elliot has got himself one of the best. He must be paying well.'

'Rich guys,' Neil said, letting out a sigh. 'I have to admit, we don't have much to go on yet. One thing is sure, though, we won't get a confession out of Elliot easily. He's clearly someone who is able to remain calm under pressure.'

'A little *too* calm,' Pauline said, 'don't you think?'

'Absolutely. I'd expect a little more grief from somebody whose girlfriend had just decided to take her own life out of the blue,' he said. 'In fact, I'd expect someone in that position to be on the verge of a nervous breakdown.'

Well, I wouldn't have. Because I know exactly the type of person Elliot Gardner is, and I know he wouldn't have given a shit about anything except his own skin, and of what was going to appear in the news the following morning.

1

For the longest time after leaving Elliot, I saw myself as his victim. That would be the story most people would want me to tell - the story of an innocent, young girl, abused by a privileged and self-important man – but it's important for you to remember that *I chose* Elliot; chose to get swept up by him. It was this choice which had ended up with me living in Amsterdam, almost a year after our painful and disastrous breakup, alone and in poverty.

I was working a dead-end job in a bar, and renting a cheap flat with a girl called Svetlana, who had come to Holland from the Czech Republic to study. Svetlana was, for want of a better word, a cam-girl. She had a regular show twice or three times a day, which helped pay her way through university, and as such I would regularly hear moaning and other strange noises emanating from her bedroom door as I tiptoed past. As for Svetlana's past, she kept her cards close to her chest. I knew, or at least had a good idea, that she was heterosexual. But Svetlana didn't really have any boyfriends around during the whole time that I lived with her.

One day, a few months after I moved in, I asked her, 'Svet, don't you miss having male company from time to time?'

'Male company?' she said, as though the concept was completely foreign to her. 'If anything, I have too much male company. I barely get any time to myself.'

'You know what I mean. What about companionship? Don't you want to find someone to settle down with one day?'

I saw a slight but noticeable change come over her face. 'I suppose, maybe,' she said, 'one day, if I meet the right person. But I don't believe in looking for companionship so desperately. That's just what men want, and it can lead you to make some bad decisions. Do you know what I mean?'

'Yes,' I said. I knew all too well what she meant. 'I just wondered how you deal with the fact that you're alone. I was so used to having lots of people around back home: friends, parties, but ever since…'

'Elliot…'

'Ever since Elliot, things are very different,' I said.

'I used to feel like that, a long time ago,' Svet said. 'If I went to the seaside with a man, I would always have a good time. But if I went alone, I would feel sad the whole time I was there. It felt like there was no purpose in me being there, unless there was somebody else to share it with. Do you know where that comes from, Poppy?'

I shook my head.

'It's because you don't value yourself enough.'

'Oh, I know *that*,' I said.

'No, you don't. What *you* need is somebody to tell you that you look nice, or that you're making good decisions, or to agree with you that the sunset is beautiful,' Svetlana said. 'And if they don't, you worry that maybe you don't look nice, or that you're not making good decisions. You even worry that maybe the sunset isn't beautiful at all, but that it is sad. What you need to do, is to stop delegating this responsibility to somebody else.'

'What responsibility?'

'The responsibility to decide what's valid, and what's not. You have to realise that the sunset is whatever you want it to be. And that's enough, just for your feelings to exist, without the validation of anybody else.'

'I suppose you're right,' I said. Svetlana poured us both a cup of coffee as we spoke. 'But still, I do feel lonely. I miss having somebody to be with. I miss sex!'

'Pssh,' Svetlana replied. 'There are ways to keep *those* urges away.'

So, for the next few months of my life, I followed Svetlana's advice to be a happier person. I went on romantic walks and nights away, even though I didn't have anyone to share them with, and I watched all of the happy couples walking past without a care in the world. I read books, and painted, and I bought myself a tomato plant, which I sat on the kitchen windowsill, and watered it every day.

I could tell that Svetlana saw a difference in me, too. On my birthday, she brought me a cake with twenty-five candles on it. I burst out in heaps of laughter when I opened up my present from her. Of course, it was a vibrator.

For the first time in a while, I thought I was moving on. But the past has an awful way of creeping up and surprising you when you least expect it, and what came next would change everything forever.

'*Instagram influencer and male fashion designer, Elliot Gardner, told police he had 'absolutely no involvement' in the death of twenty-two year old Rebecca Doherty, who fell from the balcony of his apartment during the early hours of last Saturday morning...*'

I couldn't believe what I was reading. There, in glorious high definition, was my ex-boyfriend Elliot Gardner. Seeing it made all of the hairs on my neck stand on edge. The photo was one which I recognised well. I had been there, at the time when it was taken; it was the photo Elliot used for his personal website, as well as his profile picture on his highly-popular Instagram account.

I sat on the edge of my bed, staring in horror at what was unfolding on the TV.

'*Police say at this stage they are trying to ascertain the exact circumstances surrounding Rebecca's death, and have asked anyone who might have heard anything on the night in question to contact investigators...*'

This wasn't how things were supposed to happen, was it? When I'd made the decision to move to Amsterdam, my aim was to start a new life and forget all about the past. In fact, a lifetime would have been too short to have never heard about Elliot Gardner again.

And yet, hadn't I known, in a way, that I couldn't escape what had happened between him and I just by running away to another country?

Svetlana found me in my room, sobbing away with the blanket pulled up to my shoulders, an empty box of tissues sitting beside me on the bed.

'Oh no! What's happened here?' she asked, sitting down beside me.

'It's…it's nothing,' I said, hesitantly, but Svetlana looked less than convinced. 'Okay. You don't need to look at me like that. Do you remember that I said I had a boyfriend back in England?'

She nodded. 'Elli-oht.'

I picked up my phone and showed her the story, which had made the front page of BBC News. Svetlana scrolled through for a second, almost as dumbfounded as I was.

'*Absolutely no involvement.*' Those were Elliot's words, which were being quoted alongside the story of a young woman who had died in suspicious circumstances at Elliot's apartment building. The text was accompanied by a couple of pictures of him; the first, a picture of him topless, at a birthday party on board his yacht, the *Silver Spirit*; the second, a photograph of Elliot suited at a fancy dinner party. Then, Svetlana stopped. There was another picture further down, towards the bottom of the piece.

The face of the girl standing beside him, Elliot's girlfriend at the time, had been blurred out, but her resemblance was still recognizable, at least to us.

'My God,' she said. 'That's you.'

Seeing that photo was like looking into a magic mirror, but one which only showed you bad things. I fought away vivid memories, feeling his presence all over me, like sticky treacle. They'd *blurred my face.* Somehow, that made everything worse; somehow, his image being plastered across the front page of the news with his yachts and fancy clothes, while I remained a mere smudge under the censor's thumb, added even more insult to injury.

'Come here.' Svetlana hugged me tightly. I fought back the tears and tried to compose myself. 'That poor girl. Do you think he did it?'

'I... I don't know. He did have a temper,' I said. I hated the way I'd just phrased it – like I was talking about a six-year-old who threw his toys a little too hard.

'That piece of shit. I hope he rots in jail, where he belongs,' Svetlana said, and I looked at her in shock. According to the television, nobody knew what had happened in Elliot's apartment that night. And yet, it was the word of a wealthy man, very much alive, versus the story of a younger girl who was not alive, and who had died in the company of Elliot, with no other witnesses. People would swiftly come to their own conclusions. 'What?'

'Nothing,' I said. 'It's just…a lot to take in.'

'I'll bet. How long has it been, since…?'

'Just over two years,' I replied. 'I can't help but feel like I'm entangled in this somehow. That maybe, it shouldn't have been her, it should have been…'

'*No*. Don't you dare let somebody like him get inside your head,' Svetlana said to me. 'Look at me. Now, you're not responsible for Elliot's actions, okay? He is. So you're going to put all of this behind you, and forget about it, because you deserve a happy life. Do you understand?'

'Yes. Thank you,' I said, although I didn't really believe what she was saying. I did not, deep down, believe that I was in any way more deserving of a happy life than Elliot, or Rebecca, or any of the rest of his other rich and famous friends.

'Good. Leave the past where it belongs, Poppy,' Svetlana said. I reassured her I was alright until, finally, she left me alone in my room.

But the truth was that I was far from it. This was the first time, since moving to Amsterdam and leaving everything behind, my parents, my sister, and everyone else, that the past had reared its ugly head in my rear-view mirror. It was payment owed for all of the good times I'd had, for every glass of champagne I'd drunk with him, for every holiday I'd been on and every expensive handbag I'd bought with his money. It was the price I had to pay for ignoring the truth about Elliot for so long.

Suddenly, the plan to regain control of my life seemed utterly in jeopardy once again.

Elliot would have all of the stops pulled out for him. He would hire the most expensive legal team in the country. I knew that he would do anything in his power to assert his innocence. He would discredit any witnesses which came forward, call into question the evidence which the prosecutors brought forward against him, and work the media. That was the Elliot I knew, and from what I saw on the news, he hadn't changed a bit.

'Our client asserts his innocence in these tragic and unfortunate circumstances,' said Elliot's lawyer on Sky News and CNN. I watched all of this begin to unfold, with horror and curiosity, unable to tear myself away from it, as all of the memories about he and I started to worm their way back in.

2

It was my eighteenth birthday. That was the official reason for us going out for a meal: Mum, Dad, me and Skylar, my younger sister, but I knew that the real reason was because Skylar had just achieved straight A's on her mock GCSE's.

Some younger sisters bask in their elder's shadows, but in our family, things were always the other way around. Despite her age, Skylar was always miles ahead: at school, with sports, and especially with boys. I, on the other hand, wasn't naturally clever or sporty or popular. Skylar even looked the part. She looked like those pretty, confident girls I watched on TV programmes like *Made in Chelsea* and *The Only Way is Essex*.

Mum and Dad, meanwhile, were still reeling from the breakup of my last, short-term relationship.

'I'm surprised you didn't invite Harry, Poppy,' Dad said, scanning the menu and glancing briefly across at me. Skylar tried her best to conceal a guilty smile, revelling in my misery. 'It could have been a good opportunity for you two to try to make amends.'

'Poppy doesn't want to make amends,' Skylar butted in, 'not even if Harry Morgan was *way* out of her league to begin with.'

'Stop antagonizing your sister, please,' said Mum. She looked at me with pity; a pity that I hated even worse than the scowls of rivalry from my sister, or the out-and-out scorn of my dad. 'It's her decision, and I'm sure she had a perfectly good reason to call things off. Didn't you, Poppy?'

I lowered the pages of the menu which I had been hiding behind and tried to smile. Harry came from a family of solicitors. His parents lived on a posh estate next to the local country club, a couple of miles down the road. To my parents, earning his affections was the most important thing I had achieved in my eighteen years on this Earth.

'Yes, of course,' I said. 'Harry and I were too... different. He took himself extremely seriously all of the time.'

'And so he should, with a family reputation like his to upkeep,' said Dad, who apparently had no interest in taking my side on the subject. Dad had loved Harry, tall and handsome, Harry with his well-to-do upbringing and his deep, gentle voice. While the rest of us had our parties at a cheap pub around the corner, Harry spent his time in five-star restaurants and country clubs. He was the first person in our year of school to own a car (an Audi, no less!), and on paper, at least, he was everything that a girl could want.

But thinking of what I'd become in ten or twenty years' time, imagining being introduced to guests at fancy dinner parties as *Harry's Wife* – well, that had been too depressing to consider.

'You know, I'm actually quite happy with my decision to break things off with Harry,' I said. 'But if you like him so much, Dad, then you're free to have a stab at him.'

'Poppy!'

At that moment, as if to save me from an evening of aggravation, the waiter came to the table and took our orders.

'So, Skylar's netball team has reached the Greater Manchester quarter finals, hasn't it?' Mum said to Dad, trying to change the subject.

'Wow! Really, that's fantastic.'

'Coach says we may even be in with a chance of winning this year,' smiled Skylar.

'That's what he says every year,' I chipped in.

'Well, I doubt that *you'd* know anything about it. To be in with a chance of winning you first have to make the team.'

'Will both of you please stop your squabbling? This is supposed to be a family celebration,' Mum said, lowering her voice. 'Poppy, there's no need to be jealous of your sister. I understand that you're still a bit sensitive about Harry, but we need to be supportive of each other. Now, why don't you both make amends?'

Skylar and I both apologized to each other, waiting until Mum and Dad's eyes were averted to continue trading silent insults via lip-reading.

Skank.

Four-eyes.

Failure!

I wasn't an *actual* failure, of course. On the contrary, I had an average but perfectly acceptable set of GCSE results; enough to get me into college and justify those five long, miserable years at high school. From the outside, I was just an ordinary girl, and that to me, was the main problem.

There wasn't a single interesting thing to say about Poppy Taylor.

In hindsight, maybe I would have had a nice life with Harry. Maybe I didn't give him the credit he deserved and did, indeed, throw the best opportunity of my life away, just to spite my parents.

'Well, there will be plenty of decent boys at college, won't there?' said Mum. As I tuned back into the conversation, I was dismayed to discover that I was once again the topic of discussion. I'd missed them all talking about me again as if I wasn't in the room at all.

'Whoa! There's no need for her to rush back into another relationship just yet,' Dad said, and for a second, I actually believed he was about to defend my corner. 'Besides, not all the boys at college will be like Harry. Not that I'm saying you aren't better off without him, mind you...'

'Dad!' I cursed, in between a mouthful of food. Internally, I was calling Skylar every name under the sun. She lived such a perfect life in the eyes of Mum and Dad. Couldn't she mess up once in a while, even if just to show some solidarity? 'Can we just eat? Honestly...'

'When I was her age...' Mum started off again. With friends like these, who needed enemies? Not only was I exasperated by the intense scrutiny of my teenage, non-existent love life, but now I felt an uncomfortable pain in the middle of my chest; like a tight ball. I was no longer concentrating on what Mum, or anyone else, was saying.

'That's what I mean, it's the lack of role models nowadays,' Dad was saying. For a moment I tried, unsuccessfully, to swallow.

'Are you alright?' Skylar asked. I'd managed,

ridiculously, to get some food stuck in my throat. I looked down and tried to swallow, unsuccessfully, and reached for a glass of water, nodding and smiling as best as I could.

Carefully, I drank a sip, but whatever had formed the blockage simply refused to budge. I felt utterly ridiculous. What now? My eyes widened, and I looked over at Skylar, wanting to speak but realizing, to my increasing horror, that no sound at all was coming out.

'Try having a drink, sweetheart,' Mum said, finally noticing what was going on. I shook my head, gesturing like someone playing charades at a Christmas party, and then I really started to panic, looking around frantically for help. I couldn't breathe. Meanwhile, nobody in the restaurant had noticed that anything untoward was going on at all.

Choking, I discovered many years later, is a silent killer. Many people will, upon discovering that they have food lodged in their throat, immediately head for the privacy of the bathroom, away from watchful eyes. To do so can be a terrible mistake.

In another minute or two, I would be in serious trouble. Coughing in vain, I motioned at my oesophagus. I envisioned, quite vividly, the scene of me losing consciousness in the middle of the crowded restaurant, falling to the floor in my death throes, with mouthfuls of frothy saliva.

'Oh my God. Somebody help!' Dad cried, springing into action and grabbing a passing waiter, who spilled the drinks she was carrying onto the floor. I wasn't really listening to what was going on anymore. Instead, I was thinking about ambulance times. It'd be a good eight to nine minutes before paramedics could arrive - even in the best of circumstances, and assuming an ambulance was even available - which was eight or nine minutes I just didn't have to spare.

That was around the time I realized how *frustrating*—not scary, mind you, but really bloody irritating—dying actually was. I would never get to say goodbye to Skylar or my parents or anyone else. My bedroom was in an awful state; ridiculously I wondered whether my mum would find time to tidy it up during the teary days following on from my funeral. I thought about the local community reacting to the news that an eighteen-year-old girl had been killed by a piece of chicken. How pathetic.

Most importantly, I wanted to let everybody know that during my final moments, I wasn't panicking or afraid. Dying, it turned out, was more of a gentle surprise, like getting an early Christmas present, or an unexpected discount at KFC.

Dad, not keen to give up on me quite as soon, was standing behind me, and gave me a series of violent thrusts upwards beneath my ribs. As he did so, a vague memory about the Heimlich manoeuvre came to my mind.

'Come on, Poppy!' he said. 'Don't you give up on me now!'

What I really wanted was the chance to apologize to Mum, Dad, and Skylar for putting them through this: sorry for dying on you like that, terribly inconsiderate of me I know, and especially on my birthday…

Somehow, something dislodged. What followed was the largest intake of breath I have ever taken in my entire life. My vision, which had started to blur around the edges, came back into focus, and a wailing sound—it took me a second to realize that it was coming from me—reduced the room to silence.

Everyone was looking; the waiters, the restaurant owner, who was already on the phone to 999, couples and families with children who had just been enjoying a quiet evening meal a few moments before.

I tried to say sorry, in between mouthfuls of desperately-needed air. The inside of my throat felt as though it had been scraped out with a wire sponge. Skylar was crying, and Mum was holding onto her tightly amongst the other helpless bystanders.

Then, in a final surrender of whatever remaining dignity I had, I threw up the contents of my stomach onto the restaurant floor.

When I lay awake at night, it would come back in episodes; the bruised sensation in my throat and lungs, the layout of the restaurant exactly as it was on that night, the faces of the people standing around, watching me struggle for air. I could still feel the sensation of searching for a breath and finding none. I could still see the horrified looks on Skylar and Mum's faces.

The thing with a near-death experience is that it is never *really* over. It seemed as though I was expected to carry on with my life exactly the same as it was before. Only, to me, everything wasn't the same.

'It's understandable that you feel like that,' Mum tried to console me, 'after what you've been through. These things take time. Don't worry, you'll be back to normal soon enough.'

I could hardly blame my family or friends because, after all, they hadn't been through what I had. The whole thing, to them, had lasted only a couple of minutes.

Later on, I learned that the feelings I was having were completely normal. The thing about trauma is that it rarely makes sense to other people. But it was much, much later on, at a different time in my life, when I finally understood the impact of that night many years ago – the incident in the restaurant had long been cast out of my mind by that time, replaced with other monsters.

3

Thinking back to the beginning, I certainly knew (maybe not consciously, maybe just quietly enough to ignore) exactly what I was getting myself into.

It's easy to point the finger. But who among you can say that they haven't wanted more money, a bigger house, fancier holidays? Which one of you can say, hand on heart, that he or she hasn't dreamed of a life filled with pleasure and frivolity, a world free of financial and other limitations? A world where you're special? Where people respect you and look up to you, and hang onto every word you have to say?

And how much would you be willing to sacrifice for it, if the opportunity came along? Your friends? Your family? Your own so-called moral principles?

Believe me – I don't tell you any of this to evoke pity. I've long since stopped caring about the opinions of other people or what the common view is, chattered across the threads of Twitter and Facebook and in your garish, unfunny and awful private chat groups.

Anyway, a few weeks after that disastrous affair in the restaurant, Skylar announced the news to us all that she had a new boyfriend. His name was Kieran, and the following weekend, Skylar invited him to dinner with the whole family. I tried, once again, not to think about how this success of hers would undoubtedly cast yet another shadow over my recent separation with Harry Morgan.

That Saturday, Skylar was the biggest nightmare of a sister you'd ever come across in your life. She spent all morning and all afternoon fretting over her clothes and her make-up, and although I tried to stay well out of the way, Skylar still managed to try to involve me in everything. It was as though it needed reiterating time and time again that this was her day, and we all needed (me especially) not to mess it up.

The way she was carrying on, Skylar was acting as though I'd choke to death again on purpose. I made a mental note to chew thoroughly.

At about half-past-six, Kieran's silver VW Golf pulled up outside the house. I know because Skylar had been watching the street from her window the whole afternoon, like one of those rifle-armed guards manning the towers in a Texas prison. She shouted frantically downstairs.

'He's here!'

There was a loud crash from upstairs. I was reading a thrilling and terrifying book about a young girl who was living with her survivalist Dad in the middle of nowhere, and I really didn't feel like moving from where I was sitting just then.

'I said he's here!' she shouted down again. 'Will somebody get the door please? I'll just be a second!'

Mum was in the kitchen. She had taken it on herself to cook us all up a big fancy meal, just for Skylar's benefit.

Sighing, and taking a great deal of time on purpose, I put my bookmark in place and set my book back in the shelf before going to answer the door.

I peered through the peephole. Standing on the other side of the door was Kieran. He was wearing a dark blue shirt and a pair of charcoal jeans which looked new, and the way he'd combed his hair suggested a certain care about his appearance which suited Skylar all over. Now was my moment to shine. I opened the door and stood still, trying my best to look as though I had no idea what he was doing here.

'Hi, you must be Poppy,' he said, to my surprise, extending his hand to shake mine. 'Skylar's told me all about you. I'm Kieran. It's lovely to meet you.'

'You too,' I answered dryly, walking him into the hallway and shouting upstairs to Skylar. 'Come in.' I showed him into the living room and sat opposite to read my book when without warning, Dad burst into the room, full of excitement. He took Kieran's hand and shook it firmly, extending his most overbearing smile.

'You must be Kieran,' Dad said, showing Kieran in. 'Make yourself comfortable. Would you like anything to drink? A beer, perhaps?'

'A beer would be lovely,' Kieran said. Dad went and brought him one straight away. 'You have a nice house, Mister Taylor.'

'Please. Call me Andy,' Dad said. The two of them seemed to be hitting it off straight away. I left them to it, and went to help Mum in the kitchen instead.

Dinner was carbonara with tagliatelle; a pretentious meal which we'd never have eaten normally, but which was still easy enough to prepare in under an hour. The effort to impress Kieran was hardly kept subtle. Mum had even put the 'good plates' out for tonight, I noticed, as we sat down for dinner.

'So, what type of properties does your uncle work on?' Dad asked. Kieran had a part-time job working with his uncle as a tree surgeon. Apparently, there was a lot more to cutting down trees than just swinging an axe.

'Oh, some country homes, private businesses, hotels,' Kieran said. Dad was in his element, discussing practical, manly things. 'Quite a few footballers' houses, too. You'd be amazed what you get to see tidying up the trees in Luke Shaw's back garden.'

'Luke Shaw? Impressive. Any others?'

'A few, yeah, sure.'

'That must be a decent earner, your uncle's business. I dare say he must be raking it in,' said Dad. I could never understand our family's fascination with money; we were always trying to pretend that we were much better-off than we actually were.

'Do you actually chop the trees down?' I asked. 'Like a lumberjack?'

'Yes, of course,' Kieran smiled. Skylar glared at me from across the table. 'If they're sick, that is. You have to cut down a sick tree, or the disease will spread through all the rest. If you don't, then during a strong wind a tree could come crashing down on someone's head. Football career over, just like that.'

'You know, there are too many office jobs nowadays. People sitting around on computers all day,' Dad said. 'When I was your age, I had a part-time job at the bakery. It's good for you to do some good, proper work. Earn yourself a bit of spending money.'

'I'm thinking of getting a job soon,' I said. At this, everybody around the table looked surprised, except for Kieran. That was mainly because the idea had just popped into my head out of nowhere, and out of my mouth before I'd really had chance to think the whole thing over.

'Well, this is news!' said Mum. 'What's brought this on?'

'Oh, I just thought it'd be good to get out there a bit, gain some work experience, you know,' I continued. 'And that way I'd also have a bit of money of my own to spend, and it'd get me out of the house a bit more, too.'

'That's a really good idea, Poppy,' Dad said. Internally, I did a little celebratory cheer. 'Would you like me to speak to a couple of people at work? Put out some feelers for you?'

'No, thank you,' I replied. 'It's not that I don't appreciate you wanting to help. But I'd rather try and achieve something on my own first, if that's okay.'

'That's really noble of you,' said Kieran, and I could tell that Skylar was seething in her seat. But what was I thinking? Of course, it was true that getting a proper job would help me out financially, and would probably give me some much-needed confidence in the real world. But most of all, it would show Mum and Dad that I did have an advantage over Skylar. I knew that *she* hated the idea of working.

I, on the other hand, was mature and willing enough to start paying my own way. While she went off to university, I'd be working my way up the corporate ladder, making a career for myself, and after that, who knew? I might even end up, by the time I was thirty, settling down with a lovely husband in a moderately expensive house, with the whole world at my feet.

That, at least, was the plan I had dreamed up.

If every politician, celebrity and company director had to spend six months working in a shop, I am wholly convinced that the world would be in a much better place than it is now.

Work was a designer clothes store at a local shopping centre, just a ten minute bus ride away from home. The money was okay, and the customers were fairly hassle-free, and the job itself was so easy that even a nine-year-old could have done it. There was only one major problem with where I worked.

That was the fact that, despite being surrounded by beautiful handbags, shoes, purses, coats and dresses every day, I couldn't afford to buy a single thing.

How unfair it was! I'd have to have saved an entire month's wages just to afford many of the items which we had in store.

It was Sunday, just an hour before closing time, and if things had stayed like that for another ninety minutes, the rest of my life might have been completely different. But then, something happened which would alter the course of things forever.

'Of course. What I'll do is, first thing tomorrow morning mate, I'll give my agent a call and see if we can arrange something for the next couple of weeks. Yes, I'm just going into a meeting now, so we'll have to leave things there for now. Absolutely. My pleasure. You take care of yourself. Bye bye now.'

'Can I help you?' I asked.

The man in front of me was tall and well-dressed, with combed blonde hair, and a tattoo on his neck which slightly protruded from his collar. I had the uncanny feeling that I recognized him from somewhere – from TV, perhaps – although he could have been no older than twenty-five. Despite this, the way he walked was like a much older, confident man. He slid his phone back into his pocket and smiled at me as I caught his eye, his hand resting casually on the counter.

'Hello there,' he said, 'I'm looking for a jacket, not too flashy or pretentious, but classy. I was wondering if you could maybe show me what you have in stock please?' He had a well-spoken voice, wielding a charming, almost southern accent, though he was almost certainly just local and well-off.

'Sorry, I have to work the tills,' I replied shyly. 'But there's somebody who will be able to help you find what you're looking for.' I reached for the intercom, but was instantly disarmed by the way he caught my eyes and interrupted me once more.

'Actually, Poppy, is it?' he said, reading my name-badge. 'I was wondering if you could help me out. Unfortunately, I've seen the way your colleagues dress, and, well, I'd much rather have the opinion of someone with, well… better taste.'

'Thank you,' I said, a little flattered, 'but I'm afraid I'm not allowed to. I have to stay here, in case another customer comes in.'

'Well, look around. There aren't any other customers at this time of day.'

'Well yes, but there could be. I assure you,' I said, 'that my colleague, Sarah, is more than capable of-'

'Here, let me make you a deal,' he persisted. 'If you help me pick out a jacket today, I'll make sure your manager gets a glowing review of your service, and I'm sure the commission on what I'm about to spend will be most welcome, too. But, if anybody walks in, in the meantime, you have my express permission to interrupt whatever we are doing and go deal with them. Does that sound alright to you?'

To this day, I don't know what it was about him. Was it the worry of this stranger leaving some awful review with management, thus ending my first job with a dishonourable discharge from the retail industry? Was it the way in which he - a charming and confident man used to getting his way – had strode past everyone to come and single me out? Or, was it simply that I was too awkward to say no, stemming from my natural desire to please?

Whatever it was, I suddenly found myself putting down my things, as if on autopilot and showing this stranger over to our line of men's jackets.

The man, whose name I still didn't know, followed me there and started to peruse. He tried a few on in the mirror, and commented aloud on how they looked.

'Do you think this is too flashy? Be honest with me,' he said, holding up a silver outdoor jacket which looked awful to me. I felt as though any opinion I had would be utterly worthless, and he must have sensed it. 'What am I saying? Of course it is. I can see it written all over your face.'

'No, not at all. We have some more formal ones over here, Mister...?'

'Gardner,' he smiled. 'But please, call me Elliot.'

'Elliot,' I said. 'Right then, follow me.'

Elliot followed me over to another row of blazers. Anxiously, I looked around at the front of the store. To my relief, the place was still completely empty.

'How much is this one?' he finally asked, referring to

a navy blue blazer which suited him to a tee.

I checked the label. '£195.'

'And the grey one?'

'That's... £220.'

'Do you know what? I think I'll take them both,' Elliot said. He carefully attached the silver jacket to its hanger, and followed me back over to the sales counter. I couldn't help but notice his eyes resting on me – not in a rude and inappropriate way, but certainly taking an interest in how I looked.

'Thanks Poppy,' he said, placing his MasterCard into the reader on the counter. 'You've been a real help today.'

I shrugged and smiled back as I handed him his clothes and receipt. 'Not a problem at all.'

Elliot turned to walk back out of my life just as quickly as he'd entered it, and then he stopped.

'Okay. Look, I really don't normally do this, I swear,' he said. 'But you seem really nice, and I was wondering if you'd let me buy you a drink sometime? Somewhere around here, after work, if you'd like.'

I couldn't really believe what I was hearing. The cheek of it! And yet... I'd probably been asked out no more than twice in my entire life. I had a good mind to tell him how inappropriate it was to make a girl feel pressured like that, but at the same time, I was overwhelmingly flattered by this invitation from a complete stranger. The way that Elliot spoke, the way he walked... it was like something out of another world.

'I'd like that,' I heard myself saying, cursing myself for being so easily influenced. 'But... you'll have to come back and see me next week to arrange something. I don't give my phone number out to customers.'

What was I doing?

Elliot tilted his head slightly, and then smiled from ear to ear. 'Okay then, Poppy. I'll see you next week, then,' he said.

Then, with his newly acquired purchases in hand, he turned away and strode out of the shop.

Keeping my blushing head down, I watched him out of the corner of my eye as he boarded the escalators and glided out of view. Who could believe that such a handsome and charming person had asked *me* out?

I was utterly convinced that I would never hear from him ever again.

4

I'd spent the night tossing and turning in and out of consciousness, remembering meeting Elliot long ago, and it took me a minute to realize that the cloudy, grey sky outside my bedroom window was that of Amsterdam. My sheets and pillows were damp with sweat. All in all, it had been a terrible night's sleep.

I got up, dressed, changed the bedding and watered my little plant, and shortly after there was a loud knock at the door. I paused for a moment. I wasn't exactly feeling at ease, what with all of the memories of Elliot surfacing in the past few days, and Svetlana was nowhere to be seen. Then I reminded myself that there was absolutely no way that Elliot could have escaped police custody, flown to Amsterdam, and found out where I lived, all in the space of a couple of days.

The knock came again, and I paused the TV programme I was watching (a reality show about wealthy mums in Australia) to answer the door.

'Good morning,' said the man outside, a somewhat well-spoken man in a long, grey coat, probably in his early forties. 'I'm hoping to speak to a Miss… Taylor? I was told she lives here?'

'Who are you, sorry?'

'My name is Neil Braithwaite. I'm a police officer,' he said, rummaging around in his coat pocket and producing an ID badge. Somehow, I'd known the second I laid eyes on him; his stance, the official yet cautious look in his eye. I was sure I'd given away who I was by the look on my face, but I was in no way about to tell him anything about me without knowing what was going on.

'I see. And what is it with regards to?'

'Don't worry, nobody's in trouble,' Neil said. 'I'm looking for some information with regards to a recent incident.'

'What kind of incident?'

'A murder, Miss Taylor.' At the word *murder*, I felt everything in my body suddenly run cold.

'Right, well you'd better come in, I suppose,' I said.

'Cup of tea, detective?' I said, leading him into the living room. He looked around for a second, and wandered over to the few family photographs I kept, which were sitting on a bookshelf in the corner of the room.

'No, thank you. Please, call me Neil. You have a lovely place here. May I?' he asked, indicating towards one of the framed photos. It was a photo of me and Skylar sitting next to each other at a wooden table at the fair, from a long while ago.

'Of course.' Like an experienced detective, he had a way of disarming all of the barriers I swore to keep up with just a friendly word. 'That's my sister, Skylar. Gosh, that photo must be six or seven years old, now.'

'You two seem close,' Neil said.

'We were,' I replied. 'We don't speak as much anymore.'

'I understand. Life has a habit of getting in the way, doesn't it?' Neil said, carefully placing the photograph back on the shelf.

'Look, I don't mind, but I'd rather get this out of the way, if that's okay with you.'

'Of course,' Neil said. He sat down on the armchair across from me and pursed his hands together, as if thinking of the best way to start. 'You've... probably guessed why I'm here by now.'

I found myself nervously fidgeting with my hands, and forced myself not to. 'It's to do with Elliot, isn't it? My ex-boyfriend. I read something about him on the news.'

'Poppy, how much would you say you know about Elliot Gardner?' Neil asked.

'More than I need or want to. We were together for a couple of years.'

'You've seen the news, I suppose,' Neil said. 'Elliot is, well, he's been charged in connection with the death of a girl at his apartment. She was about the same age as you. I gather they hadn't been seeing each other for long. Does the name Rebecca Doherty mean much to you?'

I shrugged. 'Not particularly. Sorry, but I haven't seen Elliot for over six months. Is there anything to suggest foul play?'

'Not much,' Neil rubbed his forehead. 'The circumstances are, well, suspicious, but neither Elliot nor Rebecca has any previous history – nothing, mind you, as of yet – and we only have Elliot's word for what happened on the night in question.'

'So, where do I come into it?' I asked. 'I gather you haven't flown all the way to Amsterdam just for a friendly chat.'

'I'm just trying to piece together information at this stage. Did Elliot ever show any...aggressive tendencies? Did he ever raise his voice, lash out, that sort of thing?'

I paused for a moment. I'd half-expected, half-known with that dreadful feeling in the bottom of my stomach, that when Elliot showed up on the news he would somehow come stampeding back into my life. But being asked such direct questions about my past was another matter altogether.

'I suppose,' I said eventually. 'Sometimes, yes. But not in the beginning.'

'Did you ever report anything to the police?'

'No. Sorry, I'm finding this a little difficult,' I said. Neil nodded empathetically, but waited for me to carry on. 'I did think about it, once or twice, you know. But Elliot was extremely charming and...manipulative. He had a way of talking me around, making me think that it was somehow my own fault. And I didn't want to create an issue at the time.'

'I see. I'm sorry to put you through this,' Neil said, 'I really am. But this girl, Rebecca, her family are relying on us to get to the truth of what happened.'

'No, it's fine. I understand.'

'I know it might be difficult to say, but... do you think Elliot would be capable of killing someone? Maybe in a temper, a spur of the moment kind of thing?'

'I don't know. I... I don't feel very comfortable speculating about somebody I... I barely even know any more,' I said. More than anything, all I wanted to do was run away. 'I'm sorry, but I'm not sure I can add anything to help with your investigation. Could he have killed someone, in a rage? Maybe. But so could a lot of people, you know? I'd love to help, really. I just don't see how I can.'

Neil put his notebook down, sighed, and looked at me with sympathy. 'I'm sorry. I do understand how difficult this must be for you. But any small insight you can give us into Elliot's character might be of help, even if it doesn't seem relevant right now.'

'I'll tell you what I do know,' I said, 'Elliot was a master at putting across an image of himself. He spent every second of every day thinking about what people would think about him, and hiding the parts which he didn't want anybody to see. So if Elliot *did* kill somebody, he would make absolutely sure he wasn't found guilty.'

'Well, that is troubling to hear. From what I understand, Elliot Gardner has hired some of the most powerful lawyers in the country to defend him,' Neil said.

'That sounds like him,' I agreed. 'From what I know, he'll charm the newspapers and the public, even buy people's silence, if needs be, to clear his own name. So you'd better have fingerprints, or some DNA or something because if not, Elliot will walk. I can promise you that much.'

Neil frowned, putting away his notebook and standing up. 'Well, thank you, Poppy. Listen, it would be great if I could get back in touch with you if I need anything more. Do you mind?'

'Of course not.' I wrote my phone number down for him on a piece of paper. He folded it up and placed it in his pocket, smiled and shook my hand.

'Great. Thank you for your time,' Neil said. 'Can I ask you one more question please, before I leave? Was Elliot a heavy sleeper?'

'I'm not sure,' I said, 'But... I don't think so. Does that have some relevance to the case?'

Neil looked up in interest, and scribbled a note down in his pad. 'It may do. I'm afraid I can't share any details right now, but... anyway, I really do appreciate you taking the time to talk to me.'

'Not a problem,' I said, my mind running around in frantic circles. There was a troubled look on Neil's face, but as far as I was concerned, I'd done enough for one day. I showed him to the door.

'Once again, thank you for your time,' he said.

'Not at all.'

'Listen, I probably shouldn't say this, but you know, men like Elliot are good in situations like this. Now I'm not saying he's guilty, but if he is, and he walks...well, all I'm saying is that a person like yourself could make a difference. If somebody was able to stand up in court and admit that Elliot was a bully, an abusive kind of person... I hope you'll think about it, Poppy.'

'Okay, I will,' I said. 'You have a good day, detective.'

'You too.' I closed the door, looking through the peephole until I was sure that he was gone.

I sat down on the sofa and closed my eyes. All of the old memories of Elliot were coming back, memories which refused to leave me alone – skyscrapers and sunny beaches, cocktail dresses and first-class seats, Monte Carlo and Santa Monica, Marc Jacobs handbags and Gucci sunglasses. It was like opening a time capsule to a history I barely recognized; a me I had promised to bury deep down, where nobody could find her ever again.

Elliot's trial wasn't just about Rebecca Doherty, I

knew – it was about much more than that. It was about people who thought that their money placed them above the law, able to do what they pleased without consequence.

Who was I? Was I the type of person who just sat back and watched it happen? What about all of the other women out there who had been the victims of men like him?

Agitated by the visit, I left home and walked until I passed through the red-light district, where scantily clad women posed in the shop windows next to the sex shops, and the tourist-trap bars along the river.

I'd moved to Amsterdam because it was a place which reserved its judgment; a place where people could live however they liked, without fear of reprisal. Back then, I had wanted to run as far away from Manchester as I could manage. But Elliot had somehow followed me here, despite being in custody hundreds of miles away. I felt his shadow watching me from the balconies of the hotels, his reflection rippling on the clear water of the canal, his eyes leering at me from every red curtain and neon-lit alleyway I passed by.

When I got home, Svetlana was in the kitchen, cooking chicken soup with mushrooms and dill.

'Hi babe, is everything okay?' she said.

'Yes, fine,' I said, walking straight past her, in the direction of my room.

'Are you sure? Let me know if you need anything.'

'Thanks,' I said. 'I'm just going to have a nap.'

'Okay then!'

I shut the bedroom door behind me and sat down, thoroughly exhausted.

After a minute, when I was sure I wasn't going to be interrupted by a checking-in visit from Svetlana, I kneeled down and reached under the bed. At the back, behind the suitcases and the spare clothes, was a small, grey box. I reached in, coaxing it out with my fingertips, and then pulled it out, brushing off the layer of dust which had accumulated on its surface.

Opening it up, I looked inside at the few memories I'd kept of that old life. There was a pair of initialled gold earrings – a garish giant letter 'P' and 'T', which I'd worn only on occasions where only the tackiest and most ostentatious outfits would do. There was a small black book of names and telephone numbers, contacts which had long since erased me out of their lives, and which I wouldn't have called upon for help even in the direst of circumstances. There too, as shiny-new as the day I'd obtained it, was my American Express Platinum card – no longer active, for sure.

Behind them all were a handful of photographs. I took them out and looked through them, one at a time.

Here was a photo of me smiling with the brattiest group of blonde, fake-breasted women you had ever laid eyes upon. Here was one of me drinking coffee with Elliot somewhere in France. I paused. Here was one of me leaning against a palm tree, sunglasses concealing my eyes, wearing short denim shorts and showing off my pale skin.

That photo was significant, because it was the earliest one of our relationship which I'd kept, and it showed a girl who was still very much in love with Elliot, a young and naïve girl whose life had not yet been turned upside down by him. It had been taken in Florida, many years ago, and looking at myself now I felt all of the memories come flooding back, so vividly that I could hear the sound of the waves and smell the Cuban sandwiches in the air.

Why had I kept these odds and ends, despite all of the bad memories attached with that time of my life? I supposed part of it was to serve as a reminder to myself of how far I'd come, to keep myself grounded, to remind myself that it all hadn't been some dream but that it had all, actually happened.

I could see him now, and hear his voice as though it had been yesterday: his casual yet confident walk, his stubbled jawline complemented by his neat shirt collar, his charismatic smile directed straight at me, as he looked into my eyes and said....

5

'You look beautiful.'

Elliot was wearing the blue jacket, the one which he'd bought during our previous encounter, and with his blonde hair combed to one side, he looked as though he had popped straight out of a male fashion magazine. I breathed in his cologne as he kissed me on the cheek before we sat down together.

'Thank you. You too. Handsome, I mean.' Elliot had chosen an expensive wine bar for our first date, the type of place I would never have dreamed of going to normally. Despite the effort I'd put in, I still felt under-dressed.

'I wanted to thank you for coming out with me,' he smiled, as the waiter came over. 'Two glasses of a good red wine, please. Do you drink wine?'

I nodded. 'It's very fetching on you.'

'What? Oh, the jacket. Well, it was hand-picked for me, actually, by a really cute girl down at the store.'

I blushed. It wasn't that the way Elliot was dressed, or the money that he seemed to have, was exactly my thing. I had, after all, already had a sophisticated and well-groomed

44

boyfriend before: Harry Morgan, whose airs and graces had seemed more stifling than attractive to me at the time. But Elliot was, well, different. He was attractive and yet, surprisingly laid back. 'Well, it looks good on you.'

'You can relax,' Elliot said. 'I know it must be awkward being asked out while you're at work. In truth, it's not something I usually would do.'

'So, why do it now?' I asked. Elliot smiled, showing a tinge of shyness which I hadn't seem from him before, before it was once again replaced by his usual, confident exterior.

'You know, I'm usually a pretty good judge of character,' he said. 'And when I saw you standing behind the counter, I thought, here's a girl who has hopes and dreams. Somebody who wants to make something of herself one day. What do you want to do with your life, Poppy?'

'Well, I'm not one-hundred percent sure, to be honest,' I said. 'I'm going to study psychology at college next year. I'd love to be a criminal psychologist one day. If not, then maybe something else. I'd love to be a singer-songwriter.' Elliot listened intently, sipping his wine and appearing positively inspired by every word I said. There was no way of denying it; he had a good way with people.

'What about you?' I asked.

'Oh, you know, the usual. I'd like to rule the world one day,' he said, and I wasn't sure to what degree he was joking. 'Doesn't everyone, deep down? But failing that, I just want to make a difference. I know that sounds arrogant, cliché maybe, but I don't mean it to be. I just want to make the best of my life, and not feel as though I've wasted any of it. I want people to say: that's Elliot Gardner, he brought a lot of good into people's lives.'

'I don't think it sounds cliché at all,' I said. 'A little

ambitious, maybe.'

'But people look down on ambition, don't they? They see it as like, you want to stab everyone in the back,' Elliot said, 'which is the very opposite of what I'm about. If anything, I want to bring other people up with me.'

'I think it's great that you know what you want,' I said. 'I guess some people never actually figure out what they want to do with their lives until it's too late.'

'Sure. I'll admit, my parents were born into money, and so I've never really had to worry about getting by,' he said. 'But I also think to myself, what's the point in just having money for the sake of it? Buying a house, raising kids, those are things you do because you're *supposed* to. But don't even get me started on my folks. Family can be a nightmare. What are your folks like?'

'Well, they're good people,' I replied, 'and we get along well, most of the time. My parents can be a pain in the ass, and so can my sister. I feel like a lot of the time I'm designated to be the black sheep of the family.'

'I like that,' Elliot said, 'here's to two black sheep, in a…flock of white ones. Something like that.'

I laughed, and we clinked our glasses together. 'To two black sheep.'

I could tell you everything about our date, but in summary Elliot was attentive, interesting, and kind. He didn't make any move on me, except for a kiss on the cheek, and I promised to see him again. Yet I had the distinct feeling that there was more to Elliot Gardner than met the eye.

But it wasn't until I got home and spoke to Skylar that I fully understood what Elliot meant about ruling the world, and how serious he was about doing it.

'Elliot Gardner. Are you sure?' Skylar said, as I sat in front of the mirror removing my make-up. Three glasses of wine had got the best of me, and although I knew answering my sister's questions would ultimately end in my own misery, I couldn't fend off her curiosity forever. Plus, there was a part of me which did want to advertise the fact that my love life was once again alive and well.

'Yes, I think I can remember my date's name.'

'*This* Elliot Gardner?' Skylar leaned over, showing me the photo which was on the screen of her phone. His face was irrefutable; those sharp, inquisitive eyebrows above a pair of striking blue eyes. In the photograph Elliot was wearing a tuxedo with a black bow-tie. Below it, the caption read:

RECIPE FOR SUCCESS:

Instagram influencer Elliot Gardner, twenty-four, shares the 6 lessons he learned from building a multi-million pound sustainable fashion business.

'Hey! Where did you get that?' I said, reaching for Skylar's phone, which she quickly snatched away. Those words were ringing around in my head, even though I hated myself for it almost immediately, *multi-million pound business...*

'Oh my God, listen to this,' Skylar said, reading aloud as I chased her around the room, trying to get a view of the screen. 'How to start your day. Though he believes in a delicate balance between work and leisure, Elliot rises at 6am every morning, and begins with a chlorophyll-rich shake of mixed greens to give him the mental performance he needs to get through his busy work schedule...'

'Come on! Stop that,' I said. Dress it up however you may, Elliot had lied to me, and now suddenly I felt like the butt of the joke.

'Is this a wind-up?' Skylar said. 'You must have known. Don't tell me you don't Google the name of whoever you're dating.' I sat down on the bed, looking solemnly at the floor. 'Oh. You didn't know.'

'God, I feel so pathetic. I mean, I wish I *didn't* know,' I said to her, 'because... how I am supposed to live up to that?' With all of his wealth and success, I knew people would see my even being asked out by Elliot as the most enviable thing on the planet.

'Your new boyfriend is *too* rich and successful? You do realize how that sounds, don't you?'

'I know, I know. It sounds stupid, but all I wanted was a bit of normality, you know? Not... that,' I said, gesturing at her phone.

'It doesn't sound stupid at all. Well, maybe a little,' Skylar said, changing her tact a little after seeing that I was visibly upset. 'You're right. Most girls our age would kill for a chance at going out with a person like that. But... maybe he didn't tell you because he feels uncomfortable about it as well. Regardless, I think you should talk to him.'

'You think so?'

'Yeah, definitely. You should see what he has to say first. And who knows, maybe you'll be pleasantly surprised?'

Skylar had a tendency of doing that - acting maturely at the moments you least expected it, contrasting my emotional instability with her calmness and tact. I thought that if *her* boyfriend was a millionaire businessman, I would have never heard the end of it as long as we both lived.

'Thanks, Skylar. He wants to see me again next week. I'll see what he has to say about all this then.'

'That,' Skylar said, 'sounds like a plan. And don't worry. I won't tease you much. Want to know why?'

'Why?' I asked.

'Because if you *do* make something of this, I'll want to be right at the top of you and your millionaire boyfriend's Christmas card list, Poppy!' she said.

Elliot agreed to a second date just over a week later. Since the conversation with Skylar, I had given none of my newfound knowledge away, and Elliot himself had kept quiet. That wasn't to say that he might not have already suspected that I knew something about his exuberant lifestyle, but he didn't know that I knew. That was to say, that in over a week of talking over text, e-mail and phone, Elliot had completely avoided mentioning anything about his current situation.

And what a situation it was! I have to thank Skylar - she did her homework. Elliot's mother ran a large and successful empire in women's jewellery and perfumes, and his father was a senior editor at a large London-based magazine. That was how his empire had first begun.

Then there were numerous articles detailing Elliot's own activities. At eighteen, he'd won a Young Entrepreneur of the Year Award; at twenty he sold his first company for a couple of million pounds. He owned a villa in South Africa, and was looking to expand his property portfolio in the next few years.

It was clear that Elliot was no ordinary young man, but rather than make me uncomfortable, each revelation made me more determined to hold him to account for at least one conversation. I chose a quiet Italian restaurant on the outer side of town. I knew it would make Elliot uncomfortable to discuss things there, and I wasn't about to give him the protection that a noisy bar might offer. I also arrived at least twenty minutes early. There was no way that I'd be walking in to Elliot already coolly sitting down with a glass of red wine with that comfortable look all over his face.

'Your table, miss.'

'Thank you.' I chose my seat so I could see Elliot the moment he arrived. *If* he arrived, that is. Ten minutes passed by, and then another ten, and there was still no sign of him.

I was utterly furious. What an utter fool I had been! Of course a person like Elliot Gardner had stood me up. He'd probably gotten bored of me after our first date and here I was, anxiously waiting for him to arrive while he was off having fun somewhere else.

As I got ready to stand up and leave, a loud roaring sound came up the road. A couple of people in the restaurant looked out of the window at the commotion. I craned my neck to see what was going on. Outside, a red sports car – a Ferrari, I found out later – swung into one of the empty parking spaces and came to a sudden, screeching stop.

The door opened, and out stepped Elliot. He was wearing a charcoal-grey suit, with expensive-looking brown leather shoes. Several people stopped and stared as he came into the restaurant and walked towards me.

For a moment, all of it made me feel as though I was floating outside of my own body. And then I remembered that this was precisely the reason I was angry at Elliot in the first place.

'Nice car. I suppose I should be impressed.'

'No, you shouldn't,' Elliot said, sitting down hurriedly, 'I'm sorry I'm late. I got here as quickly as I could.'

'Yes, you *are* late, actually. I was just about to get up and leave when you decided to show up.'

'I know! You absolutely deserve better than this. I'll make it up to you.'

'I do deserve better, Elliot.' He shifted uncomfortably in his seat, having not even had chance to order a drink yet. 'Like knowing that the person I'm dating is some millionaire playboy social-media star. At what point were you going to tell me?'

'So, you know,' he said.

'Yes, I know. Thankfully, my sister told me who you were. Have you any idea how embarrassing that is?'

'In my defence, I didn't try to hide anything from you. Search my name on the internet, and you'll see a heap of information about me,' Elliot said. 'Most of which is untrue, by the way.'

'Oh come on! I shouldn't have to find out about you from the bloody internet.'

'Poppy, please,' Elliot said, looking visibly embarrassed by my refusal to stay quiet. 'Look, you're right. I should have told you. But the truth was I didn't want anything like that getting in the way of things between us. Do you have any idea how arrogant it would come across to say hi, I'm Elliot and I have a Ferrari, will you go out with me?'

'That's the lamest excuse I've ever heard,' I said. 'Do you understand how it feels to be me, Elliot? I don't have money, or Twitter followers, or whatever other things you have. I at least have the right to know if I'm going out with somebody who is better than me in every way.'

'You think that stuff makes me any better than you?'

'Well?'

Elliot lowered his voice a little. 'God, no! If anything, it's me who should be embarrassed.'

'Really? Why?'

'Because I'm the one who is unusual. Abnormal, even.'

'I'm not convinced.'

'Look outside. I wasn't hiding anything from you, I swear. I... just wanted to have that conversation at the right moment. I didn't ask to be born into privilege, you know,' Elliot said, 'and I'm not oblivious to the fact, either. But look at things from my perspective. Usually, once a girl knows who I am, she wants to be with me for my money. I want something more meaningful than that. Wouldn't you?'

'Well, yes,' I admitted.

'The fact is: the clothes I wear or the car I drive doesn't define me as a person. Anybody who thinks that it does is an idiot. And the same applies just as much to you. When I laid eyes on you, Poppy, I didn't see you as a retail worker, I thought that you were the kind of person I'd like to get to know more. So if you want to walk away, that's fine, but if you want to get to know me more too, here I am. No more secrets.'

'Do you really mean that, Elliot?' I said.

'Yes. I really do.'

'Okay,' I said. 'But from now on, I want you to be honest with me. If I find out that you're secretly heir to the throne of Austria or something, we're finished. Do we have a deal?'

'That sounds reasonable,' Elliot said. 'Now, let's start

over. Shall we order? What would you like to eat?'

'Well,' I said, grinning, 'what can we afford?'

6

The first time I started getting a real sense of how different Elliot's life was to mine was when he took me down to London for our first weekend away.

It was a few weeks after our conversation in the restaurant. I'd kept Elliot at arm's length for most of that time, partly because I wanted to see whether he really was interested in a relationship, or whether he was just a rich kid with a new toy with which he would quickly get bored of and move on. But it was also partly to give me time to find out more about the man I was dating.

It was apparent that Elliot was more than a nice guy who happened to have some money straight away. His fashion company, Gardia, focused on designer menswear, and Elliot functioned as both CEO and part-time model for some of the clothing. As a side-gig, Elliot was a promoter on social media for various brands, including his own, though this was starting to pick up and if things carried on the way they were heading, Elliot would soon be making more from his social media channels than from his actual, physical business.

I scoured Elliot's social media posts, of which there were thousands (Elliot posted multiple times a day). And although I was blind to it at first, gradually I began to find in them all of the subtle references to the brands which he was promoting for money.

Once I became tuned to these signals, I began to see them everywhere. He would be staying at the *Royal Palms Resort & Spa* in Phoenix, Arizona, or test-driving an *Aston Martin DBS Superleggera* sports car, or wearing a *Breitling Navitimer 1 Chronograph GMT 46 Blue* watch. Nothing was unbranded or unreferenced; everything which Elliot put out on social media to the public had a *point*. All of it *mattered*. Everything was paid-for promotion, masquerading as an insight into the life of an extraordinary person.

This world was, to me, completely alien.

It was also clear that Elliot was living what most people would consider a dream life. He travelled around the world all year round, visiting luxurious places and eating fine food, and driving around in speedboats and fast cars, whilst earning revenue for doing all of those things and showing them off on Instagram and TikTok.

'So, explain to me again how this works,' I said, as we drove down the M1 in the fast lane. There was no way of denying it – sitting in the passenger seat of Elliot's Ferrari made me feel like a very important person. 'Companies pay you to wear their clothes, eat their meals, drive their cars, and so on, because you have a lot of followers on Instagram, so that means a lot of people will be influenced by what you're doing. And you have a lot of followers on Instagram because people enjoy watching you doing all that luxury stuff?'

'That's pretty much how it works.'

'Okay, but there's something I don't understand,' I

said. 'You can't just pick up the phone and say, 'hello, Armani, I'd like you to pay me for wearing your jacket next weekend?''

Elliot laughed. 'Actually, at the start, that's almost exactly what I did. But now it's different – the companies approach me instead.'

It was like a type of virtual reality entertainment, for people who dreamed that they'd be millionaires one day but never would be, paid for by the profit margins on every handbag or pair of shoes or bottle of perfume in the shops. And how could you blame him for playing along?

'I see.'

'You sound like you don't approve.'

'I'm just...amazed,' I said, trying to find the most positive word for what I was feeling. 'It's like working for a company that insists you take the week off, every week, for the rest of your life.'

Elliot laughed. 'Not quite.'

'Don't take this the wrong way, but why you?' I asked him. 'Couldn't we all just leave our jobs behind and do this for a living?'

'It's not as simple as that,' Elliot said, and I decided to leave the conversation there for now, so as not to risk offending him. It was a lot to take in. But the truth was that I was starting to like Elliot; not for all of the Bruce Wayne stuff, but because he seemed decent, and humble, and my honest opinion at the time was that he was not at all arrogant about where he was in life, or about how he got there.

Elliot owned a residential apartment right in the centre of London, overlooking the Thames. It was an incredibly posh building, with polished marble floors in the lobby, and a concierge sitting at the front desk.

The most expensive place I had ever set foot in before was a three or four-star hotel at an affordable Spanish resort. So how could I have prepared myself for what I was about to experience?

You'll forgive me, as we travelled up in the lift with its plush carpet and calming music, for being so swept away by everything. Elliot read the moment well. He kissed me there and then, and I leaned into him, filled with both an incredible excitement, and a stern warning in the back of my head not to allow anything to cloud my judgment.

'Well,' Elliot said, reaching into his pocket for a small, black key card. These apartments didn't even have keys! 'Here we are.'

I followed him inside with my suitcase, and the first thing I noticed was the view. You could see the entire London skyline from up here. The sky was a deep orange, with the sun slowly setting behind. I was amazed – Elliot got to see this breath-taking snapshot of the capital every time he went to sleep.

'That's incredible!' I said.

'It sure is. Make yourself at home,' Elliot said. 'I just need to check on my messages. I won't be long.'

The place was immaculate, and although it was clearly expensive everything was done in the best of taste. Judging from the exterior of the building, I'd expected gold taps and mahogany bookcases, but Elliot's apartment was decorated with nice, modern carpets and pictures, and the settee was a cyan fabric affair, rather than one of those enormous leather monstrosities.

The kitchen was open-plan, with a breakfast bar and a couple of stools jutting out from a black, marble worktop, above which there hung a set of flawless, polished silver cookware. Filled with awe, I poked my head in the bathroom. It had a chestnut faux-wooden floor with a luxuriously-soft white bathmat, an expensive-looking modern shower in one corner and a white, curved bathtub on the other side of the room, and was walled with grey tiles with warm lights embedded in them.

It was obvious that somebody besides Elliot cleaned. The place was filled with a lime and basil scent, and there wasn't a shred of dust on any surface.

'How much did this place cost you?' I asked Elliot, as he finished up on his work laptop.

'I… really shouldn't say.'

'Oh, go on. Half a million? More?'

'A little more,' he said, visibly uncomfortable. 'Wait, there's one more room you haven't seen.'

'Is there?'

'Right through here,' Elliot smiled at me playfully. He showed me into the bedroom, a softly lit room with walk-in wardrobes, two large pictures set above his bed, and a similarly spectacular view of London through a set of electronic, remote-controlled blinds, which he opened up as soon as we entered the room.

Sitting on a small table at the foot of the bed was a bottle of champagne, a couple of glasses, and some chocolates.

'You don't have to try and impress me, you know,' I said, although I couldn't help smiling. In fact, I cursed the stupid, gleeful look which had been on my face ever since we'd arrived here. More than anything, I didn't want Elliot to feel like he had the upper hand.

'Don't worry. I'm not trying to buy you over with

cheap gestures or anything.' It was as if he'd read my mind. 'But I'd still like to try and make a good impression, if I can.'

'I think you already have,' I said, and Elliot closed the blinds again to kiss me gently, his arms enveloping me with comforting touches as we sat down on the bed together. I was falling into his eyes, losing myself in the touch of his fingers when I heard the warning again in my head, the voice of reason telling me that here was a man I still knew very little about.

'Wait,' I said. 'Sorry. It's just...'

'Too fast?'

I nodded. Elliot smiled, kissing me tenderly, running his hand ever so lightly through my hair.

'I just don't want to get hurt, Elliot. I really like you, but I just need to be careful. Do you understand?'

'You don't need to apologize,' he said. 'Honestly. But I won't hurt you. Ever.'

'I'm not afraid. I mean, I won't be.'

'Good. Do you like ballet?'

'Ballet?'

'I believe Swan Lake is on tonight. How about it?'

Ballet? I paused for a moment. This was all so far removed from anything I was used to; London, being treated nicely, looking out on that skyline from the fifteenth floor. I was almost afraid that I'd wake up at any moment and be back at home, living an ordinary life.

'Of course,' I said, 'I'd love to come with you.'

'Great!' Elliot said. 'And then tomorrow, I'll show you my boat.'

'Your boat?' I laughed, before realising that he was serious. 'Oh my God. You really do have a boat.'

'Well, it's just a little boat,' Elliot shrugged, looking at me innocently, and we both burst out laughing at the same time.

That night, Elliot and I had sex. Although I had promised to myself that I would take our relationship at a slow pace, the simple fact was that there was no strong reason not to sleep with Elliot. I won't go into great detail about our escapades beneath the bed sheets, but suffice to say, there was a great deal of chemistry between us. Elliot was a good lover: attentive, passionate, and not at all too rough.

Sleeping with him cemented two things in place; that he and I were both very attracted to one another, and that our relationship was now official.

I was now Elliot Gardner's girlfriend – a fact which I did enjoy repeating in my head, convinced that it was for all of the right reasons, and nothing to do with his money, his charm, or with desperately trying to get away from my overbearing parents. The fact was, in my mind, that Elliot and I had been destined for each other since the very first time he walked into the store on that lazy Sunday afternoon.

But I also wouldn't forget the conversations I started to overhear walking through college, or in the shops at the weekends.

'Isn't that the girl who's dating Elliot Gardner?'

'Yeah, that's her. Poppy Taylor.'

'Can you believe her? God. I heard he's taking her to Milan for Easter.'

'I heard he buys her a Gucci handbag, like, every month.'

'Well I ain't sayin' she a gold-digger...'

On his social media accounts, Elliot remained vague about his personal life, I assumed mostly for my benefit. But then one day the story broke; Lisa Barker, a girl I knew from school, had seen me getting into Elliot's car. Soon, people from school knew, and then, almost overnight, hundreds of thousands of strangers were speculating online as to who Elliot Gardner's new girlfriend was.

'I…think you'd better look at this,' Elliot said to me one day, not too long after, before bringing to my attention to an article on his laptop. I started to read it, with a mixture of curiosity and confusion.

Who is Poppy Taylor, new love-interest of rising Instagrammer and business owner Elliot Gardner?

'What's this?'

'It's… a story which is, well, doing the rounds at the moment on a small corner of the Internet,' Elliot said.

'Who wrote it?'

'Nobody I know. Some Internet loser, envious about what they don't have?' He sighed. 'I knew that this would happen, sooner or later. I guess we probably should have had this discussion a little earlier in the relationship.'

'What are they saying about me?'

'It's not important. Just some nonsense.'

'What nonsense? Show me.'

'It's not even worth your time of day,' Elliot said, as I approached and peered closer. He tried to remove it from his screen, but before he did I managed to scan the first couple of paragraphs – enough to get the general gist of what was being said.

'*Little is known about Poppy, who hails from an ordinary two-bedroom house in Bolton,*' I read aloud, '*save for the fact that she once was the centre of attention when she was saved from* *choking on food at a local restaurant. Perhaps she will find Elliot Gardner's millionaire status a little easier to digest...*What the hell? How do they find this stuff out?'

'They have their ways,' Elliot said. 'People will come forward with any titbit of news about someone for a little bit of money. But take my advice on this one, please. There's no point obsessing over what people will write about you. Somebody will always have an axe to grind. They'll lie about you, call you every name under the sun...'

'She'll no doubt be looking forward to the future as from now she'll be swapping sausage rolls for Chanel as they...' Elliot closed the window on me while I was reading. 'As they what?'

'The best thing to do is just ignore it.'

'I know that. I just don't know why they have to insinuate that it's this Oliver Twist, rags to riches thing...'

'Because that's *all* they have. Trust me. I'm speaking from experience. You can't win. Ever. Put on a pound, and they'll say you have a weight problem. Lose a pound? They'll call you bulimic. Dress too well and you're pretentious; too casually, and you're an alcoholic,' Elliot continued. 'Right now, the only thing they have to go off is the money thing. These people are bloodsuckers. They've followed me around, making up lies, for as long as I can remember.'

'That's awful,' I said. 'How do you put up with it?'

'Well, I try to avoid doing anything too embarrassing. And I dress well, look after my figure, and treat the rest of the comments like water off a duck's back. After all, what do a bunch of strangers know?'

'You're right. Your opinion is the only one which matters to me,' I said. 'Although from now on, I am not leaving the house without makeup! And losing a tad of weight won't do me any harm.'

'Exactly. Don't worry, you'll get used to it.'

There is one good thing about this, you know.'

'What's that?'

'At least the know I'm your girlfriend now,' I said, and we both smiled. Nothing Elliot ever said made me feel uncomfortable. The bond we shared was like a shield which protected both of us from anything out there in the big wide world.

7

The trial of millionaire social media star Elliot Gardner is due to begin next week at the Old Bailey. Gardner, 27, is accused of murdering his girlfriend, 22-year-old Rebecca Doherty, following an argument at his residence during the early hours of the morning. Appearing before television cameras, Elliot Gardner stated that he had 'absolutely no involvement' in the death of Rebecca Doherty, who fell from the fifteenth floor following a scream reported by neighbours. If convicted, Gardner faces at least fifteen years in prison.

Speaking outside the court yesterday, Gardner's defence barrister, Quentin Lautkin QC, said, 'my client has no recollection of the events which led to Miss Doherty's tragic death. This is a distressing case for everybody involved, but we are confident that the evidence will attest to the innocence of Mr Gardner.'

Meanwhile, protestors are planning to gather outside the court next week as the trial has gone viral across Instagram, with hordes of Gardner's supporters taking to the social media platform to call for his immediate release.

One supporter said, 'Nobody can say for sure what happened. But what I do know is that Elliot would never hurt anybody. It is so upsetting to see somebody hauled in front of the courts for a crime he clearly didn't commit.'

Others, however, were less supportive.

Caroline Fletcher, the Labour MP for Plymouth, Sutton and Devonport, and a long-time campaigner for women's rights, urged those supporting Mr Gardner 'blindly' on social media to reconsider their positions.

'People think that because they've seen somebody on a video or seen them on Instagram that they know that person, which is preposterous. What we have in this case is the death of a young woman which needs to be fully investigated and brought to a conclusion by the Crown Prosecution Service. It is sadly the case that many young women's deaths still go unsolved. In this day and age, it's more important than ever that people know that justice will be served.'

For more about the trial, including our live updates from Monday, please visit our website.

I wanted to avoid Svetlana as much as I could, because as our living conditions would have it, she and I were destined to cross paths sooner or later. It was the weekend before Elliot's trial and so, while she was occupied with her online clientele, I walked gingerly downstairs and slipped out of the house.

It was dark outside, and I saw Elliot everywhere; reflected in every street lit puddle, his voice speaking to me above the noise of the cars driving past and the overheard conversations from the shops that I passed. When I got to the main road, I flagged down the first taxi I could, and headed for the airport.

The driver's dark eyes watched me, glancing between the road and the rear-view mirror.

'Are you okay?' he asked, noticing probably the worried look on my face, and the fact that I didn't have any luggage with me whatsoever.

'Yes. I'm fine.'

He was fishing for a story, but I had no intentions of letting my guard down with a total stranger. He nodded, smiled, and went back to driving, while I thought about – of everyone in the world – Skylar. We hadn't spoken for months, no, years.

When everything with Elliot had come crashing down, so had things with her, and with Mum and Dad; it was a complicated, messy affair. But before that, something else had happened with Skylar, something which had changed her life dramatically. I didn't even know where she was living now. All I had was her phone number; a phone number which, so far, I hadn't dared to phone or text.

Now, unable to prevent myself floating back into the world of Elliot Gardner, I wished more than anyone, that I had her to talk to.

'Good evening,' I said to a woman at one of the ticket desks inside. She flashed me a look of suspicion while I continued. 'I'm looking for a ticket to London at short notice. Tonight, if you have any. Do you think that would be at all possible, please?'

'Tonight?' she said, after a brief pause. 'Wait a moment please… We do have a flight available in a couple of hours. Unfortunately, it's more expensive to book at short notice. The cost would be 295 Euros. Would you like me to look for a cheaper alternative?'

'No, that will be fine, thanks.'

'In a hurry?'

'What? Oh, yes. I have a family thing to take care of.

It's just come up, at short notice.'

'I hope it's nothing bad,' she said. I handed across my passport, paying for the ticket on my credit card, which had taken the brunt of my bad decisions of late.

'Oh, no,' I smiled haphazardly. 'It's...'

'Sorry. I shouldn't have asked. Here you go. Gate 12. And I hope you manage to get things sorted out.'

I thanked her, eager to get on my way as soon as possible.

To my horror, just as I was folding up the tickets neatly in my pocket, I found Elliot strolling across the airport to greet me.

He was wearing a *Giorgio Armani* cashmere suit, in grey, and was carrying a small leather briefcase in his hand. Elliot looked at me across the arrivals lounge, through the crowd, as he strolled in my direction. My spine froze up, and I felt a wave of nausea take over me. He smiled. I blinked, and then I realised that it wasn't Elliot at all; just a French-looking businessman on a work trip, just a stranger whose eye I'd happened to catch.

The look on my face must have been of pure terror. He quickly looked down at his feet and carried on walking past me, and I made my way up the escalators towards the departure lounge, where my flight to England would soon be waiting.

Putting together all of the memories was like placing the pieces of a broken vase back together. At first, I'd found it hard to remember any of the details about my time with Elliot, or about our relationship, but with Elliot's story all over the news, it had all started flooding back in; from meeting him in the store to that first weekend away in London, and now the memories wouldn't let me have ten minutes of peace.

As I sat on the plane, flashbacks came to me from different parts of our relationship. I'd heard of people losing their memory before, but this was something different. When I focused hard enough it was all still there, waiting to be uncovered. It was like I'd fallen asleep at the wheel and had woken up to a pair of bright headlights straight in front, a loud, blaring horn as ten tonnes of metal rushed at me...

If that was buried deep in the memories of my subconscious, then could something else be, too? Something important enough to make a difference at Elliot's trial?

He'll get away with it, you know.

There it was again; the voice of doubt in my mind. No matter what I did to bat it away, it nagged at me incessantly.

But there'll be evidence, surely? People don't commit suicide by jumping to their deaths following an argument in the middle of the night.

What evidence, Poppy? A conveniently highlighted bruise on Rebecca's wrist, a boot mark on her backside? There's likely not to be any evidence at all. You know that. So it'll all go down to the opinions of a jury...

A jury which will see straight through a narcissist like Elliot.

Really? Can you be so sure about that? Has anyone ever seen 'straight through' Elliot Gardner? Did you? Men like Elliot can be extremely cunning. Well-spoken. Well-rehearsed. So, how confident are you in the investigative skills of twelve random men and women off the street?

The voice of doubt had a good point. If Elliot was able to make himself appear like a genuinely grief-stricken boyfriend whose life had just been turned upside down, it was difficult to see how some juries would convict him. There again, there were several factors which worked against Elliot. His money. The fact that he looked good, and in control, was enough to make some people mistrustful of him. Still, Elliot practically owned a degree in social psychology.

The legal system will do its job. Elliot hasn't got a chance of getting away with this.

And if it doesn't?

Well, what if he walks? What does any of this have to do with me, anyway?

Because if you don't do anything, Elliot will get away with it all. With everything. Is that really what you're prepared to let happen, Poppy? After everything you've gone through, are you going to let him walk off into the sunset, happily ever after?

I didn't have an answer to that.

8

As Elliot and I started spending more time together, the rest of my life started to feel toned down to a dim murmur.

I was supposed to be preparing for my A-level exams, but instead nearly every weekend I was with him, except for the odd times when he was away on business. Not that my parents noticed. They were so over the moon with him that they didn't even stop to question why I'd stopped working Sundays at the clothing store.

'He seems absolutely lovely,' Dad said upon meeting Elliot, although he rarely visited the house. 'Polite, handsome, well-dressed, you know...' with not-so-subtle hints that I had chosen a boyfriend from an appropriate social class once again.

In the weeks and months which followed, Elliot took me everywhere. We went hot-air ballooning in the Lake District, driving fast cars around the Silverstone Circuit, and for my personal favourite, he arranged for us to meet the big cats, up close and personal, on a special tour of Dartmoor Zoo.

How could my otherwise plain and simple life live up to any of that? For me, normal life was a place where absolutely nothing interesting happened at all. By contrast, what Elliot and I shared was real; it was *connection*. None of the things he treated me to were shallow wastes of money. They weren't just *things*. They were experiences; memories I would never forget.

Skylar's curiosity about Elliot and I, meanwhile, had reached an all-time high. Although she and I had never actually been that close, in the past few weeks she'd been prying all of the time, messaging me out of the blue to ask how things were going, and liking and commenting on all of my new pictures. Finally, I agreed to meet her for a coffee next weekend, when both of us were free, and Elliot was away on another business trip.

I expected her to be brimming with jealousy, and why not? The week before, he and I had eaten at Gordon Ramsay's Michelin-star restaurant in London; a place so prestigious I could have only dreamed of going in prior to my relationship with him.

Everywhere we went, Elliot insisted on the full VIP experience. When we ate out, he ordered salmon and langoustines, filet mignon, tagliolini with white truffle sauce and artisanal bread with foie gras. We drank espresso martinis and gin infused with flakes of 24 carat gold. We relaxed in hot Jacuzzis, and we never, ever waited in line for anything.

'My God, Poppy Taylor,' Skylar said, 'You're even beginning to *sound* like a Cheshire housewife.'

'I'm serious. We've always been brought up to believe that everything rich people do is sinful,' I said. 'That somehow, it's despicable to want to go on a nice fancy holiday, or to be treated extra special when in fact, that's what we all want at the end of the day.'

'What are you trying to say? Please don't tell me you think you deserve all of this.'

'What? No, that's not what I'm saying.' This wasn't like the Skylar I knew, who was always looking after number one. 'It's not like that. But why should we feel guilty for not wanting to stand around in line all of the time, for not wanting to settle for second best? That kind of guilt is like a... like a coping mechanism we've been brought up with.'

'Right. And I suppose the fact that Elliot is paying for it all doesn't make you feel guilty in the slightest.'

'I contribute, thank you very much.'

'Really?'

'Yes, really!'

Painfully, though, Skylar had struck a nerve. Elliot never made me feel guilty about the dynamic of our relationship. But I did have fearful questions running through my head: why had he chosen me, of all people? And what if he got bored of me one day? I sipped my coffee and smiled intensely.

'How are things with Kieran, anyway?'

'Things are good,' Skylar smiled back. She never seemed to have a care in the world. 'He's looking at applying to Manchester University. After that, we'll probably wind up moving to Dubai.' I nodded, half-asleep, knowing full well that anything she said had to always be taken with a pinch of salt. 'Have you looked at universities yet? I'm going to see which ones are worth applying to this year.'

'You're only sixteen, Sky,' I laughed.

'Well, you have to be proactive with these sorts of things, if you want the best chances. It's all about beating the competition. Look at you. I bet you haven't even started your applications yet.' The tediousness of formal education was enough to make me want to dig a hole in the ground and jump right into it.

'I'm... not thinking about university right now,' I said. 'Six months is a long time. I don't know, I might take a gap year or something. Spend a year working, and then see what I want to do.'

'Oh,' she said, and paused for dramatic effect. 'Can I say something? I'm a little bit worried about you. I hope you remember that there was a time *before* Elliot.'

'Jesus, Skylar.' It had only been a matter of time until she launched her attack on our relationship. 'I don't think I need life lessons from my little sister, thank you.'

'I just don't want to see you put all your eggs in one basket, that's all.'

'Trust me. I know what I'm doing. When you're older you might realise that life isn't all about exams and accolades and...and P.E. kits.'

'Fine,' she said, resignedly, in a way which roughly translated to *don't say I didn't warn you*. 'Well, I suppose I should give you one other piece of news. I think I'll be moving out in a couple of months. You can finally have the big bedroom back, if you want.'

At this, I was genuinely shocked. 'With Kieran?'

She nodded. 'His dad's already picked out a few potential houses for us to look at.'

'Wow! That's a big step,' I said, amusing myself with the irony of how, two minutes before, *she* had been the one warning *me* to take my time with Elliot.

'Well, sometimes you just know, don't you?' she said. 'I couldn't ask for a better boyfriend than Kieran. He's exactly what I've been looking for in a potential partner.'

'Congratulations.'

'Thank you! I'm really looking forward to this next stage with him.'

Partner! Next stage! Skylar had skipped out all of her teenage years and gone straight to her forties, it seemed. But I could agree with her on one thing. 'Sometimes you just know,' I murmured. And with Elliot that was how I felt; that there was a large possibility of me spending the rest of my life with him.

'Keep them closed,' Elliot said, parading me down the hallway and into the hotel room which we'd been staying in just outside of Bristol, with his hands over my eyes. 'It's just a bit further along.'

I couldn't help laughing, almost tripping over my own feet as Elliot got the door for us and ushered me inside.

'I can't see anything!'

'That is the general idea,' Elliot teased. 'Okay, now in front of you on the bed is an envelope. Just reach down, it's right there.'

Giggling, I put my hands onto the soft sheets of the bed and felt around. I felt the sharp pointed edge of a paper envelope and picked it up.

'Can I open my eyes now?'

'Not yet. Open it, first.'

Feeling around the edge of the envelope, I slid my finger underneath the flap and opened it. Inside, I touched some smaller pieces of paper. To my blind hands, they felt like Monopoly money, but I had no idea what to expect when I opened my eyes. Elliot took his hands away.

In front of me was a pair of tickets. In honesty, it took me a moment to register what I was looking at, but then I read:

15th Jun   Flight EI2951
Manchester (MAN)
To-
Miami (MIA)
SEAT 3A   Miss Poppy Taylor
SEAT 3B   Mr Elliot Gardner
FIRST CLASS

'Oh my God,' I said, not quite sure how to react. 'Are you serious?'

Elliot smiled, clearly excited for the both of us. 'Mhmm. I hope you don't mind, but I wanted it to be a surprise. You don't mind, do you?'

'Mind?' I laughed. 'Elliot, I'm thrilled. It's just that...' I held back the sudden onset of tears, which had bubbled up to the surface to my own surprise. Elliot put his hand on mine, and sat down on the bed next to me.

'Sorry. It's just that nobody has ever done anything like this for me before,' I said, dabbing the corner of my eye like an idiot.

'Please don't apologise!' Elliot said. 'I just hope I made a good decision.'

'You really have. Thank you,' I said, squeezing his hand. 'But, hang on a minute. June? That's only a couple of weeks away!'

'Does that create an issue?' Elliot asked, suddenly looking nervous. I could tell he had been full of trepidation towards springing a surprise holiday on me. I could only imagine how he had debated it back and forth in his head for the past few weeks.

'No, not at all!' I said, simultaneously thinking of my exams, and of the time I had marked out to view university prospectuses, and of all the boring humdrum of planning out the rest of my normal life, which Skylar and other people seemed to adore. I quickly glanced at the return ticket. Well, what was so wrong with going away for thirteen days?

'I'm just going to need to buy some new outfits. And go on an immediate diet!'

Well, what was the point in all of that, anyway? People like Skylar and my parents always did what they were supposed to do, in their permanent efforts to maintain appearances. They never took life by the reins. And what did people regret more in the long run – taking risks and enjoying life, or playing it safe and never having any fun?

I looked into Elliot's eyes, which I could see were full of love and appreciation for me.

'Thank you so much,' I said, kissing him and pulling him into my embrace, as we both fell onto the bed together.

Sooner or later, everyone has a major disagreement with their parents. It was the plot and basis of every Disney movie ever made, but Disney characters never questioned whether what they were doing was the right thing. Was I sure that what I was about to tell them was the right thing to do?

'Hello, Poppy. Have you had a good time?'

'Hi Mum,' I said, 'Dad. Could I have a quick talk with both of you please?'

Not quite listening on the other side of the room, Dad

suddenly shot me a glance.

'Of course. What is it?' Mum asked. Dad turned the TV down. They were both staring at me intently, and I realised with hilarity what they both must have thought of straight away.

'I'm not pregnant! My God. You should see the look on both of your faces.'

'Well, it's not unheard of, you know,' said Mum, 'Especially when you and Elliot have been so... close lately.'

'Come on Poppy, don't keep us in suspense!'

'Okay, well look, this isn't easy for me to say.' I looked down awkwardly at the floor. 'But with everything that's been going on recently, I've been thinking about everything. And the more I've thought about it the more I've realised that...I don't want to go straight to university. I know, I know you both really want me to go. But I need to take some time out from studying, to really consider all of my options.'

'Oh,' Mum said, 'I see. Well.'

There was a silence which caused me to want to keep talking, and thus dig my own grave even deeper. 'I don't want you to think that this means that my mind is made up. But lots of people take a gap year-'

'A gap year?' Dad finally spoke. 'You can think twice if you think you're going to go travelling around like some hippie student through Thailand or Australia. You know those people get abducted, don't you?'

'I don't think she means that. Do you, sweetheart?'

'God, no! I don't want to have some year of sponging around and pretending to be cultured. What I mean is, I'd rather use some time away from studying to properly look at my options, speak to employers and so on, maybe do an internship. That way, I'll be better informed to know what to study and why.'

'Well that sounds pretty sensible to me,' Mum said, placating Dad as she always did by trying to get him to see my point of view.

'It sounds like an excuse to me,' Dad said. He rarely spoke to me like this, and I had never heard him address Skylar so directly. 'Now, I can't help but notice that you've let your college work slip recently. Spending lots of time with your boyfriend...it concerns me a bit. You need to remain focused on your future.'

'What's Elliot go to do with this?' I said, suddenly feeling on the defensive.

'I'm just saying that you need to...'

'I'm *not* going to make the wrong decision just because it's what you want me to do, Dad. I've been thinking about this for a long time, and I'm not rushing into some course I'll regret signing up to.'

'You know me and your father only want what's best for you, Poppy,' Mum said.

'I know that. But I know that what's best for me right now is to take some time to get everything in order. I'm not asking for permission from you, but I hope you'll respect my decision. I'm not some stupid little girl who's throwing her life away, you know.'

Mum and Dad paused for a moment, and I felt proud that, for the first time in my adult life, I had not only made a decision of my own but stood up for myself, too.

'We'll support you, whatever you do, Poppy,' said Mum. 'But, I think your Dad's right. You need to make sure that you keep an eye on your future.'

'We don't want you getting all swept up in this

romance with Elliot, that's all,' said Dad.

'Well, seen as we're on the subject, there's something else, too,' I said. 'Elliot has invited me to go on holiday with him next month, to Florida. For thirteen days.'

'Next month?'

'I know what you'll say, but I'll be taking my revision materials with me. I just thought I'd let you know.'

Dad, clearly experiencing a challenge which he had never come across before, looked incensed. 'You're taking this too far,' he said. 'I'm putting my foot down.'

'Oh, come on! For as long as I've known, Skylar's been allowed to make her own decisions,' I said. 'She decides to move in with Kieran and you don't say a word. I want to go on *holiday*, and…and all hells breaks loose!'

'Skylar's moving in with Kieran?' Mum exclaimed.

'This is ridiculous. Sit down, Poppy,' Dad said. Defiantly, I turned to walk away.

'You're right, this *is* ridiculous. I'm going to my room,' I said, storming out.

In one swift and rather unbloody battle, Mum and Dad were no longer completely in control of my life. What a liberating feeling that was! And now that I was no longer under the immense pressure of having to go to university in the autumn, I would be able to spend more time with Elliot. With my newfound freedom, I planned to use that time to learn about the wider world, to reflect on my two years of college, and to decide what it was that Poppy Taylor wanted to do with her life.

9

The trial shouldn't have taken more than a week, under normal circumstances, but it seemed as though Elliot was determined to make a show of it.

All that is necessary for evil to triumph is for good people to do nothing, so the saying goes, but it also helps to have a bunch of enablers to come crawling out of the woodwork, looking to further their own careers off the back of it. Elliot had drafted in as many people as he could to take to the stand and attest to his good character. And each and every one of them were the worst sycophants money could buy.

Some of them were doing it for money, or in exchange for Elliot's favour. Some of them were doing it to stay relevant. And some of them were simply doing it for fifteen seconds of fame. But all of them were hungry for power.

Exhausted, I looked at myself in the mirror.

'You don't have to do this, Poppy,' I said. 'You can just walk away right now.'

Except, I couldn't, no more than I could have stopped myself getting in the taxi and driving to the airport and booking a flight back to London, getting straight off the flight in the early hours of the morning, and stumbling into the nearest Premier Inn with nothing more on me than some make-up and a change of clothes.

A thudding headache resounded at the back of my head. I was flying on autopilot; compelled by some need which overwhelmed all of my other senses. It was far beyond simple curiosity. This was closer to an obsession.

Instead of sleeping, I had researched everything I could about Elliot's case. By his grandiose posturing, Elliot was managing to turn the murder trial of a young girl into a theatrical show for the amusement of the public. He had released several statements to the media since his arrest and subsequent bail, and I wasn't sure if they were designed to influence a potential jury, or even potentially to get the case thrown out of court due to the amount of media attention it was getting. But by striking first, Elliot was ensuring that the job of the court would be to unwind a narrative which had already started to take root in the minds of anyone who knew about the trial.

I read on, horrified by the cold, and calculated strategy that was unfolding right before my eyes.

Elliot kept on repeating the same messages again and again. He insisted that Rebecca had jumped to her death during the middle of the night, while he was sleeping, but following a minor argument an hour or two before. He stated that they had been in a 'good' relationship. He said that he abhorred violent men, and that he would never conduct himself in a violent way towards women. He believed in the justice system, he said, and he was confident that in the end, 'truth would prevail'; that a jury would see sense and set him free.

'I'm truly heartbroken for Becky and for her family,'

Elliot said to the television cameras, his face solemn and heartfelt, like a Shakespearean actor delivering his monologue. 'This has been an incredibly painful process, and I want to get to the truth as much as anyone. I hope that this trial will help put things to rest, so that those of us who were close to Rebecca can try our best to… to move on.'

Most frightening of all were the thinly-veiled attacks upon Rebecca. All of Elliot's statements, all of his lies, were carefully placed towards the suggestion that *she* had been going through a lot of stress recently, that *she* had suffered with alcoholism and depression in the past – all of it directed towards the suggestion that Rebecca was a woman capable of doing something drastic. A woman who, I reminded myself, had lost the ability to even respond to all of the allegations now heading her way.

It was standard Elliot Gardner, drawn straight from the millionaire defendant's playbook. The implication was that painful revelations about Rebecca's mental health would be revealed in the trial, and that despite the desire of Rebecca's family to have somebody to blame, the reality of Rebecca's death was that it was an unfortunate, unforeseeable tragedy.

Do you expect to walk free, Mister Gardner?

What of the allegations that you and Rebecca Doherty argued on the night of her death?

'I'm sorry, I can't answer any more of your questions for today.'

Will you be leaving the court an innocent man, Mister Gardner?

Anything to add, Mister Gardner?

Mister Gardner!

I exited the news report I'd been watching, taking in

the implications of what it would mean for Elliot to succeed in pulling the wool over everybody's eyes.

If it worked, Elliot would be free to do whatever he liked. If he was found not guilty, off he would go, with all of his entitlement and his millions of pounds, to bed and destroy some other vulnerable, unfortunate twenty-something with high hopes and low self-esteem.

Because that was where I came into things, wasn't it? I had been Elliot's first victim; what he did to other women, he had practiced on me. And at the time I had failed to see past Elliot's façade; the charming, introspective, thoughtful and well-spoken Elliot, a man who bore confidence and humility in equal amounts, and was incredibly attractive for it.

I had failed to see his dark side until it had almost left me for dead.

And although I'd managed to leave all of that behind, our fates were bound together. Because when you were involved in something, that meant seeing it through to the end, didn't it? You couldn't just walk away from the scene of a crime, even if you weren't the guilty party.

You had to see things through.

I knew I had to look into Elliot's eyes, so that he could see there was a person in the room who hadn't bought into all of his bullshit over the years. I had to look him in the eye, above all, so that he would know that his power over me had been revoked.

'I have to,' I said. The girl I saw in the mirror said nothing. She had been through a lot of transformation over the years. Some of adulthood had been cruel to her, and she bore the scars of it in her eyes, but behind that, she was fierce and strong and ready.

I turned away, left the hotel room, and headed

downstairs towards the foyer. It was early morning; a new day. I stopped off quickly for a double-espresso, drew in a deep breath, and set off – in the direction of the city centre, towards the court where the murder trial of Elliot Gardner was about to begin.

Elliot's trial had become an epicentre of drama, and had attracted hordes of protestors, activists, and busybodies, who all seemed to be very angry about one thing or another. As I approached the court there was an ever-increasing crowd outside, and a small group of police officers, who were trying to keep the peace.

As I drew closer, I could see that one of the groups of protestors – the smaller group – had been segregated from the main crowd, and were hiding behind the protection of some improvised police barriers. They were carrying placards, shouting and jumping up and down for the television cameras, while the crowd which had filled the street pushed toward them, stopped by a line of police who had blocked the way.

A girl walked up to me. She was carrying a tote bag full of leaflets and God-only-knew what else.

'What's going on?' I asked. I noticed that a lot of the people here were young, trendy types; veterans of this sort of thing. At the front was a lady with a megaphone, whom I did not recognize.

'Those shills have come out to defend a conman and a murderer!' she said, indicating to the smaller group who had congregated near the entrance to the court. 'Look at them. Defending a man who they know is guilty. But they don't care. We're here to show that privileged white men like Elliot Gardner need to pay for their crimes. Would you like a leaflet?'

'No... thank you,' I said, suddenly feeling slightly disgusted with the way this had all spilled out into the public domain.

'You're not one of those 'free Elliot' types, are you?'

'No.'

'Good. The last thing a monster like him needs is support. So, are you with us?'

'Look...' I started, wanting to get away. I had to make my way through to the front of the crowd.

'What's your problem?' asked the girl, who was now eyeing me up curiously.

'Look, get away from me, okay? You don't know a damned thing about Elliot, or me, or anything. You just want to turn everything into your own stupid fucking platform.'

'Hey! You can't speak to me like that,' she cried, as I barged past and made my way towards the police guarding the main entrance. I didn't have time for this. Ignoring her, I carried on as her voice grew louder in outrage:

'Get back here! Murderer!'

The air was tense, and I briskly kept on walking while behind me, the confused and angry voices fading away. In front of me were the police officers. I noticed one of them glance my way as I approached, then turn to face me as I got right up to the cordon; a big man, wearing a helmet and looking as though he was expecting things to kick off at any second.

'And where do you think you're going?' he said.

'Hello,' I said, 'My name is Poppy. I need to be in the courtroom today. I'm linked to the case.'

Raising an eyebrow, he looked at me. 'No one's allowed in or out of here today. The court is closed to public viewing. I'm afraid you'll have to take it up elsewhere, miss.'

Calmly, I tried to compose myself. 'It's really important that I get to the trial.'

'Are you deaf, love? The court is off limits. Or do you expect us to let all of you crackpots in at once? Now, I'm going to have to ask you to step back, okay? If you have anything else to add, you can speak to the court registrar. *Tomorrow*. Is that understood?'

This couldn't all be for nothing. Could it?

The policeman beckoned me to step back, and I obeyed, falling back into the folds of the crowd. They were heaving and shoving towards the front towards the police, and now there were more officers arriving on the far side of the street, equipped with riot gear and horses, ready for some kind of charge or assault on the crowd if things got any further at hand. I darted through a gap to the side and slid away from the main entrance, angry and frustrated beyond belief.

'God damn it!' I said aloud, to no one in particular.

Just then, as I had lost all hope of seeing Elliot's moment in the spotlight, I spotted a familiar face walking towards the back of the large, concrete building of the court. It was Neil, the police detective who had showed up at my apartment in Amsterdam a few weeks ago. He was carrying a black briefcase, wearing the same grey coat, and although he looked a little neater than our previous encounter, it didn't take me more than a second to recognize him.

He was walking briskly with his head down, probably to avoid drawing attention from the throng of people outside the court-room. And clearly, he was heading inside.

'Detective!' I shouted. 'Mr Braithwaite! Wait up!' I sprinted up the street, clothes and hair flying all over the place, and caught up with him.

Neil looked up, astonished. It must have taken him a minute to recognise me.

'Miss Taylor,' he said finally, glancing at his watch uncomfortably, and thinking about how to manage this unexpected interruption. In that moment, if any response could have been less committal, I know he would have chosen it. 'What a surprise, running into you here.'

'You're on your way to testify, aren't you?'

'I...,' he started, 'Yes, I am. And I'm running late, so I'm afraid if you need to talk to me, it'll have to wait for another day.'

'Look, I've thought about things for a while, and, well, I've changed my mind. About the case. About Elliot. And I'd be happy to testify, if you think it will help. I think it *will* help, actually. Do you understand?'

Neil folded his hands and looked me in the eye. His eyebrows showed an earnest expression of familiarity and trust, so what he said next took me by complete surprise.

'I'm really sorry, Poppy. I'd love to help you. But, the trial is about to start. The case has already been put together by the CPS, and adding another witness at this stage wouldn't bring anything new to the table. I understand that testifying against Elliot might have brought you... some closure. But I'm afraid you're too late. I'm sorry.'

'I see,' I said, reeling back from this final kick in the teeth. But deep inside, I knew that Neil was right. I had waited too long.

'You're right. It's my fault. I should have listened to you earlier, when you came to see me in Amsterdam,' I said.

Neil shrugged. He wasn't judging me, but at the same time, both of us knew that I had dithered and delayed. He smiled at me as if to say, *everybody makes mistakes.*

'Promise me one thing, at least?'

'What's that?'

'Promise me you'll ensure that Elliot gets what he deserves.'

'Look, we have a really strong case. The evidence against Elliot Gardner...well, it speaks for itself. I hope you'll take some solace in that. I'm really sorry you can't be a part of this. I'd better be off. Don't want to be late, do I?' Neil smiled, briefly touching my arm. It was a moment of intense human connection, a spark from across the void, and for a second, I felt re-assured.

I exhaled deeply, saying goodbye to this chapter of my life forever. There were missed chances, perhaps, but at least I had faced my demons, I decided. At least, after all of the ups and downs, there was that.

I turned and started to walk away.

'Miss Taylor, wait!' said Neil. He jogged back up the pavement toward me, and, a little confused, I tried to smile at him.

'Did you fly all the way over just to be here today?'

I shrugged, shyly. 'I just wanted to be of help, that's all.'

'I understand. It means a lot to you, seeing Elliot answer for his actions, doesn't it? I can only imagine what you've been through,' Neil said. 'Well I can't make any guarantees, but I can see if the registrar will permit you into the courtroom. Not as a witness, mind you. You won't be allowed to speak, just to observe. What would you think about that?'

'I'd be…that would be really good,' I said.

'Great! Come with me, and I'll see what I can do. Hurry! Before any of those damned protestors catch onto us.'

'Thank you so much,' I said to Neil, as we paced hurriedly towards the rear entrance. Neil said nothing. He obviously didn't want to get too friendly, and besides, his mind was probably more focussed on the important case we were both about to enter.

10

The sun glinted off the water, and the warm breeze whipped up my hair around my face, causing it to fly around in an uncontrollable frenzy as I posed, uncomfortably, next to the Bayfront Park Fountain in Miami. I was standing in a plaza just off the seafront, surrounded by the tall glass buildings of downtown Miami and a never-ending crowd of sun-kissed, roller-blading, hot-dog-eating beach people. They walked past without as much as a glance at Elliot or me.

'Can we stop taking pictures now, please?'

'If we must,' Elliot said. 'But you look so gorgeous today. Miami suits you.'

Ordinarily, I would have blushed at such a comment. But maybe it was the heat, or maybe it was the fact that most of the photos Elliot had taken so far were just of me standing on my own. I scowled at him instead.

'Alright, I'll put the camera away. I didn't mean to make you feel uncomfortable.'

'I'm sorry, it's not that,' I said. 'It's just...can we get one of us together? Please?'

Almost embarrassed that he'd made such an obvious mistake, it was Elliot's turn to turn red. 'Of course! I'd love to…let me just find somebody to take it who isn't a hobo or whatever. This camera was expensive, you know.'

He went off approaching people on the boardwalk, and I took in a deep breath to compose myself. Of course, I didn't mean to be so ungrateful or short with Elliot. But I was suffering from a little bit of jet lag, and something else – some other sort of lag, the lag of a person who was used to camping trips and cheap B&Bs, who suddenly found themselves experiencing first-class flights, and room service, and a view of the entire Miami shoreline from her hotel room – might feel.

'Come on, Poppy, get yourself together,' I whispered under my breath.

He soon re-appeared, accompanied by a backpack-wearing student with bleached-blonde hair, who he'd poached from the boardwalk. Carrying his skateboard under one arm, the young student gave me a shy wave before Elliot showed him how to turn on the camera and operate it. 'Here you go!' he said. 'It's the button on top. Make sure you take quite a few.'

Elliot came over to me, put his arm around me, and smiled for the camera. Staring at this stranger with his bright orange shorts and his darkish smile, I couldn't help but feel wholly uncomfortable.

'Smile, guys!'

Click!

Click!

I tried to smile as naturally as I could. Elliot wasn't looking at me. Instead, he was focusing directly on the camera. I turned and kissed him on the cheek for the remaining few pictures.

'Thank you,' I said, giving his hand a quick squeeze afterwards. 'I really appreciate it.'

'Okay, let's see,' Elliot said, as he retrieved the camera, frowning as he looked through the photographs to make sure they were alright. The student, who clearly didn't know anything about, or care about, photography in the slightest, looked on bemused. 'Hmm. How about we do it again but pivot slightly... Poppy, can you move over there a little bit?'

'What, here?'

'Left a bit more... okay! Perfect.'

'What was wrong with the others?' I asked him, when he came back over.

'The lighting was a little bit off. Now, keep the camera straight,' he said to the young man, 'and I'll stand on the other side of her this time, okay?'

'Sure, whatever dude,' said the student, more than a little impatiently.

All of a sudden, we were being photographed again. Caught off guard, I tried to smile as best as I could. But it was no use; straight away I felt the muscles around my eyes tightening up, my lips pursing into an utterly forced smile. Elliot, on the other hand, looked completely natural. He looked past the camera and into the middle-distance, as though he was contemplating something really important, and he looked good.

'You happy now? I'm done. Here you go, man,' the student said, handing Elliot back the camera. He threw his skateboard onto the ground, leapt onto it, and rode away down the boardwalk, out of sight.

'I'm so happy you're here with me, Poppy,' Elliot said, putting the camera away carefully, after inspecting it for damage.

'Me too,' I said, smiling back at him. 'So what are we going to do, then?'

'I have a few friends here in Miami who I'd like you to meet this evening. But first, I'd like to take you shopping.'

I laughed out loud. '*You* would like to go shopping?'

'Well, let's just say…jeans and hoodies aren't exactly the fashion here. You have to loosen up a bit, you know?'

'Oh, so my clothes aren't good enough for Miami?' I laughed. To tell the truth, half of the things in my suitcase were from places like Primark or H&M. Elliot looked at me deadpan for a moment, which made me laugh even harder than before.

'Alright, alright. But *you're* paying.'

I hated the way it had come out like that, like I was already some kind of trophy wife whose husband bought her designer dresses and handbags as part of their ongoing romantic arrangement. But Elliot didn't seem to mind.

'Come on, let's hit the town,' he said, lowering his sunglasses so that his eyes were out of view, and taking my hand as we walked back across the park to where the taxis were waiting.

Almost three thousand dollars later (Elliot insisted on spending so much, while I, mortified, protested again and again in vain), Elliot took me back to the hotel to get ready, while he went and picked out a hire car for the rest of the week. He had helped pick out all of the clothes I was going to wear: a couple of mini dresses and halter-neck affairs, a ridiculously overpriced pair of platform sandals, a *Jacquemus Le Chiquito* light-green leather handbag, and a bottle of *Gucci Bloom* eau de parfum. While I did protest at a couple of things, I was completely surprised how much Elliot knew about fashion. He took me from shop to shop, asking me to try things on and commenting honestly on how they looked, and putting up with me endlessly complaining about why I couldn't wear a simple top and skirt to meet his friends at their condo on the south side of Miami beach.

'Are you sure all of this is necessary?' I had asked, at around the time of Elliot's fifth purchase of the day. My feet were already starting to ache from walking around all of the shops.

'It's not necessary,' Elliot said. 'But, I enjoy buying you things. And besides, you want my friends to have a good impression of you, don't you?'

'So if I don't wear the right clothes, they won't have a good impression of me?'

'No. It's not that at all,' Elliot said. 'They can be a little... judgmental at times, I'll admit. But you wouldn't want to look out of place, would you? I just want you to fit right in and feel comfortable. I'm sure they'll really like you regardless. Trust me, okay?'

Elliot told me his friends in Miami were fellow influencers and social media stars – the kind of people you see pulling pranks and performing outrageous stunts on YouTube. And while I knew that Elliot had my back, I felt like I was about to walk into a dragon's den with my pale skin, off-white teeth, and a whole heap of psychological complexes.

Elliot's friends lived in a small, exclusive clique known as the *SoFI* area of Miami beach. *SoFI* stood for *South of Fifth*, a neighbourhood made up of yuppies and new money, with condos in the area ranging from (as I looked up on my phone) between half a million, and 30 million dollars.

From these condos there were magnificent views of the entire Miami beach, from North Bay down to Fisher Island and the luxurious *Key Biscayne*, with the Florida mainland on one side, separated by a small strip of water – with the sparkling Atlantic on the other side.

Elliot rented out a blacked-out Range Rover with all of the mod-cons. He could probably feel the nervousness radiating from me, like the coolness radiating from the air conditioning onto my snow-white face.

'Try to relax,' he said, reassuringly. 'I won't let anything bad happen to you. It's just a party.'

'I'm relaxed,' I replied, unconvincingly. I felt awful; on the verge of throwing up, but I had to do this for him.

We drove down the length of Miami beach until we reached the southernmost neighbourhoods; a maze of palm trees, tiled courtyards and two or three storey, bleached white houses with rooftop gardens and verandas. Every house had a high wall and was surrounded by CCTV cameras, which seemed to watch me with their impenetrable gaze. Finally, we pulled into a Venetian-looking courtyard, through an electric gate, which Elliot had an automatic pass to open, and parked up.

We got out of the car and walked up to a light-wooden door, with inset glass rectangles and a modern, chrome handle. Next to it was an audio buzzer.

'Who the fuck is that?' asked a voice. Elliot looked at me and rolled his eyes, as if to minimize the damage. Maybe he was just as concerned, I suddenly realised, with the impression his friends would make on me.

'It's Elliot,' he said. There was a click as the door unlocked, and then, taking my hand, Elliot showed me inside.

There are hardly words to describe my first

impressions of the house. It was like scuba-diving, and seeing the colourful diversity of a coral reef for the first time.

Inside, we were greeted by a lavish, white room with French windows on the upper level. There was a pristinely polished wooden floor adorned with rugs, and large pieces of art hung up on the wall, in the centre of which a modern glass staircase, with shiny silver balustrades, made its way up to the second floor. Though it hadn't looked it from outside, inside the place was huge and well-lit, with plenty of natural light. There were sculptures and potted plants neatly arranged around each room, in the same way you'd expect to find a show-home decorated for sale, and I felt like my clumsiness would cause me to knock something over at any time setting foot in the place.

At the far end of the room, watching a huge television attached to the far wall, were a trio of people.

'Heeeere he is!' cried a blonde-haired man, who could've been no older than twenty-five. He leaped up from one of the oversized sofas and shook Elliot's hand. I recognised his voice as being the one from the buzzer. 'And you must be Poppy. Awesome to meet you.'

'Poppy, this is James ... and this is Sophie, and last but not least, Courtney.'

'Hi, I'm Sophie,' smiled a pretty blonde girl, wearing a lot of makeup. She took a step forward and kissed me on the cheek, and I was suddenly overcome with the scent of expensive perfume. Feebly, I kissed back. 'It's soo lovely to meet you!'

'You too,' I said.

'Hey,' said Courtney. She had straight, dark hair, and a bit of a vacant look on her face, as though she didn't really care about anything which was going on. She looked me up and down for a second. 'I'm Courtney. Is it your first time in

Miami?'

'Yes, it is.'

'We just flew in yesterday,' Elliot added.

'That's great. Well, don't worry, my head was a bit blown too, when I first came here. You'll fit in just fine. Would you like a drink? A cocktail?'

'That would be great, thank you.'

'Super. Let me grab hold of my useless boyfriend for a second,' Courtney said, before shouting up the stairs with a volume that made everybody wince. 'Eric! Will you get down here? You've been dicking around up there for a whole half hour already.'

'Eric's a video game streamer,' Elliot explained to me, 'He's completely addicted to his computer. James and Sophie are both YouTubers. And Rish… well, you'll find out all you need to know about Rish soon enough.'

'Guy's fuckin'…HILARIOUS,' James chortled, receiving a quick scowl from Elliot in my periphery.

'So, what kind of YouTubing do you do, James?' I asked, trying not to sound condescending, but immediately failing at doing so.

'A bit of everything, you know. At the moment, I'm doing a couple of collabs. Have you heard of the Slow Motion Show? I'm going to hang out with them in a couple of weeks. Sophie mainly does reaction vids, makeup tutorials, that sort of stuff. Elliot's talked a lot about you, you know. Never thought I'd see him settling down. I tell you, you must be something pretty special.'

'Don't be fooled by James,' Elliot interrupted. 'He's a very smart guy, a very shrewd businessman. Not many people make their first million by the age of thirteen.'

'Is that true?' I asked.

'There he goes, changing the subject,' James deflected. 'But way to go guys, I'm serious. I'm definitely picking up positive vibes from you two already.'

Finally, there was some commotion from upstairs. With a camcorder in his hand, down came Eric – a guy with baggy shorts and a fringe which almost covered his eyes entirely. Accompanying him was an Asian with spiked hair, who I assumed to be Rish. He ran down the stairs two at a time before noticing me and Elliot, launching into a superhero pose at the bottom.

'Oh my God, I recognise you!' I said. Last year, there had been a video on Facebook of someone randomly going up to people in a busy city centre and falling asleep on them for a prank. The kid in those videos was Rish.

'Rishi Binni Prasanna Phalguni,' he bowed.

'Bullshit, that's not your real name,' said James.

'Yes it is, I cannot believe this racism, oh my God,' Rish replied. 'Three years and you don't know my name?'

'Say it again.'

'Rishi Binni Prasanda Phalguni'

'You said 'Prasanna.'

Rish burst out laughing. 'Stop embarrassing me in front of my new friends, man,' he said.

'Will you make us a couple of cosmos, Eric, dear?' Courtney asked, as the group all started chatting loudly. Elliot seemed extremely comfortable in this group of boisterous, over-the-top personalities. I was taken aback to see this other side to him. I stood awkwardly, listening to the back and forth of the conversation until Eric brought the drinks back, and Courtney leaned over to speak in my ear.

'Would you like to take a look at the upstairs

balcony?' she said, looking me straight in the eyes. 'There's a lovely place to sit and enjoy a drink. You can get a great view of Miami, too.'

'That sounds nice,' I said. In truth, I was terrified to be separated from Elliot, but I also didn't want to offend any of his friends. I turned to let him know where I was going. Engrossed in conversation with James and Sophie, he nodded at me and carried on talking.

'Come on,' Courtney said, 'it's this way.' I followed her upstairs, along the hallway and through another room, through a sliding door which led out onto the rooftop sitting area.

There was quite a view from that rooftop. Up here was a decked area for sunbathing and lounging, with a built-in hot tub and bar. I wondered briefly who would use it in such an exposed place, within view of the other rooftops. Next to the deck were a couple of deckchairs and a glass coffee table, with a folded up parasol in the centre. We sat down.

From here you could see right across Miami, the tall skyscrapers lined up along the main beachfront, and across the buildings of this part of the neighbourhood, the small shapes of roads adorned with palm trees, with tiny people shapes walking up and down the promenade, difficult to make out.

'So,' Courtney said to me, sipping her drink. 'Let's have a talk.'

11

'So, how are you doing?' Courtney asked me, once the two of us were alone. I still found this whole scene bizarre and surreal; the Miami backdrop, this stranger, who I had just met, taking me for a 'girl talk' up on the rooftop, while downstairs, a group of eccentric internet stars drank and partied.

'I'm great, thank you.'

'I'm guessing you're probably a little overwhelmed. I know I was, the first time I met these guys. I could tell when you walked in – please don't be offended – that here was somebody just like me. Somebody normal, thank God,' she laughed, tossing her hair back. I noticed that Courtney was wearing very little makeup compared to the others, but her face was very naturally pretty. 'How long have you and Elliot been dating now?'

'A few months now. What about you?'

Courtney sipped her drink. 'It's been three long years with Eric,' she laughed. 'Every day just as crazy as the first. I met him at a party. He seemed pretty normal then, back when he was just starting out as a gamer. And what's wrong with playing a few video games once in a while, right? I didn't really think anything of it for a while. But then Eric decided to quit college all of a sudden and make videos full-time. Now, he has over five million subscribers. Can you believe that?'

I shook my head, saying that I genuinely couldn't. 'Is that what you do, too? Make videos?'

'Me? God, no. I'm studying to be a veterinarian. I know what I want to do, and no amount of pestering from Eric or his friends is going to change that.'

'You sound like you've got your head screwed on.'

'Sometimes,' Courtney continued. The brightness in her eyes had faded at the bottom of her drink, and I felt the sea-breeze send a chill over my shoulders. 'The truth is that Eric and his friends are fine in small doses. But all of the memes, and the larking around, can really get to be...'

'Childish?'

'I was going to say wearing, but you're right. Half of the time it feels like being a primary school teacher. I guess, though, that you don't have that problem with Elliot. He's much more...serious. And the two of you seem to be getting along really well so far.'

'Well, yes, we are,' I said. Courtney looked at me intently, and I felt as though I was obliged to go on. 'Well, don't get me wrong. At first, I was a little intimidated by the money, and the fashion, and the business trips. But Elliot really treats me well, like an equal. I probably wouldn't be here if he didn't, to be honest.'

'Of course. If you don't mind me asking, has he mentioned anything about next steps – moving in together, that sort of thing?'

'We're getting there. But, why all of the questions?'

'I'm sorry. I didn't mean to make you uncomfortable,' she smiled, placing her hand on my shoulder. 'I'm just being curious, you know, looking out for a new friend.'

'Do I need looking out for?'

'To be honest, it's a relief, running into somebody like you around here,' she said, deftly swerving around the question. 'Most of the people I have to hang around with are other internet 'celebrities' I can't stand. You'll discover soon enough that one of the drawbacks of being with a guy like Elliot is that you'll run into a lot of fake friends. But if you ever want somebody to talk to, if you have something you need to get off your chest or whatever, I'm here for you.'

'Thank you,' I said. 'That's really kind. I'm curious. How long have you known Elliot?'

'Hmm. I'd say it's probably close to a couple of years now? Just as friends; of *that* I can assure you. He first came up here to Miami, just after Eric and I moved here from Connecticut. We met at one of James and Sophie's famous all-day house parties. We all thought it was so cool, having a British friend and all. A lot of people will gravitate to you over here because of the accent. They certainly gravitated to Elliot – that's one of the reasons behind his success over here, for sure.'

'Any jealous ex-girlfriends I need to beware of?'

Courtney suddenly burst into laughter. She almost spat out her drink, and then composed herself with a deep breath, before turning to me.

'I'm sorry. It's just a funny question to me. The thing is, I've not known Elliot have a girlfriend since I've known him, let alone a serious one.'

'No girlfriends at all?'

'Nothing committed. Of that, you're definitely the

first. Here, before I forget, let me give you my cell number.'

'Thanks. Here's mine.'

'Remember, any time you need to speak to someone, I'd be happy to, okay?'

'Of course,' I said, a little embarrassed by her boldness. 'It's been lovely meeting you, Courtney. But we should probably go and see what our boyfriends have been up to.'

'Boyfriends!' Courtney smiled again and laughed, before regaining her usual disinterested stare, as we prepared to head back downstairs. 'God forbid. The moment I pass veterinarian school, I'm going to marry myself a doctor.'

And a part of me thought that behind that laugh, there was a very determined girl who might do good on her threat, one day.

Downstairs, more people had turned up, and the party was in full swing. There were a variety of people milling around the house, most of them between the ages of eighteen and twenty-five, and I had the feeling that James and Sophie's neighbours were probably used to the noise by now.

What was different than any other party I'd been to were the number of devices on show. Nearly everybody there stood or sat, almost comically, with a phone either in their hand or sitting next to them on the table. In the dining room, a blonde girl in a *Marc Jacobs* dress was scrolling through her Instagram feed whilst talking to her friend, who was also flitting between half-listening to the story she was telling, and texting somebody herself; I watched her for a second, her head jumping between the two things going on and registering neither very well.

In the kitchen, Eric was making cocktails by floating shot glasses in pints of various alcohols, while somebody streamed the whole performance, live, to their online fans.

As Courtney and I walked downstairs, my eyes were drawn to the screen of a phone belonging to one of a group of girls who were chatting beneath us, as she sent messages on WhatsApp to somebody about the person she was actually standing with, pretending to like:

Yea she is trying 2 talk to me now and act like nothing has happened. What a bitch!

'Who are all these people?' I whispered to Courtney.

'They're all different really. Some of them are friends of James and Sophie – fellow YouTubers, vloggers and stuff. A few are socialites and the kids of rich New Yorkers, who are on… well, what you'd call a permanent spring break. Do you see the girl there, standing with the guy wearing glasses over by the counter?'

I nodded.

'That's Pandora Van Der Bakker. She's a promoter for *Estée Lauder*, the skincare and make-up company, as well as being one of the most important social managers in New York. As I happen to know, she manages some of the biggest Internet stars on the East Coast. Standing next to her is Tristan Hughes. He's a fashion influencer, like Elliot. And he's a *major* hottie,' Courtney said.

I looked over. The man standing next to the girl called Pandora (who instantly stood out from the crowd) wasn't too eye-catching at first, but then he turned and I saw exactly what Courtney meant. He was mid-sentence, adjusting his glasses in a cool and yet determined way, and showing off a set of perfectly straight white teeth as he smiled. Having spent the time I had with Elliot, I could see how much the two of them had in common: the careful composure, the way they dressed, the way they stood and smiled...

He was mid-sentence. 'Of course, in such a difficult situation, one is forced to improvise. That's what I mean. I can scarcely remember the last time that a planned trip to the Caribbean actually *went* as planned...'

They even sounded the same! Looking at Tristan was like looking at one of Elliot's classmates, if Elliot had been to a special school for influencers. The way he stood, hips slightly bent, lips just ever-so-slightly pursed, as though poised to speak. It was part of a performance, like an outfit you put on before going to a party.

'Ah, there you are,' came Elliot's voice, aptly timed, from over my shoulder. I turned around and saw that he was standing with someone – a woman in her mid-thirties, with short brown hair. 'I told James that if I let any of these god-awful people steal you from me, I'd never forgive myself.' He looked at Courtney and smiled. 'I see you've been getting better acquainted. That's wonderful.'

'We've certainly set the world to rights,' Courtney smiled at him.

'You don't say. Poppy, there's somebody who I'd like to you meet. This is one of my agents, Kamara.'

'It's a pleasure to meet you,' she said, extending her hand to me. I shook it apprehensively. With her formal handbag and her black dress, Kamara didn't look at all like most of the people here. In fact, she looked like the type of person who would have avoided a party such as this one like the plague.

'Nice to meet you,' I said.

'Kamara is in charge of everything I do while I'm in the States. She's my eyes and ears over here. She keeps me in touch with all of the fashion developments going on, companies, promotions, and so on.'

'I try my best,' she said, with a fake bashfulness which suggested she knew just exactly how important she was to Elliot. 'Elliot says it's your first time in Miami? You just *have* to take a walk through the Design District. If you like your architecture, it's a must-see.'

'We'll be sure to check it out.'

'Fantastic. Well,' she said, turning to Elliot, 'I'll let you know as soon as I have an update from *Hugo Boss*. And if you can look through that paperwork, as soon as you get a chance, I'd appreciate it. It was nice meeting you, Poppy.'

She kissed Elliot on the cheek, and then came to me. Not quite knowing what to do, I carried out the pretentious cheek-kiss without a hitch, despite the fact that there was nothing in the world I wanted to do less. Kamara turned and walked back out through the hallway and let herself out of the house.

'You must be getting pretty tired, I expect,' Elliot said, taking me to one side. 'How about we finish these drinks and get out of here?'

'Are you sure?'

'Please. These parties are so exceedingly dull to me. We've made an appearance, but there are about a million better things we could be doing than listening to the bourgeoisie complaining about how unreliable room service is. Unless you want to stay a little longer?'

'No, I think I've seen quite enough for one day,' I said, more than a little exhausted.

'I'm really grateful for you coming today,' Elliot said, as we took our coats, said goodbye to a few of the guests, and made our way outside.

'Of course,' I said. 'So, you have an agent just for the

U.S.? I didn't realise how much work went into your business.'

'It's difficult staying on top of everything going on thousands of miles away. Kamara looks after my relations with publicity agents, and lets me know whenever there might be an opportunity I might be interested in. And she also keeps me on brand and connected with everything that's hip and cool. If everyone on the East Coast is suddenly into soy milk, or basketball shoes, or bonsai trees, Kamara lets me know.'

We set off, driving back across the sea to the Miami mainland. Deep down, I felt so glad to be free of all of the noise and chaos of James and Sophie's party.

'And you have more than one agent?' I asked.

'I have a few, yes. But the truth is, Kamara is really in a league of her own. I'm thinking of firing my UK agent, actually. I was managing everything on my own before, and I know I was doing a damned sight of a better job than she is.'

'She?'

'Oh, don't be suggesting anything,' Elliot said, 'it's all strictly professional. But it's something I've been meaning to do for a while. When we get back, I need to sort out some alternate representation out for my work in the UK.'

12

The moment he entered the courtroom, Elliot looked around, and his eyes suddenly latched on to me from his position at the front of the room. He looked at me through all of the people, as if, for a moment there were only the two of us there.

I froze, transfixed, like a rabbit in headlights.

More and more people filtered into the courtroom, squashing and barricading me into place on the bench I had chosen. If I had thought that sitting at the back, nestled in amongst the spectators, was going to allow me to keep a low profile, all of that had just flown straight out of the window.

I don't know what went through Elliot's head in those few moments. I don't know if he felt any emotion at all; if his conscience panged at the sight of my face still alive, still breathing, the face of someone who knew Elliot for who he was. Whatever he felt, he and I sat transfixed, eyes interlocked, for what felt like a century.

'Please be seated, the court is in session for the case of the Crown vs. Gardner,' came the voice of the clerk.

And then it was gone, and he looked across at the judge to confirm his name and that he understood the nature of the charges, and so on. People shuffled uncomfortably in their seats. I had never stepped foot in a courtroom before, but I could quickly glean a sense for who was sitting where – the prosecution and defence, the journalists and family members, and finally – the jury.

Here were the twelve men and women upon whom the fate of Elliot Gardner would rest. And although they didn't know it, they might as well have been presiding over me as well.

I looked them over each in turn. There was the thirty-something year old man with the light-blue shirt, who could've been some sort of manager – I imagined him taking the dog out for a walk, dropping the kids off at football practice in some type of big car with plenty of boot space. Would he see himself reflected in Elliot's neat hairstyle, his expensive suit and his well-spoken manner? Would the woman sitting next to him in her fifties see past Elliot's lies and understand him for who he really was? What did I think of the older, thin-looking man who was looking down at his feet – was it antipathy for men like Elliot in his expression, or a hatred for the law and everything it stood for?

Looking across the twelve people who had been plucked at random from the public to take on their civic duty gave me no indications whatsoever.

At the front of the room was Elliot's lawyer, Quentin Lautkin QC, an impeccably-dressed barrister with a straight back and long legs, and sitting next to him was a blonde woman, possibly another barrister, who was shuffling through her folders of paperwork on the desk in front of them. Parallel to them were a couple of lawyers for the prosecution. I could spot the difference between the two legal teams straight away, and I wondered just how much Elliot was paying for one of the most prestigious legal organisations in the country to represent him in court.

There were also a series of people sitting behind them, in the first couple of rows. I supposed that these would be the witnesses; a coroner, perhaps, or a forensics professional for the prosecution, and, well... Elliot's witnesses could be spotted from a mile away.

'You are charged with murder under the common law, in that you, Elliot Gardner, did on the 3rd April 2018, unlawful kill Rebecca Jane Doherty at your place of residence, with malice aforethought. Do you understand the nature of the charge?'

'Yes,' said Elliot. He didn't look my way this time around. 'Yes, I do.'

'How do you plead, guilty or not guilty?'

'Not guilty,' he said.

'Very well,' said the clerk. 'You may be seated.'

The biggest day of my life so far was about to begin.

As the jury were sworn in, I kept my eyes fixed firmly on Elliot, and for the first time in his life, he looked rattled. I'd seen him at professional photo-shoots, public events and private parties – always smiling, always acting like the most confident person in the entire world. And yes, he was still smiling. But I could see moments when the smile dropped and was replaced with something else. I could see moments when Elliot, at just over six feet tall, looked incredibly small.

The prosecution made their opening statement to the members of the jury.

I won't bore you with the detail, but the narrative was something like this: 'Elliot Gardner is a man who thinks he can get away with anything. He enjoys the high life – fast cars and expensive clothes. He is, in fact, so brazen, that he thinks he can get away with murdering an innocent girl, by pulling the wool over the eyes of everybody in this courtroom.'

'But if Elliot thinks he can run away from owning up to his responsibility for Rebecca Doherty's life, he is wrong. The evidence will show that Elliot and Rebecca were alone in his apartment, and that Rebecca was pushed – forcefully – from his balcony overlooking the Thames.'

'We know that Elliot and Rebecca had an argument that night. What we won't likely ever know are what the final moments of Rebecca's life looked like. To repeat: there were only two people in Elliot Gardner's apartment that night. Only one of them can be here today.'

'The other, Rebecca, is not with us. You – the jury – must find justice for her.'

It was a passionate plea, and Elliot sat through it all with his face fixed firmly; not too hurt as to appear guilty of what he'd done, and yet not so unphased as to look as though he wasn't taking any of the allegations extremely seriously.

The people in the jury sat and listened intently to the prosecutor, who walked up and down the courtroom frowning and speaking as though we were all good friends who knew right from wrong, all good and honest citizens – all except for Elliot, that is.

'Very well,' said the judge to the prosecutor, when he had finished. 'You may proceed in calling your first witness to the stand.'

'Thank you, Your Honour. The prosecution calls PC Claire Gasforth as our first witness.'

'And do you recall what Mr Gardner was wearing at the time of his arrest, Miss Gasforth?'

'Yes,' she replied. She had her eyes fixed firmly on the prosecution barrister, only glancing up momentarily to take in a view of the people sitting at the back of the courtroom. 'He was wearing a blue shirt, grey trousers, and a pair of brown leather shoes.'

'Did you make a note of Elliot's clothing in your report?'

'At the time, it wasn't my priority, no.'

'But you remember clearly what Mr Gardner was wearing?'

'Yes,' she replied. 'I spent some time with him in the police car, and it's part of our job to make a mental note of the appearance of any of our potential subjects.'

The prosecutor was taking his time, showing the jury the facts which he wanted to them to see in a methodical, structured manner.

'In hindsight, *was* there anything notable about Mr Gardner's appearance at the time of his arrest?' he asked.

'Yes, slightly. I found it unusual that a person who had been woken from his sleep, and had called the police immediately upon waking, had been able to put so much effort into his appearance before we arrived at the scene.'

'Thank you. Do you recall the time of the arrest, Ms Gasforth?'

'Yes, it's written in the arrest report. 1.52am.'

'And the 999 call was made at...let's see...' the prosecutor took his time looking through an assortment of papers in front of him, with an almost amusing level of theatre. '1.38, is that correct?'

'To my knowledge, yes.'

'So that's fourteen minutes between, if we are to believe Mr Gardner's statement, Rebecca Doherty falling to her death, and Mr Gardner's arrest. Do you think it would be possible for a person to get dressed, to the level in which Elliot Gardner presented himself to the police, in that amount of time?'

'I would find it unlikely. It would be possible to throw on some clothes, perhaps,' she added, and I felt with an increasing level of horror that the case against Elliot was already looking extremely flimsy.

'Did Mister Gardner say anything to you in the car?' asked the prosecutor. Was this really all they had to go on – some aspersions about Elliot's dress sense? There was absolutely no way a jury would convict on the fact that Elliot was wearing freshly ironed clothes. Even I thought it likely that Elliot would pick out something decent to wear if he knew the police, and possibly journalists, were about to turn up on his doorstep.

'Yes, he did. He said that he never thought she – Rebecca, that is – would do something like this in a million years.'

'So he was sure, then, that Rebecca had committed suicide, despite the fact that he was supposedly asleep at the time of her death?'

'Yes, he was quite clear about that,' said PC Gasforth.

'Thank you. I will now pass you over to my learned friend for further questions,' said the prosecutor.

I wrung my hands in despair. Everything so far had been completely circumstantial – a series of rumours about a man acting suspiciously – all of it discountable and none of it worthy of passing sentence upon. If things carried on like this, Elliot would be a free man before the week was over.

During the first break of the day, I wandered out into the main corridor of the court and looked for Neil. The courthouse was a hubbub of activity; barristers and the members of the public from the viewer's gallery rushed to the toilets and spilled out into the dining area. I didn't know where Elliot or the members of the jury were. It seemed as though they had been kept separate to the rest of us, probably for their safety and security reasons.

Sitting at a small table at the end of the room I spotted him, coffee and papers in hand. He was poring through a set of documents in front of him while another man, who I recognised as the lead prosecutor, ate a sandwich, and listened to him speak.

I was making my way through the lingering people towards him when a hand touched my arm. I turned and

114

looked in shock. The face of the girl in front of me was one I recognised well from Elliot's past. It was Sophie Romana, who I had first met at the party in Miami. As usual, she was wearing her makeup to high heaven, and she flashed me a deadly smile.

'Oh my God, I thought it was you!' she said, her cheeks glowing as she did so. 'This is pretty wild, isn't it? What are you doing here?'

Glancing over in Neil's direction, I turned back to her with a vacant look.

'I'm just watching the case,' I said.

'Right, right. Are you living here now, then?' asked Sophie. Her attempts at fishing for information were about as subtle as all of that concealer work.

'No, I'm just visiting.' Just over her shoulder, I saw Sophie's boyfriend, James, grabbing them both a coffee. 'What about you? What are you two doing here?'

'Well, we were asked to come. By Elliot. I can't imagine what it's like, being thrust into that courtroom setting, you know?'

It suddenly hit me, and I broke the air with a dry laugh. 'You're here to testify, aren't you?' Of course she was; it all fit together. 'Because that's what people like you do, isn't it? You all stick together, no matter what, no matter whose innocent lives are caught in the crossfire.'

Sophie kept her composure together. She smiled at me so intensely that I thought the vein would burst in her forehead. It was as though all of the energy concentrated into that fake smile and fake persona was enough to break through a sheet glass window. 'You've got it all wrong, sweetheart,' she said, 'because Elliot Gardner *is* innocent. And there's proof. It's really sad that things didn't work out between you, but that isn't a reason to go around slandering people, you poor thing.'

'I really don't care what you think,' I said, 'and I don't have anything else to say to you. Okay?'

'Of course,' Sophie said, preparing to move out of my way, but not before unleashing one final salvo. 'The thing is, we all heard about what happened between you and Elliot. And, well, it's pretty disgusting, really. Elliot has worked really hard to get to where he is, okay? So if anybody should really be up there on the stand, defending themselves, it should be you.'

'You're wasting my time. *Move.*'

'Right, right, you have somewhere important you need to be.' She giggled, and I barged past her just as James was coming back to the table. With people like that, any attempt to engage was a waste of effort.

I found Neil going through the next stage of questioning with the prosecutor. He was too engrossed in his work to look up.

'Detective, you *have* to let me testify.'

'Poppy. What the hell are you doing?'

'What are *you* doing, Detective? I might not be a lawyer, but Elliot is going to walk. Let me testify,' I said. 'Some of the things I have to say will be damning, to say the least.'

'This isn't how things work, Poppy. I told you. You're too late.'

'Come on. You don't have a case, and you know it.'

116

'I'm sorry,' Neil said, 'but the judge won't allow new evidence into the case unless it is absolutely pivotal. That means CCTV footage of the murder, DNA evidence, not some more character testimony. Do you have any of those things?'

I shook my head.

'I've already done you a favour by getting you into the courtroom, Miss Taylor. Now, I need to concentrate on my work. Understood?'

'Understood,' I sighed, storming away from him in frustration to order myself a coffee. Sophie and James had disappeared. It was raining outside. I took my coffee and sat by the window, taking a few painkillers to help the raging headache I'd developed. I felt like a helpless spectator to the whole case; stuck behind a screen, watching all of it unfold like some cheap court drama on TV.

Except here, things were different. On TV, everyone knew who the villain was, but here the possibility that Elliot was just an innocent, hard-working man caught up in a tragedy was still a possibility to many people watching.

That's the problem with real life; that evil doesn't come up to you with a funny moustache and a maniacal laugh. It comes with a smile and a suit, and it flatters you and insists you have nothing to worry about. And it buys you flowers, and tells you that you're important to it, at least for a while. It stands in front of television cameras and judges and juries, and tells its story, and asks for sympathy, all the while looking out for one thing: its own survival. And if you spare it a minute to recover and gather its strength, it will come back to feed on you again and again and again.

I had learned all of this the hard way. I wished I could share my knowledge, wished that I could scream out loud to everyone who knew Elliot: kill it, kill it, *KILL IT while you still can!*

But on the trial continued, without my input.

13

It was fair to say that things with Elliot were looking up, and life was moving along pretty fast. The trip to Florida seemed like a dream, fading from my memory almost as rapidly as the tan-lines on my arms and legs, and falling back into old routines felt like taking a step backwards on the life-line of Poppy Taylor. But just as I was getting worried that I'd start regressing to my primitive form, climbing back into my chrysalis like some kind of reverse-metamorphosis, Elliot picked me up with a new and exciting proposition.

It was like he plucked the fear straight out of my mind and solved it, in his usual, Elliot-like way.

'You want me to become your agent?'

'Yes, of course,' he said. I was genuinely stunned, not because I doubted Elliot's commitment to our relationship, or his desire to keep things moving forward, but because I didn't think there was even a remote possibility of me being able to do a decent job of agenting in a world I barely understood.

'Wow. I don't know,' I said.

'You don't?'

We were sitting upstairs in a Kensington coffee-shop, and Elliot was shopping around online for a yacht. Exactly how much money Elliot had at that point, I wasn't aware of. It was all just a bunch of zeroes to me; numbers which went up and down (mostly up) in several bank accounts, and which so exceeded anything I had expected in life up until that point, that from my point of view, it might as well have been an unlimited pot.

'I'm flattered, please don't get me wrong. But I don't know anything about the work you do. It feels like too much responsibility. I'd only mess it up.'

'That's nonsense,' Elliot said. 'I trust you more than anybody, and you're an excellent judge of character. You're good with people, you're smart, and – most importantly of all – you'll know when to say no to a bad offer. Those are the exact traits I need in an agent. The rest of it can be picked up in time.'

Elliot was on the look-out for a fifty-foot boat with two decks; a flybridge yacht for private trips, tanning, and hosting small parties on board for his most exclusive friends. He said that forty-foot boats were okay, but that a fifty-foot boat would really give him many more 'dividends' from a social point of view. 'You know all about *this*…this stuff,' I said, pointing at the screen, 'I wouldn't even know where to start.'

'You can pick all of it up on the job. And I'll still be managing the business. All you have to do is keep on top of what all the other obnoxious, popular rich-kids are doing on social media, and keep me in the know. Keep a track of a few diaries and telephone numbers...'

'Well, I did say to my parents that I'd find a job this year,' I admitted.

'Exactly. You get to help me out, and learn a bit about the world of online influencing at the same time. It's win-win! I'll pay you a proper wage, no bullshit – you'll be able to put it on your C.V., and I promise you, *that* will open up opportunities for you. So, what do you think?'

'I'd love to. Thank you. For trusting me, I mean.'

'Of course I trust you. Don't be silly.'

'I just don't want to let you down,' I said.

'You won't. Believe me.'

The thing was, not doing a good job as Elliot's agent wasn't my main concern. What did bother me was the possibility of Elliot and I having a professional relationship which got in the way of our actual relationship. All it might take is one wrong deal, one clumsily worded Instagram post or disastrous phone-call to ruin everything we had built so far.

Almost right on cue again, Elliot seemed to voice my thoughts out loud. 'And don't worry. I'd never let work stuff cross over into our personal lives, or anything like that. If you really don't like it, we'll just go back to the way things were, and I'll find someone else to do it.'

'I'm glad about that. But you have to really help me out at the start, okay? Because I don't have the slightest clue what I'm doing.'

'Of course. We'll do it together. It'll be great fun.'

'And no witty remarks about me being your secretary, either,' I added. 'I'm not bringing you cups of coffee and asking if there's anything else you would like, all the time.'

'Alright, alright! But I do think you'd look exceedingly sexy in a skirt and tights…'

'Great. I can feel a sexual harassment case coming on already.'

'Please,' Elliot laughed. 'You and I both know that with a legal team like mine, you'd have to put up with all of the sexual advances I decide to put my mind to…'

'I don't doubt it,' I laughed, and he put his arms around me and kissed me.

In theory, working for Elliot was the perfect arrangement. I now had a job which would keep me busy, provide me with some invaluable experience into the interesting and undoubtedly useful world of social media influencing, and which kept my parents off my back for at least another year. I also got to spend more time with Elliot, instead of him disappearing off on trips without me all of the time.

In return, Elliot now had an agent who was solely devoted to him rather than being shared across a group of clients, and, most importantly, an agent he could trust to *always* be on his side.

Elliot sorted the paperwork out a week or two later. He gave me a proper job contract, a company laptop, a company phone, access to his address book and diaries, and, most impressively - all of the passwords to his various e-mail accounts, bank accounts, and social media accounts.

Suddenly, I was in control of Elliot's personal and company Facebook page, his Twitter profile, and his Instagram and TikTok accounts. It felt like being given the nuclear codes to an entire country. Hundreds of thousands of people waited, eagerly, on tenterhooks, to see what I posted. Before that point, I wasn't even sure whether the people on my own social media accounts had truly cared about anything I had to say.

So, where do I begin to tell you about the weekly schedule of influencer-extraordinaire Elliot Gardner?

On Monday, Elliot wakes up at seven o'clock – not six, as he boasts in interviews – showers, watches the BBC Breakfast Show, and makes himself two poached eggs with a toasted bagel, and a cup of freshly brewed filter coffee - no sugar, a dash of milk. There is no chlorophyll kale shake, no protein powder, but Elliot does take breakfast incredibly seriously. He says that the key to poaching an egg correctly is to lightly simmer slightly-salted water, give it a gentle stir, and slide the eggs into the centre of it from a large serving spoon, so that none of what he calls the 'fluffy bits' disintegrate and swirl around the pan.

Then, he does an early-morning e-mail round at around 8.30: organizing upcoming events, sending article pitches to friendly media organizations, staying in touch with 'important people', and replying to adhoc enquiries about him endorsing a particular product, or working with this company or that. He absolutely, resolutely refuses to look at social media before ten in the morning. Elliot says that social media should be treated with as much caution and respect as heroin, and used in similarly controlled doses.

After a fleeting browse, Elliot will work on his business administration – settling debts with suppliers, filing information with his accountant, and so on. He has lunch later – not usually until around half-past-one. On Monday afternoons, Elliot usually has a 'influencer-slot', where he'll dress up, go out somewhere, and make a video to post across his social media channels.

He finishes work early – sometime around four – Monday evenings are always quiet affairs. Elliot enjoys having a long, hot bath with lavender salts. He says it helps him unwind.

'Do me a favour, will you?' he asks me from the bath. 'Would you see what I've got on for Tuesday? And if I'm double-booked, just push something back to next week for me.'

Not wanting to let him down, I go through his diary and shuffle a few of those appointments around for him.

Tuesdays are Elliot's business-orientated days. He will typically have two to three meetings relating to fashion – with suppliers, customers, publicists, or with one of two managers who take care of the day-to-day running of things, now that Elliot has decided to spend more time as a figurehead of the company. For a few of those meetings, Elliot invites me along, introduces me (as his girlfriend rather than his assistant, thank God) and asks me to take notes.

He has a quick lunch, or sometimes decides to work through it. Elliot says that Tuesday is the most productive day because most normal people don't really get started with work until Wednesday. He says that this gives him a solid one-day advantage over most other self-employed people.

On Wednesday morning, Elliot wakes early. He swims or cycles, depending upon his mood or the weather. Elliot has a waterproof FitBit, which he uses to keep a track of his heart-rate, his calorie intake, and his sleep patterns. He has a yearly private health check-up, a quarterly dental appointment, and a private physiotherapist.

The rest of Wednesday is typically spent producing content, whether that's by going out and about for photo opportunities, or by making a casual-looking 'home-video', which in reality is anything but. The entire thing will be scripted in advance, and Elliot will do anywhere between five and fifteen takes of a video before he's happy with it.

Once the content is ready, Elliot uploads it onto his accounts, and saves a copy onto his private hard drive. On that hard drive is every photo Elliot has ever taken, and every video he has shot, along with all of Elliot's business documents. They are stored so that if Elliot ever needs to go back to something, he already has a copy to hand. That can come in useful when a company wants to re-run an ad campaign, and Elliot wants to make sure that what he runs this time is new and fresh. It's also a good audit trail in case of any legal disputes along the way.

'Hey,' Elliot asks me, 'Did you get the latest finance report from Sinclair?' Sinclair is Elliot's accountant.

'Is it January's? I think so. Yes, I have it here.'

'Could you save it on the hard drive for me please? There's a folder on the drive. Make a new folder for each month please, so I can find it easily.'

'Okay. Did you want me to do anything else?'

'If you could call Kamara tomorrow, that would be great,' Elliot replies. 'Ask her when're we likely to be able to do the three-piece promo for *Aristocracy London.*'

'Roger that.'

'Fantastic, thanks Poppy. You're doing a really great job,' Elliot says, and carries on going through analytics data on his laptop.

On Friday morning, Elliot checks his e-mails and works through lunch. He uses Friday to plan ahead – not only the week ahead, but the entire month – in case he needs to arrange flights and hotels in advance. He doesn't actually arrange the flights and hotels himself; he phones somebody to do it, but the principle is the same.

When it comes to the weekend, Elliot likes to remain productive, even if he spends little time on his work. He will swim, row, or spend the afternoon at a horse race, a barbecue, or at a garden party (and when I say barbecue or garden party, I mean the kind with a guest list, professional caterer, and live entertainment). He will never miss an opportunity to network, introduce himself to people, and share contact numbers for future business. He also plans out the following week. Many of Elliot's brainwaves come to him at seemingly random moments, when his mind is at its most relaxed:

'Do you know what I've just thought, Poppy? I wonder if Richard Islington might be interested in a summer jacket range. Could you make a note for me to speak to him on... Tuesday?'

'I don't really like being your secretary at the weekend, Elliot,' I say, all of a sudden. My own forwardness frightens me, and I immediately regret opening my mouth. But something in Elliot's tone worries me, and that worry is stronger than the urge to do nothing, for some reason.

'Excuse me?'

'You know. I feel like at the weekend, we should be equal,' I continue speaking, horrified as I do so. 'I'm sorry. I don't mind helping you out at all, but it's just the way you speak to me sometimes. I should have probably brought this up a different way.'

'It's fine. I'll do it myself,' he says.

'You're not angry at me, are you?'

Elliot says nothing. He storms away to retrieve his computer from the house. I sit alone, and wait for him to come back.

14

It was Tuesday, and Elliot was in a series of meetings in his study, while I ran around trying to juggle a million different responsibilities as his agent. I had agreed to post something on Elliot's social media accounts twice a day for the next week in order to promote a new brand of men's moisturizer, as well as some jackets and shoes from Elliot's own brand clothing line. As well as this, I maintained a list of upcoming events which Elliot might be interested in attending, kept track of some of his rival influencer's accounts (of which, believe me, there were many), and pulled together many invoices and contracts relating to the business. I placed all of these in a ring binder for Elliot to review on a weekly basis.

And, alongside all of this, I answered Elliot's business phone.

'Hello, Gardia?'

'Oh, hi Poppy. It's Courtney; we met in Miami. How are you doing?'

'Hi, Courtney! I'm doing well, thank you. Elliot's keeping me busy.'

'I bet! If I can offer one piece of advice, don't let work get in the way of you two and your relationship. Boundaries are super important, in my experience. How are you finding the work side of things?'

'Well, it can be exhausting,' I said, 'but surprisingly, I am actually starting to enjoy it. Making contacts, staying on top of the latest trends... sorry, you must excuse my manners. I'm going on and on. Was it Elliot you were looking to speak to?'

'It's great to hear that you're doing so well. I just wanted to let him know about something coming up in Daytona. It's a spring break thing with some concerts, some VIP parties, a few big names. The sort of thing anyone who's anyone will be attending.'

'Well, that sounds great! 'Do you need me to take a few details down?'

'No need to. Just tell Elliot to check his e-mails, okay?'

'Sure. I'll do that.'

'Great! Listen, I'd love to catch up some time. You have my number, okay? Give me a call. Speak soon, Poppy!'

I quickly grabbed a pen and jotted down on a piece of paper:

Courtney – email – Daytona spring break VIPs.

Of all of the things which Elliot had given me access to, the only thing which was still distinctly private was his e-mail account.

Why did that bother me so much? I had access to Elliot's Facebook account, his Twitter, and virtually everything else. I knew his whereabouts nearly all of the time, and despite his charm, there was no reason for me to suspect Elliot of hiding anything major from me, which I'd need to know about. Except for the Infinity London thing, I'd never had a moment's suspicion about his loyalty to me. And yet, at times, I still felt as insecure as when he and I had first started dating.

Ah, yes. Well, there *was* the Infinity London thing.

Infinity London was a VIP event which Elliot had been going on about for months, and he wanted me to accompany him to it. It was like Miami all over again, except this time it wasn't just a casual party with friends. There was a more than unconfirmed rumour that Niall Horan might be in attendance. Elliot sold it to me as both a girlfriend's duty and an agent's work obligation, pick your poison.

'I've told you, Elliot, I really don't mind supporting you with all of this stuff. But I'm really not sure that it's the right place for somebody like me,' I told him.

'What does that mean, Poppy – *somebody like you*? Plenty of different people will be there. Managers, assistants, agents – just like you.'

'I don't want to go as your agent, Elliot.'

'Then don't, for fuck's sake. Go as my girlfriend. It'll be a fun night. I'm really not seeing what the problem is.'

'I don't get what there is to not get. I already do a lot of things for you and your business. But this…feels too much. And I don't understand why it's such a big deal if I don't want to go.'

'Because-' Elliot paused. 'Actually, do you know what it is? It's about us doing things together. Isn't that what you want? You're always going on about us doing things together, spending time together. I get a once-in-a-lifetime opportunity to take you to one of the biggest events in

London, and you want to stay at home.'

'That's not exactly what I meant by spending time together, Elliot.'

Elliot held his head in his hands for a moment, then stood back up and walked to the far side of the room. 'You see how much effort I put into this business. The networking, the incessant presence on social media… how do you think it looks if I turn up to a big alone?'

'See! That's all you ever care about. How things will *look*. What about *me*? What about what I want to do with you?'

'What *do* you want to do with me?'

'Well… I can't just answer on the spot. Something that isn't work-related, for a start.'

'I have been focusing too much on my work. I'll admit that. Nobody is without their flaws. But honestly, if I don't make a good impression at Infinity, it's throwing months of hard work out of the window. I need you there, Poppy. But I won't force you to do something you don't want to.'

'I…'

'I've asked you, and you know how important it is to me. It's up to you, at the end of the day,' he said, turning away from me to look out of the window of the apartment.

What choice did I have, after that? If I refused I would be a selfish little girl, throwing my boyfriend's dreams and hard work into the bin for my own petty wants and needs, and he would bear it all with a smile. He wouldn't be angry, just disappointed, and that would hurt me all the more than going actually would.

'Fine,' I said. 'I'll go. I know how important this is for you.'

And so everything would have gone as planned, until

Mum rang me up the following morning to ask that I come home right away, because there was something important we all needed to discuss about Skylar.

'What is it? She's alright, isn't she?' I asked Mum over the phone. She had a tendency to get flustered, and all that I'd managed to discern was that there was some sort of problem to do with my sister.

'What? Oh. Yes, well... sort of. I mean, there's nothing to panic about,' Mum said. I could tell by the way she spoke that there had already been a great deal of panicking done on her part. 'But it'd be a lot easier to explain in person. Skylar is going to need all of our support, as a family...'

'What do you mean? Is she okay or not?'

'Yes, she's perfectly fine. But would you be able to pop by this weekend? Just for a cup of tea, and a quick chat...?'

'I don't know.' There was vaguely, at the back of my head, a notion that there was somewhere I needed to be.

'I don't want to sound like a nag, but me and your father never see you anymore. You're always in London, Paris, Miami...'

'I thought you'd be glad! You were the one who always told me I needed to get out there and see the world.'

'And I am,' Mum said, 'but it'd really mean a lot to me if you could come and visit. Skylar's a bit of a mess, to be honest. I don't really want to get into it over the phone.'

'Is she?' I couldn't imagine anything about Skylar being 'a bit of a mess'. I have to admit, part of me was immensely curious as to what on Earth could have been going on.

'Things are... a little tense. 'I tell you what, I'll bake

you something as a little treat. Coffee and walnut cake – your favourite. Please, Poppy.'

My hands were a little tied. I hadn't been home for what must have been several months. By the time I'd accepted Mum's invitation, hung up the phone, and gone back to look at Elliot's schedule, it suddenly hit me.

Infinity London!

How could I have been so stupid?

Well, it *was* a family emergency, after all. I hoped and hoped that Elliot would understand.

When I saw him coming out of the office, I tried to let him down as gently as I could.

'-and according to my Mum, it's something fairly serious, although she wouldn't tell me over the phone. So I said I'd go and then when I hung up the phone I realised that it was this weekend. I'm such an idiot.' Elliot was watching me closely, waiting for me to finish. 'But I haven't been home for so long, and I was thinking...'

'You were thinking to go and see them.'

'Yes.'

'And not to come with me to Infinity.'

'I'm so sorry, Elliot, it's just that-'

'No, no, it's my fault,' Elliot said. 'Here I was thinking that you would actually put me ahead of some family drama. I'm the idiot. God! I can't believe I actually thought you would come after all of that conversation last time.'

'I don't think that's really fair,' I said, 'not when something unexpected comes up...'

'And what has come up? Well? What is it that's so important it can't wait a couple of days?'

'I'm not sure.'

'But you were sure enough that it warranted cancelling our plans, weren't you?' He started pacing around the hallway, scratching his head. 'God, I am so dumb for thinking you wouldn't try something like this.'

'Something like what?'

'Some… pathetic excuse. I knew straight away that you wouldn't come to Infinity with me. I knew it! And the thing is, you don't even know what's going on at home. You just jumped on the first opportunity you could to let me down.'

'Look, I am really sorry. But I know Mum wouldn't ask me to come if it wasn't important.'

'I suppose your mind is made up, then,' he said, putting his hands in his pockets. 'What's even the point in discussing it? I'll go on my own. Thanks a lot, Poppy.'

'Elliot, wait…'

'Wait what?'

'I could call her back. I'll tell her I'd forgotten that we had an urgent thing this weekend. She'll understand, honestly.'

'That's not the point. You never wanted to go to Infinity in the first place. You've chosen to go and spend time with your family. So it's decided. I'll be going on my own.'

'But I thought you wanted me there!'

'Yeah, well, now I don't. I need to go out,' he said, walking past me to grab his coat. 'For a walk. I'll speak to you later.'

'I'm really sorry,' I said again. But Elliot didn't want to hear any of it. He slung his coat on, checked his hair in the mirror, and shut the door forcefully behind him as he exited the apartment.

All hell was breaking loose when I got home; Mum and Dad looked like they had aged twenty years, and Skylar was nowhere to be seen. It seemed as though Elliot and I hadn't been the only ones arguing recently.

'Hi Mum,' I said, giving her a quick hug while my dad, who knew how situations of this sort were best handled, gave us some space to talk. 'How are you doing? Where's Skylar?'

'She's out for the day,' she replied, 'hopefully, getting sometime away from the house will do her some good. It's been frightfully awkward around here, but I said you were coming, so maybe we'll get an appearance this afternoon. I'm so glad you're here!' Mum made us both a cup of tea and finally we sat down for our talk.

'So, are you going to tell me what all of this is about?'

'You do know how to put me on the spot. 'Skylar's...well, there's no other way to put it really. She's pregnant, Poppy.'

I could scarcely believe what I was hearing. *What?* 'Pregnant?'

'That's right. Would you believe it!' Mum said, and then her smile gave way, and I could see how badly this had affected her. 'Your father's hit the roof, of course. Opened his mouth before he'd had chance to let things settle, which made matters worse. We found out a few days ago, and it's been bedlam ever since. Doors slamming, shouting matches. The works.'

'Oh my God. No wonder you're stressed.' I couldn't imagine the havoc it would have caused if I had announced to everyone that *I* was pregnant, let alone Skylar. Skylar was practically a household celebrity. It followed suit that any drama which happened to her was ten times more volatile than anything which happened to me. 'What about Kieran? What's he had to say for himself?'

'Well, that's where it gets even more complicated. Kieran says he doesn't want children. He says he's far too young for that kind of responsibility. And I'm tempted to agree with him, you know. College, university... you can't just throw all of that away to become a parent.'

'I think you're right. But that makes things simpler than ever. So what's the complication?'

Mum avoided eye contact with me. 'The problem,' she said, 'is that somehow your sister has got it into her head that, well, getting rid of it isn't the right thing to do.'

'Are you serious?'

'Absolutely. Kieran's family have said that he is to have nothing to do with Skylar, or this situation. I... get where he's coming from to an extent. Skylar is far, far too young, but she's got some notions in her head right now which, I must admit, me and your father don't really understand.'

I knew what was coming next before she even opened her mouth.

'Would you... talk to her?'

'Talk to her? What on Earth do you expect me to say?'

'She might listen to you. Goodness knows, we've tried, Poppy, we really have. Maybe she needs to hear it from somebody closer to her own age. I really don't know. But if you can do anything, anything at all, know that me and your Dad will always, always be grateful to you.'

'I can't promise anything,' I replied. 'I'm not even sure I'll be able to tell her what to do. But maybe I can figure on what's going on in Skylar's head right now, at the least.'

'Great. Why don't you send her a quick text and let her know you're home? It might be best if you went out somewhere for a chat, away from here. What do you think?'

I nodded, taking my phone out of my jacket pocket. A missed call flashed up on the screen. It was Elliot. I ignored it for now, too busy with other thoughts, and I composed a message to Skylar as my Mum left the room and cleaned the pots. There was a lot to take in all at once. My brain felt overwhelmed, and I had absolutely no idea what I would say to Skylar the next time we crossed paths. If what Mum said was true, then she was scarcely the Skylar I knew anymore; all of that had changed in the space of the few months I had been away from home.

15

I agreed to meet Skylar, after she finally responded, at a park not too far from home. It was neutral ground, and I got the impression that in this particular situation, to Skylar, I felt like just another enemy. She was already sat down by the time I got there, at the top of a small hill, staring down at her phone on a park bench, alone.

Perhaps it was the coat she was wearing, or the way her hair was blown around her in the breeze, but something about Skylar looked different; I was reminded, somehow, of a little figurine in a watercolour painting in the way she was sitting. I approached her cautiously, holding in front of me a pair of Styrofoam coffee cups. Skylar looked up at me and half-smiled.

'I got you a cappuccino,' I said, sitting down on the park bench next to her. Skylar put her phone back in her purse and drew in a deep breath.

'How are you doing?' she asked.

'I'm alright, I suppose,' I replied, not entirely sure that I was actually telling the truth. 'Work has been keeping me really busy. I've been avoiding Mum and Dad a bit, since deciding not to go to university this year. You know how they can be.'

'Oh, God yes.'

'They're worried about you, you know.'

Skylar turned her head away.

'Honestly, they are. I know our parents have unusual ways of showing it sometimes,' I continued. 'And I'm worried about you too, Sky. You can talk to me.'

'I wish I could believe you, about Mum and Dad, I mean,' said Skylar. 'But I've had enough of them, to be honest. I am so sick to my teeth of having their judgmental opinions forced upon me. Did you know that Dad threatened to kick me out of the house?'

'He what!?'

'It's not fair, Poppy. Nobody is listening to me, as per usual. I have enough problems to deal with, without them giving me more hassle.'

'Come here,' I said, outstretching my arms to Skylar. She set her coffee down on the floor, and leant across into me. I hugged her tightly. My sister and I hadn't hugged like that for years, and when she sat back up I noticed a wet tear glistening on her pale white cheeks.

'Why don't you tell me what's happened with Kieran?' I said.

'I can't bear to talk about him,' Skylar said, drawing in a deep breath. 'First, he says he loves me, and then he says that maybe we aren't right for each other after all. And then he gets really annoyed, tells me to not to ruin his life and to stay away from him and his family. Tells me he won't have anything to do with his own baby, even if I do decide to keep it.'

'And is that what you've decided to do?'

Skylar paused. 'I don't even know yet. Nobody has even given me the mental space to make such a decision. I'm surrounded by people telling me what I should and shouldn't do, 24/7. And this is a personal decision, you know?'

I nodded, and Skylar went on. 'It's not like buying a car or something. You can't just... decide something like this based on whatever takes your fancy that day.'

'It's a big decision,' I agreed. 'But, if you don't mind me saying, you must get where Mum and Dad are coming from.'

'Of course I do! That's what I find so frustrating. I don't need telling about all of the perils of becoming a young, single mother. It's fucking offensive, to think that I haven't thought of that stuff. That isn't to say it's an easy decision, though. I have to think about...about whether I believe in abortion or not, for example. And about how I could end up, in ten or twenty years or so, sitting on a queue for IVF treatment, wondering why on Earth I threw the chance away when I had it? I got pregnant, and now my boyfriend wants nothing to do with me, and that's far from ideal. But calling it a *mistake* requires, well, a certain level of know-it-all, I think.'

I thought about my decision to put off university for a year, and to go and work for Elliot. 'I understand what you're saying. I think they are just very, very afraid of you making a decision which you'll regret. But it is your decision. Nobody else has the right to make it for you.'

'Thank you. You're the first person to treat me like an adult about this.' Skylar gave me a smile.

'Ordinarily, I'd be the one who would be screwing my life up, according to Mum and Dad,' I said. 'I'm forever hearing, why don't you be more like Skylar?'

'Well, you might not be hearing that for much longer.'

'Whatever you do, you'll always have my support. I mean that.'

'Thank you so much. You seem to be doing really, really well, anyway,' Skylar said. 'How's the business?'

'Things are good, I think,' I said. 'Elliot can be a bit temperamental, but he has a hectic job which doesn't help. He's taught me all sorts about the business world, which is great. And I've met a lot of interesting new people.'

'You're really lucky. I follow Elliot on Instagram, you know. So whenever he's out and about I go and have a look, and I either see you, or I'll think to myself, I bet Poppy might be with him, taking the photos.'

'That's so cute,' I said. And then I realised that at this particular moment, I didn't have a clue where Elliot was and that I certainly wouldn't be the person taking any of the photos tonight.

'Are you okay? Is something bothering you?'

I shook my head, giving Skylar a bright smile. She had enough of her own issues to worry about right now.

'I'm fine, honestly,' I said, taking a sip of my coffee, and changing the subject of the conversation back to Mum and Dad. In life, I often found that the best way to avoid talking about myself was to focus all of the attention towards someone else.

We walked home together, just as it was reaching teatime, but Skylar went straight upstairs to her room without talking to anyone. Mum flashed me a look as if to say, well, had I made any progress with her?

I shrugged my shoulders, sat down, and looked for a message from Elliot.

My phone was completely blank; there were no direct messages of any kind, no missed calls or notifications from Elliot whatsoever. I took my time composing a message to him. I wrote:

I'm sorry we argued before. I hope you're okay and I look forward to seeing you when I get back. Lots of love, Poppy x

I waited a while for a reply, but there was nothing. No sign from him whatsoever. Finally, I gave up and went to bed.

I had almost managed to get my stuff, tiptoe downstairs for some toast, and let myself out of the front door, before Mum spotted me getting ready to leave. She must have been up early. Skylar, I assumed was still asleep. I had tapped her bedroom door lightly before going, but had received no response.

'You're leaving so soon?'

'I have to, I'm afraid,' I said. 'Sorry. I didn't want to wake anyone.'

'Oh, you didn't,' Mum said, 'as a matter of fact, I' always up early, these days. Must be something to do with my age. So what came of your talk with Skylar?'

'I had a talk with her,' I said, pausing for a moment to reflect on my words. 'She's grown up a lot. I think the most important thing for you to do is to listen and support her. It sounds as though she has a lot on her plate, at the moment.'

'Yes, she does. I'm very worried about her. And so is your father, you know. We both just want what's best for her, at the end of the day.'

'I know. But lecturing her about the dangers of having a child is the last thing you want to be doing right now. If you're not careful, you'll end up pushing her away.'

'I'll...have a word with your father. See if we can make things up to her. Do you think that would be the right approach?'

I was slightly taken aback; it wasn't like my parents to ever ask me for advice on something. Most of the time, I had been the subject of their lectures and lessons, in the same way that Skylar was now.

'Yes, I think that would be right.'

'Wait, before you go,' Mum said. She went through to the kitchen, and brought me out a small wrapped parcel, with a blue ribbon on top. 'It's not much, but I got you something.'

'Thank you! You shouldn't have.'

'I hope things are going well for you. It's hard to keep up with all of the travelling you've been doing. How's Elliot?'

'He's...great!'

143

'That's good to hear. I know it's hard to keep in contact, what with his business and everything else going on. But don't be a stranger, okay Poppy?'

'I'm sorry. I'll make more of an effort to stay in touch. I've just been really, really busy.'

'There's no need to apologise!' said Mum. 'Now go on, you don't want to miss your train. And, thank you. For talking to Skylar. I know she'll be very grateful you came.'

'That's what sisters are for,' I smiled. 'I'll give her a ring in a couple of days, and see how she's doing.'

'Alright. Love you lots.'

'Love you too, Mum.'

She gave me another hug and saw me out of the door. As soon as the front door closed behind me, I set off at a quick pace in the direction of the train station.

Elliot was still not answering any of my messages. It would be at least a few hours until I got down to London, and in the meantime, I didn't have the slightest clue where he was, or if he was okay.

'Elliot, it's me. Just checking to see if you're okay. Give me a message when you get this,' I said, recording a message on his voicemail. Grabbing my suitcase, I jogged towards the train station, clipping the wheels along the bumps and cracks of the pavement until I broke into a light sweat.

Why was I panicking so much?

There were a couple of reasons which sprang to mind, but I think that mostly part of me was deeply afraid that I needed Elliot far more than he needed me. Instead of engaging with me, Elliot had simply managed to shrug me off, and was going on living his life without me.

It was the oldest trick in the book, of course; show a lack of interest in someone, and they're bound to chase desperately after you even more than they were doing before. But it was working.

The train ride back to London was nail-biting. I spent it tapping my feet, checking my messages, and staring out of the window, desperately wondering what his reaction would be, the next time he and I were face to face again.

16

'Excuse me, Miss?' came a voice from the darkness. I opened my eyes and stretched, looking into the face of a kindly court worker who had woken me from a deep sleep.

'Yes?'

'You can't sleep here. Sorry.'

'Alright, alright,' I said, picking up my things and pulling myself up from the quiet corner of the court restaurant. I had a terrific headache, and God knew how much time had passed since the case had ended for today. Dealing with the emotions of Elliot's trial was proving to be exhausting.

With some difficulty, I recalled the rest of the events of the afternoon. There had been several more witnesses called forward by the prosecution. Firstly, there had been the autopsy report, showing that Rebecca had died from her injuries from the fall, but nothing else. It was hypothesized that a man of Elliot's size could have pushed Rebecca from the balcony of his apartment without it leaving visible evidence on her body; a point which even the judge needed to point out to the jury was an imagined scenario, and nothing more. Then, two people were brought to the stand – a man and a woman, who lived in neighbouring flats to Elliot's. The man lived in the flat next door. He had just arrived home from a night out in London when he heard the couple arguing.

'And what was it they were arguing about, if you may?' asked the prosecuting barrister.

'It sounded like they were arguing about an affair, or, should I say, an alleged affair,' the man replied. 'I heard them shouting at each other, pretty loudly. I must admit, I turned the TV down to have a listen. They were going at it for about ten minutes. Then it went quiet.'

'Could you be more specific?'

'Well, it sounded like the girl, Rebecca, she had found out that he, Elliot Gardner, was e-mailing other women, texting, something like that. She sounded like she'd had enough of it. She was telling him that she was going to pack her stuff and leave.'

'Did you hear Elliot's response to this – to Rebecca saying that she was going to leave?'

'Yes. He said 'you're not going anywhere'. 'Sit the eff down,' something like that,' said the man, who was looking across the court as he did so.

'Is there anything else you can tell us? Any details you can remember, no matter how small, may be of use to the court,' pressed the barrister.

'Well, just snippets, really. Elliot, Mister Gardner, sounded very angry. 'Swear to God', something like that. I heard Rebecca call him a couple of names, a cheat or a liar, something like that. I also heard the sound of something banging on the floor for a moment. It could have been anything, really. A chair being moved, or a door closing, or something. I didn't think it was anything important at the time. It was only when the police came that I wondered if it was something more sinister.'

'Thank you, I have no further questions for you at this time.'

After that, things had quickly started to fall apart. First of all, the cross-examination of the male witness revealed that he'd had at least seven or eight pints of beer that night in a nearby club. That equated, the defence barrister reminded everybody present, to fourteen or sixteen units of alcohol – an amount which placed him far beyond the legal limit to drive.

And of course, if a man wasn't trustworthy enough to get behind the wheel of a car, was he trustworthy enough to recall the misheard snippets of a heated conversation through the walls of Elliot's building? He insisted he did, but neither the lawyers nor the jury looked very convinced.

Soon, it was time for the other neighbour to provide her statement. She lived in the flat above; she too, had heard the details of Elliot and Rebecca's argument that night, but she also recalled hearing a scream in Elliot's apartment at the exact time that Rebecca allegedly fell from the balcony.

'Was the scream inside, or outside the apartment, Mrs Baker?'

'I… don't know. I'm sorry.'

'And did you hear anything prior to the scream? Was there any more conversation in the run up to that event?'

'No. Nothing.'

'And after?'

'Nothing at all. The place was deadly silent,' said Mrs Baker.

Mrs Baker's testimony did two things, both of which

were equally important to the trial. First of all, she confirmed that Rebecca was alive *after* the argument, during which almost an hour had passed. That also meant that the bang which the previous witness had heard was probably nothing; Rebecca died in a moment, rather than as the result of an extended situation of violence against her.

Secondly, she corroborated the statement provided by Elliot regarding the time of the victim's death. That was important, because it proved that Elliot was, at least on some level, telling the truth about the time of the fall. There were no unexplained gaps of time during which he could have hidden evidence or tampered with the scene, save for the brief window before the police arrived.

None of this cleared Elliot, but it didn't exactly expose him, either. The big question which lay before the people of the court was this: if Rebecca had decided to kill herself, then why scream? Had the scream come after jumping from the fifteenth floor, or had it come as someone was pushed, or thrown, from the building?

Without any decisive answers as to what truly happened, I could tell it was going to be a nightmare for the members of the jury.

Could anyone say that Elliot had, beyond all reasonable doubt, killed Rebecca Doherty? I thought that I could. But that was because I knew Elliot, knew what he was capable of, whereas judging an unknown person from the stand was a much more difficult matter. I could hardly blame them for thinking that there was a very significant element of reasonable doubt to be deliberated on.

And then, just as I was starting to lose interest, Elliot himself was asked to take to the witness box.

As he stood up, I could feel Elliot watching me, not

with his eyes necessarily, but acutely aware of where I was sitting. Aside from the look at the beginning, Elliot had avoided looking across at me at all. He swore himself in and sat down, calm and composed. Firstly, it was the turn of the prosecution barrister to cross-examine Elliot's testimony.

I watched on, eerily amazed at the calm manner in which Elliot presented himself to the jury and to the court.

'Could you please tell us, in your own words, what you remember about that night?'

'Yes. I'll try. Becky…Rebecca and I had been to the Libertine Club that night, we stayed until around midnight. We left because I had an early morning appointment with a couple of charitable organisations which I was looking to support as part of my business.'

'Ahem.' The barrister cleared his throat. 'If you could stick to the facts of the evening, please, Mister Gardner.'

'Of course, my apologies,' Elliot said. 'So, B-Rebecca and I took a taxi to my residence. We arrived home at around…12.35am. Rebecca had had quite a lot to drink. She began to throw around accusations that I was having an affair. Obviously, that was very frustrating to deal with, so we shouted back and forth for about, twenty minutes or so.'

'Were you having an affair, Mr Gardner?'

'No. Absolutely not.'

'Then what evidence did Miss Doherty say she had?'

'I'm not sure. Some… e-mails, or something. She was very loud. You'll forgive me for not paying her much attention. All I wanted to do was to calm her down.'

'Did you say, and I quote, 'sit the fuck down'?' asked the prosecutor.

'I can't say for sure. I might have said something like that. Rebecca was inconsolable. She picked up my laptop computer and threatened to throw it out of the window.'

'Were arguments like this a common occurrence for the both of you?'

'I wouldn't say common. But they weren't uncommon.'

'Had she accused you of cheating before?'

'Me? No, of course not. In my line of work, in the fashion industry, it isn't unheard of to have enemies. I can only assume that someone must have got to Rebecca. I've always been loyal to her.'

'Mister Gardner, can you please tell us what happened *after* the argument?'

'Yes. Rebecca was adamant on taking her things and leaving. It was the middle of the night. I thought that would be a bad idea. I was concerned for her safety. So, I convinced Rebecca to stay until the morning. Once the alcohol wore off, I thought she might be in a slightly different frame of mind,' said Elliot. 'I agreed to sleep on the sofa. I said goodnight. But that…that was the last time I ever saw her.' He rubbed his hands over his eyes, looking down at the floor for a moment. The prosecuting barrister, obviously aware not to give Elliot's performance any credibility, simply waited for him to continue.

'I woke up some time later. My recollection is a bit hazy of those first few minutes. I remember hearing something from the direction of the room Rebecca was asleep in. I was frightened; worried that someone had broken in. So I got up out of bed and knocked on the door. I waited a minute, then knocked louder. There was no answer.'

'You went from the living room, where you were sleeping, to the bedroom. You're absolutely sure about that?'

'Yes,' said Elliot.

'And then you opened the door? Tell us what you saw.'

'I...I opened the door slowly. I could tell straight away that something was wrong, because the room was ice cold. As I looked at the bed, Becky was nowhere to be seen. I saw the open door to the balcony. I panicked. I ran to the balcony, still looking for her...and then I looked over the edge. I saw... sorry. I saw...' Elliot put his hand out for the edge of the witness box and grabbed onto it tightly. Even his skin seemed to turn white. He looked up at the judge for some sympathy. The judge simply continued looking back. Elliot wheeled around, first glancing at the jury, and then at the uncompromising stare of the prosecuting barrister.

'I can't keep doing this anymore!' he finally cried out, and then burst into floods of tears, his broad chest heaving up and down as he sobbed into his masking hands.

'Oh, please,' I said out loud, from my position in the public gallery. The person next to me turned and looked at me as though I was from another planet.

They weren't actually falling for this, were they?

Of course they were. Even if not consciously, even if it only took place on some hidden place of the psyche, Elliot's plan was working. It was hard to disbelieve a person showing such credible reactions; just like the way you lost yourself while reading a book or watching a blockbuster Hollywood film. Elliot's words had transported everyone into a scene which he had created.

All he had to do was strike first. Create the narrative. And then it was a case of disproving him, of casting doubt on an already existing theory. It was what Christianity had managed to do, and nobody had managed to disprove that for two thousand years.

'I have no further questions,' said the prosecuting barrister. If that was supposed to be a grilling, then Elliot remained severely undercooked. 'Please remain in the witness stand, my learned colleague will have some more questions for you.'

Elliot nodded meekly, like a predator waiting for his prey to edge a little closer.

Like everybody else in the court, I had no knowledge at the time of the tiny piece of evidence which was about to turn Elliot's trial upside down.

'Do you recognize this, Mr Gardner?'

The defence barrister was holding up a small plastic bag with EVIDENCE written on the side. Inside of it was an inconspicuous looking, small black wristwatch.

'Yes. It's my FitBit,' Elliot said. 'I use it to keep a track of my heart, my workout sessions, and so on.'

'Have you ever had it modified in any way?'

'What? No.'

'How often do you wear it?'

'All the time, pretty much. It's fully waterproof.'

'Even while you sleep?'

'Yes. Even while I sleep. I use it to keep track of my REM activity. Sleep patterns, and so on.'

Of course, it was so like Elliot to be so self-obsessed that he kept a track of absolutely everything! But then, that would mean... I had an idea where this was going, and I didn't like it one bit.

'Were you wearing this watch on the night of Rebecca's death?' asked the barrister, his face calm and composed. He looked like the most confident person in the room at that moment.

'I think so. Yes.'

'Ladies and gentlemen of the court, may I please present to you the slide marked A.' In the front of the court, a clerk wheeled a white pull-down board to the centre of the room and locked it into place. A projector whirred into life, flickering a pale white square of light onto the board. The defence barrister walked over and placed a piece of paper onto the project, which was then flung up onto the board for everybody to see.

The chart on the screen was a simple line graph, with lots of up and downs on it. It looked like a seismograph, but I quickly realised that it was a series of heart readings. Along the bottom axis were a set of times... 10pm, 11pm, 12am, and so on. The vertical axis showed Elliot's heart rate, measured in beats per minute, or bpm.

It took me half a second to register the graph, move my eyes along the horizontal axis, and realise what the data was showing. Half a second to question everything I thought I knew.

'Mister Gardner,' said the barrister, 'What time did you say you awoke to sounds coming from Ms Doherty's bedroom?'

Elliot didn't even need to answer. The answer was right there for everybody to see. The courtroom started to murmur, and the judge fidgeted restlessly in his chair. 'I think it was around half past one,' he said.

'If I can direct you, Mister Gardner, to the graph here, you will see a sudden increase in heart rate between 1.35 and 1.36am. Would you say that corresponded with you waking from sleep to the noise you say you heard?'

Elliot looked at the graph. His face had changed; it was obvious to me even from a distance that Elliot felt like a huge weight had been lifted up off him all at once. And that was, I reminded myself, a reaction which I'd expect the Elliot I knew to show. But something on his face was worrying me so, so much.

He looks so genuine! So absolutely genuine! He could win an Oscar!!

'I'm not an expert,' Elliot said, 'but I'd say so, yes.'

'And, Mister Gardner, here, at the 1.36 mark, your heartbeat increases considerably – from 90 to 150 beats per minute.' The barrister hadn't needed to call a cardiovascular expert or any other witness in order to present this cataclysmic piece of evidence. All he needed to show was that the data corroborated Elliot's story to an unrelenting degree. 'Do you know why that would be the case?'

'Yes,' replied Elliot. 'I would say that would mark the point at which I noticed the balcony door was open.'

'Thank you. Please remind us - at what time did you call 999?'

'It was… 1.38.'

I didn't know whether, in order to put on the most convincing show known to man, Elliot had convinced himself that he truly wasn't guilty. But there was some part of him which truly possessed that belief; I could see it written all over his face.

'Why the two-minute delay, Mister Gardner?'

'It… took me a minute to pick up the phone. My hands were shaking,' Elliot said, with the clearest and most honest of composures.

'Thank you. I have no further questions.'

It didn't matter whether there were potential holes in Elliot's story. What mattered was the performance. The graph. Elliot *couldn't* have killed Rebecca Doherty – he was asleep, and the evidence was right there proving it beyond doubt.

I stood up there and then, my own legs starting to tremble. A couple of people looked around at the sound in the quiet courtroom. I felt, like a sharp knife slicing through the air in front of me, Elliot's eyes fall across me. I picked up my bag, pushed my way through the row to the end, and hurried out of the courtroom into the open corridor.

What did I believe now?

'Are you alright, miss?'

'Leave me alone!' I said, clutching for the wall and pushing past, forcing my way through to the fresh air outside.

What on Earth did I actually believe after that?

17

The rest, as they say, was history. I watched the outcome of the remainder of Elliot's trial on the news, but I didn't need to be a clairvoyant to know that he was going to be found innocent of Rebecca's murder.

The jury deliberated for only twenty minutes.

Twenty sodding minutes for a girl who had been humiliated and accused of being a suicidal alcoholic, while her body had been scraped off the cement right outside the apartment block of Elliot Gardner!

Triumphantly, Elliot finally had his field day in front of the television cameras.

'I hope that now, Rebecca's family can finally get some closure and peace,' he said. There was no statement from Rebecca's family. They were probably going through a whole heap of complicated emotions, as they tried to process the unbelievable conclusion of the court.

FASHION AGENT, 23, FELL TO HER DEATH, JURY FINDS, was the first headline I saw.

INFLUENCER ELLIOT GARDNER FOUND NOT GUILTY BY UNANIMOUS VERDICT, read the other.

On my way out of London, I stopped at a pharmacist and asked for the best headache cure available over the counter. She gave me a packet of Nurofen and, when I insisted upon needing some help to sleep, some valerian root tablets to be taken at bedtime. I took them both, and headed for the nearest train station. By the time I got onto the platform, I was already drowsy. I got on the train towards Manchester, found my seat, and then fell into a deep sleep until I arrived back home, to look for Skylar.

Following the haziest blotches of my memory, I stepped off the bus which had taken me the rest of the way here, and looked around. I barely knew this part of Manchester; a few run-down streets of terraced houses opposite a row of derelict corner shops, covered with graffiti. I crossed the road and walked along the edge of a green which bordered a line of small houses.

I found the house I was looking for towards the end of the row, and, with some trepidation, I knocked on the front door.

The house looked shabby from the front. The tiny wall which separated the garden – if such a word could be used – from the street, was crumbling, and the door was in desperate need of a fresh coat of paint. Dandelions had crept their way up through the cracks in the paving and showed their frayed, happy little heads. The view through the window was blocked by a couple of dirty, off-red curtains. This looked like a place which most of my old friends, from the time I was with Elliot, wouldn't have been caught dead in.

I was thinking about what to say when somebody opened up the door.

'Oh,' Skylar said. She was wearing her hair up in a bun, and her face, devoid of makeup, showed how taxing the past few years must have been. My hands fell awkwardly to my sides.

'Hey, Skylar.'

'You were about the last person I expected to see today,' she said. 'Well, I suppose you'd better come in.'

I followed her into the living room. The floor was strewn with various piles of laundry and mislaid items; a stack of brightly coloured bricks, a train set, and a soft teddy. I sat down on the free bit of settee that was unoccupied and thought about what to say first, folding my hands. In from the kitchen came a little boy in a bright yellow shirt. He looked at me.

'Poppy, this is Harvey,' Skylar said. 'Say hello, Harvey. Poppy is my sister. Your auntie.'

'Hewwo, Auntie Poppy,' said Harvey.

'Hi!' I said. He smiled, and then ran to Skylar, who picked him up in her arms and sat down across from me.

'How old is he?'

'He's three. He'll be four in April.'

'I can't believe it,' I said.

'Yeah, well neither can I,' replied Skylar. She looked tired, worn, and not at all over the grudges which she'd clearly developed towards me. 'I heard about Elliot. You must be thrilled.'

'Not exactly,' I said. 'Look, I feel like there are some things we need to discuss. I know I haven't been there for you. I can only imagine how hard it must have been, raising him on your own.'

'The truth is, I don't need your sympathy, Poppy. So if you came here to make yourself feel better, then I'll have to ask you to leave.'

Harvey pulled at Skylar's blouse. She let him down to play with his toys.

'No, that's not why I came,' I carried on. 'But I've been putting this off for too long. You have a right to be angry at me. I don't expect you to forgive me, but all of this time, I wanted you to understand why I upped and left. I thought that maybe… with all of this stuff on the news, that, well, it might help.'

'Well?'

'Well, what?' I asked.

'You may as well try to explain. Because I've thought about it a lot, Poppy. And there are things I don't understand,' Skylar said.

'Like what?'

'When you started going out with Elliot, you knew what you were getting yourself into. You knew what kind of person Elliot was, didn't you?'

'A little. But believe me, I had no idea how things were going to turn. People like Elliot… they have a way of concealing the truth from everyone. Of putting across a certain image, of manipulating everyone around them.'

'You make it sound like Elliot cast a spell over us.'

'That's what it felt like. I tried to talk to Mum and Dad, Skylar, I really did. But nobody believed that things were that bad…to the extent that they were.' I paused. 'I felt like I was screaming at the top of my lungs, and nobody was listening. It was enough to drive anyone to insanity.'

'You could have talked to me. But you didn't. You just packed your things and left.'

'I didn't think you'd listen! Not to mention the fact that you had enough stuff to deal with already.'

'So you just…abandoned your family? I was worried sick to death about you. Then we found out you had moved to Amsterdam and you weren't coming back. Meanwhile, Elliot told all of us you'd lost your mind. It was hard not to believe it. You ignored all of my messages, Poppy.'

'I… I know.' I said. 'I'm so, so sorry.'

There was a moment of silence. So much time had passed, I realised, and Skylar had moved on from me, moved on from the drama of Mum and Dad, and made a life for herself on her own. I looked down at my fingernails. All of this probably felt like a step backwards for her.

Skylar must have been deep in thought.

'So,' she finally said, 'you think he killed this girl?'

'Yes,' I nodded. 'I've had some time to think between the trial and here, and in fact, I'm almost completely sure of it. Elliot…has been on a trajectory, for as long as I can remember. He started off with small things; little misdemeanours. And he's been getting away with them, and getting away with them, and each time his behaviour has been reinforced, and become worse.'

'He was found not guilty.'

161

'I know. But all that means is that he's managed, somehow, to beat the system. So now, Elliot thinks he can get away with absolutely anything. Who knows where he'll stop? I feel partly responsible. I feel like if I'd have spoken up, if I'd have put a stop to things earlier...'

Skylar shifted uncomfortably in her seat. 'I don't know, Poppy. I can believe that Elliot was a bad boyfriend. But a murderer? Are you absolutely sure?'

'Yes.'

'How can you be?'

'I suppose in order to explain that, I'd have to start by telling you about things that summer, after I visited and talked to you in the park.'

'Things seemed pretty good between you and Elliot then. I remember, you seemed happy,' said Skylar.

'And well, things mostly were. Mostly. But already the signs of Elliot's controlling nature were starting to show.'

'How? What signs?'

'You know, little things. Condescending comments. As a boss, Elliot became almost unbearable. He was obsessed with the details of his work. If I messed up, he would remind me about it for days and days. When I came to see you, I was supposed to accompany Elliot to some fancy night out in London. He wanted to make sure he was seen with me, and I didn't want to go. So, when I decided to come home for the weekend, Elliot lost his temper.'

'I guess you preferred keeping things to yourself then,' commented Skylar, 'because when I saw you in the park, you seemed absolutely fine.'

'That was when things started getting really bad,' I recounted, lost in my own thoughts. I was starting to feel sick to my stomach. 'When I got back to London. That was the time when...'

'When what, Poppy?'

I felt the old familiar feeling of my windpipe closing up again. 'Give me a minute,' I said. The ceiling was spinning, and I clutched my head as another migraine came along. 'I think all of this about the case has been getting to me recently. I can't remember the last time I had a good night's sleep. Anyway, I was saying?'

'You were telling me about when you got back to London after that weekend.'

'Right,' I said. 'So the thing was, when I got back to Elliot's apartment it was empty, and...

...Elliot was nowhere to be seen. The bed was neatly made, with no signs of having been slept in; all of the kitchen utensils were stored neatly in place, and the apartment smelled fresh and clean throughout. I checked the bedroom. Elliot's laptop was lying on the desk, closed. I thought about checking it, but the fear of being caught stopped me from doing so. I still felt like I had to make things up to him, and I wasn't going to jeopardise that by looking through all of his personal effects.

Instead, I looked through my phone to see if there was any clue as to Elliot's whereabouts. He had been offline, both on WhatsApp and Facebook Messenger, for over fifteen hours. In his profile picture, Elliot was posing in a suit and sunglasses; his typical image.

I didn't know anyone else who had been to the Infinity London event. Well, not well enough to go asking questions about where my boyfriend had disappeared to. But then I remembered the number one rule of minor celebrity life which Elliot had taught me: *if it doesn't go on social media, it didn't happen.* Infinity was something which people wanted to be seen at. Sure enough, a quick navigate to the official Instagram page left me with hundreds of pictures to go through.

Sitting on Elliot's chaise longue, with the TV on quietly in the background, I started to sift through them.

The event was sponsored by a well-known energy drink company, and everybody seemed to be casually holding cans of it, pretending as though that was the way things always were. I saw a young indie band, who were just coming out of irrelevance and whose first album had just started to gain traction overseas, standing next to London's biggest names in the influencer scene; people Elliot and I both knew well. There were young people of all sizes and shapes, socializing on what looked to be a good-mannered, business-orientated night out. Infinity London was an affair of glitz and glam. I shuddered at the thought of myself there, treading through those B-list names and trying to fit in to the conversation.

Suddenly, I stopped. There, in all of his public facing glory, was Elliot. He was grinning, with a bottle of beer in his hand, but that wasn't what caught my attention first. What did was his company.

On each side of him was a girl, pretty, blonde, each in their early twenties, as well as a couple of miscellaneous friends, but what I focused on most were the girls. His hand was on the waist of one of them, and he was smiling straight into the camera. Smiling at me. I didn't recognize who they were, but the picture was enough. So, this was why Elliot hadn't come home.

It was obvious; obvious what he had been up to, and obvious that it was my fault. I should have been there, because if I had, none of this would ever have happened.

I waited a while, stewing in my thoughts, until I heard footsteps coming down the hallway. A key turned in the door, and I froze stiff. Dried tears were stuck to my cheeks. Elliot walked in and saw where I was sitting. He walked straight past me and hung up his coat in the bedroom, before coming back out and sitting near me.

'Hello,' he said, after what seemed like a lifetime.

'Hi.'

'Did you sort out whatever thing it was you had to sort?'

'Yes, I did, thank you.' I swallowed, hard, wondering what would come next.

'Good.'

There was another moment's silence. Elliot seemed not to care.

'How was the event?' I asked finally.

'Fine.'

'Fine?' I scrutinized every aspect of his body language. Elliot exhumed nonchalance from every pore, it seemed.

'Yes, fine.'

'Where have you been?'

'Oh, I stayed at a friend's last night. Have you been waiting long?'

'No,' I said. 'What do you mean, stayed at a friend's?'

'I mean exactly what I said.'

'Oh.'

'Is there a problem?'

'Yes, actually, there is a problem, Elliot,' I said. 'I haven't heard anything from you for almost fifteen hours. I come home, and you're nowhere to be found. And you tell me you stayed with a friend? What friend, Elliot? Why didn't you let me know? How am I supposed to have a clue where you've been last night?'

'This is ridiculous. I don't have to justify my whereabouts to you.'

'But I have a right to know where you are and what you're doing.'

'And I have told you. The party finished late, so I decided to stay at a friend's instead of coming back here. You're being possessive and controlling. And frankly, Poppy, I deserve better.'

'Where did you stay last night?' I persisted.

'At Robert Greening's place. Do you even know who that is? No. So what on Earth is the point in telling you?'

'And what about these?' I asked, showing Elliot the pictures I had discovered online. I saw his face take a moment to process the information in front of him, but he remained both unphased, and on the offensive.

'What about them? You're being absurd. Am I not allowed to be photographed with people anymore?'

'No, it's not that at all,' I faltered. In my head, confronting Elliot with the pictures had made so much sense. He'd clearly transgressed, and he would come clean to whatever he'd done, or at least spend the rest of the day apologizing to me. None of that was happening; the script I had formulated in my head was being drastically deviated from.

'But look at these. *Look* at them. What am I supposed to think? You should have messaged me. I still don't have a clue where you were last night.'

Elliot stood up. 'Did I know where you were last night either?' he exclaimed. 'No. Did you know where I was. Yes, actually. You knew *full well*—he emphasized this part, pointing an accusational finger—' that I was at an important event last night, and you even have the photographic evidence to prove it. What the fuck are you accusing me of, exactly? You've put two and two together and made... seventeen! And do you know what is so exasperating about this situation, Poppy?'

I didn't say a word.

'What is so fucking *stupid* about all of this is that you could have been there last night. It's *you* who disappeared off on *my* important weekend, but it's me – who has done nothing wrong – who is having to stand here and defend myself!'

'I'm sorry,' I said, standing up to try to make things better. I put my hands out meekly, arms outstretched, to try to give him a hug. Elliot wasn't making eye contact. He was looking across the room, out of the window, and when I tried to speak again he flinched as though I had been holding a gun to his head.

'I'm really s-' I started.

Elliot's arm flew around in a second. His open hand caught my cheekbone with a sudden crack, which turned the world into a dizzy blur of stars. I shut my eyes, grabbing at the fabric of reality without success, and then the pain came suddenly after, stinging and numb, as I re-opened them. I was sitting on the edge of the settee, confused and hurt.

There were tears running down my cheeks, but I wasn't sobbing. The room was, in fact, eerily silent. For a moment I wondered if time had stopped.

And then, Elliot was next to me, his arm wrapped around me, his breath in my face, still with a mild undercurrent of alcohol wrapped up within it. He was apologizing frantically. He was stroking my hair, and putting his hand on my shoulder, but I felt as though I was wearing a suit of heavy armour and none of his human touch was getting through. I was paralysed; unable to say a single word.

'I shouldn't have done that. I'm so sorry,' Elliot was saying. There was a look of real panic on his face, and it made him look more human than I think I'd ever seen him before.

'Don't touch me,' I mumbled, still dazed and coming to grips with what had just happened.

'Are you alright, Poppy?' he kept repeating, 'Are you alright? Poppy, I'm so sorry. I'm so, so sorry,' and I don't know how long he kept it up, but it must have been at least a couple of hours before I plucked up the courage to open my mouth again in his presence.

18

'I had no idea,' Skylar said, comforting me as I finished my story. 'You poor, poor girl. I had absolutely no idea. Did you tell anybody? Anybody at all?'

'No, I didn't. It's difficult to explain. Even though Elliot had done something bad to me, I didn't want to do anything bad to him. I guess…I guess that's what people like him rely on.'

'And you felt like you had caused the issue by coming to see me that weekend.'

'Well, not exactly,' I said, recalling the sudden terror with which Elliot's rage had appeared, out of nowhere. 'But Elliot's explanations did make sense. I had the issue, not him. And if I didn't trust him, well then, I had the option to go with him to Infinity.'

'So, did you ever find out if he'd… you know?'

'Cheated?' Harvey was eating dinner in his high chair. I wondered what Elliot's friends would think of a dinner of chicken nuggets and potato waffles.

'No. The thing with a relationship like ours, any relationship really, is that you have to have *some* trust. I didn't have any evidence that he had been up to no good. So, I let it go,' I said, sighing. 'Like so much else.'

Skylar drew in a deep breath, gazing at the living room carpet. 'I think I understand a bit more,' she said, 'about what you must have been through. Not all of it, you know? But I can, like, see the tip of the iceberg, if you know what I mean.'

'Thank you. That means a lot.'

'There's something else you should know, Poppy.' She ensured that Harvey was out of earshot, and then leaned over to me. 'I'm afraid that I wasn't honest with you, or Mum and Dad. About Kieran, and about...you know.'

'No, I don't know. What are you talking about?'

'He...isn't Kieran's,' Skylar whispered.

'What!?'

'I know. I know. It's kind of a long story.' *Not Kieran's? How was that even possible?*

'The short version is, I slept with somebody else.'

'But my main question is, why? I thought things were going great between you two.'

'It seems as though we're both capable of pulling the wool over each other's eyes on that front,' Skylar said. 'The thing was, that by the time I decided that I didn't really like Kieran, Mum and Dad were already enamoured with him. So... staying with him felt like, the right thing to do. I should have been more honest about how I felt. But I was young and immature. I confessed to Kieran, believe me – that wasn't an easy thing to do. But, somehow, I managed to hide the horrible truth from our parents.'

Suddenly, something clicked into place. 'So that's why, when you got pregnant, he suddenly wanted nothing more to do with you.'

It was Skylar's turn to look guilty.

'Well of course, Kieran wasn't going to support a child which wasn't his. But I couldn't tell Mum and Dad that, could I? And you know when a lie runs out of control and grows and grows?'

'I know all too well.'

'By the time I thought I should tell Mum and Dad the truth, the lie had grown so big that it was monstrous; it had grown a life of its own. So, rather than face the truth I let them think that I had decided to just raise Harvey on my own.'

'But that raises an even bigger question, Skylar. Why would you decide to keep it? After all, knowing you weren't even carrying your boyfriend's child?'

Skylar shrugged, helplessly. 'I ask myself that, a lot. But, well, look at him. My life might not have turned out the way people expected, but hardly anyone's does. Some people get their lives cut short by some hideous disease. I got Harvey. And not a day goes by that I regret having him.'

'That's very mature of you,' I said. 'And he looks really happy.'

'So what are you going to do now, now that the trial's over?'

'I guess I try to carry on with my life. Go back to Amsterdam, and pray that Elliot doesn't show up looking for trouble. He saw me in court, you know.'

'He wouldn't be so stupid. Besides, I'll bet you're pretty difficult to find.'

'You never know. And Elliot… goes back to abusing women. Before long, he'll probably bump off another one. Now that he's been found not guilty, he believes he'll never be convicted. All he needs to do is produce another load of spurious evidence to distract the jury…'

'Spurious evidence? Like what?' Skylar asked.

'Oh, ridiculous stuff. Supposedly, Elliot's FitBit watch shows that he must have been asleep right before the point where he killed Rebecca. And apparently his story, in which he wakes up in the middle of the night, finds that his girlfriend has mysteriously flown off the balcony, and immediately rings the police, is backed up by the evidence.'

'And you don't believe that?'

'I don't know. Maybe Elliot found a way to manipulate the evidence. Or, maybe he set an alarm, woke up and threw Rebecca Doherty straight out of the window. What I do know is that when a girl dies in strange circumstances, and she just happens to live with an abusive narcissist, it doesn't take a genius to work out what's happened. I just wish that the jury could've seen that, too.'

'It sounds like you need to let it go, Poppy,' Skylar said. 'I'm saying that as your sister. This isn't your fight any more.'

'So whose fight is it? Who will step in and make sure that another woman doesn't die at his hands, Skylar?'

'You have to trust that in the end, Elliot will get what's coming to him.'

'And what if he doesn't?'

'I don't know. But if you spend your life worrying about Elliot, and obsessing over what he's going to do next, then you're letting him win. The best thing you can do is to live a good life. Move on. That's the best way of proving beyond a doubt that all of Elliot's controlling bullshit doesn't define you.'

'You may be right – as usual, Skylar,' I said. I looked at the clock on the wall, finished my tea, and fetched my bag from the side of the settee. 'Listen, I'm sorry to leave so soon. I really am. But if I'm to get a flight back tonight then I'd better not leave it too late.'

'It's fine. I understand. But, do me a favour? Stay in touch this time. I'll write down my number for you.'

'Thanks, Sky.'

I gave her a hug, and folded away the small post-it with her phone number in my coat pocket.

'One more thing. If I speak to Mum and Dad, what shall I tell them? About you, I mean.'

I paused for a moment. 'Tell them I'm doing well. Tell them I still need more time, and when I'm ready to, I will reach out. Is that okay?'

'Of course.'

'Come here, you.' Skylar wrapped her arms around me, and I squeezed her back tightly. 'I mean it, don't be a stranger,' she said.

'I won't.'

'Harvey, your auntie's going now. Say goodbye, Harvey!'

'Ba-bye.'

'Ba-bye, Harvey!' I parroted back. Skylar smiled. Despite her financial situation, she seemed wiser and happier, a much more mature person than I'd known her to be before. That was what Mum and Dad had never understood. Part of growing up was learning to live for yourself.

Skylar had told me that living my life worrying about Elliot was a way of letting him win. So, as I left Skylar's house and made my way to the airport, I fought away every thought and memory of him as they crossed my mind.

I fought away the temptation to look for Elliot in the airport, or to see him climbing out of every taxi or hiding in every alleyway I passed.

I resisted every paranoid thought I that somehow, Elliot would be waiting for me in Amsterdam, or that he'd have broken into my home and left a note, or that he was lurking around every corner with a knife in his hand.

Still, when I got home the following day I made sure to circle the building once, and do a sweep of the place when I had made sure that nobody was watching the property from outside.

It was, after all, better to be safe than sorry.

Svetlana was gone.

I'd thought nothing of her absence when I arrived home, putting it down to her just being out for the day, but after five or six hours had passed I was beginning to wonder where on Earth she could be. I tried to leave a message on her phone, but the single grey tick on-screen revealed her absence.

How long had I been away? Was it four days, or five? Six? Seven?

Svet hadn't been online for almost seventy hours. Even for her usual air of mystery, this was unusual, and I tried to fight away the thought that something bad must have happened to her, and remind myself that people did, on occasion, make other plans. It was just as likely that she had decided to go and visit home, or was spending a few days with a new love interest. I reminded myself that it was in fact I, not Svetlana, who had disappeared into the blue, without leaving a message, and so I didn't exactly have the right to start criticizing her for doing the exact same thing.

And yet, try as I did to forget all about her, none of my worries were assuaged. Svetlana's door was closed to. I tiptoed towards it and placed my ear against the door. There wasn't a sound.

Deep down, something in my mind somewhere wondered, *could this have something to do with Elliot?*

'Hello?' I said aloud, looking for her.

Nonsense. That's ludicrous, Poppy, I corrected myself. Elliot had nothing to gain from doing anything to Svetlana, and he probably didn't even know where I lived. Paranoia over the case was tearing my life apart. Angry with myself, and yet still worried to the pit of my stomach, I opened Svetlana's door.

Her room had been ransacked.

There were clothes all over the floor, and by the looks of things, whoever had been here had been in a significant hurry. The drawers had been taken out of the dresser and were scattered, upside down, on the floor, along with their contents. The bedside table was on its side, and her papers and other belongings had been strewn all across the room in chaos. It was as though a whirlwind had ripped through here, taking her along with it. And I didn't have even the slightest clue where to begin investigating what had happened.

'What have you gotten yourself into, Svetlana?' I whispered, stepping carefully into the room.

Svetlana's bed was tucked into the corner of the room, leaving plenty of space in the centre, but now nearly all of it was occupied with clothes and loose documents. Against the far wall, I could see the tools of her webcam trade; a large mirror and tripod, a standing make-up lamp and a backdrop which she had fashioned into a kind of stage area, and a box of sex toys. I cleared a bit of a path, putting her clothes onto the bed and scanning the papers as I picked them up.

None of it was very telling; just some bills and some other documents in Czech and German; no passport, and certainly nothing that gave anything away as to where she might have been. And yet, in and amongst the debris was something which gave me a bit of information – about 450 Euros, neatly stacked and tied up with rubber bands. She hadn't been robbed, then.

I was on the verge of giving up when I spotted, poking out from under the corner of the bed, something which might give me a clue as to her whereabouts. It was her laptop computer. I slid it out from under the bed, sat down at the foot of the bed, and tried to switch it on.

The power light clicked on, and the computer whirred into life as I thought about the possibilities. Svetlana had a mysterious past, that much I knew. Could something have finally caught up with her here in Amsterdam? Or, was it more likely that some business with one of her 'clients' had gone astray? I reminded myself of the danger any woman who dabbed in sex work could find herself in. But at the moment, all I had to go off was a flashing screen requesting a password which I didn't have.

I tried a couple of things which came to mind: Amsterdam, Svetlana01, and of course, password. I didn't have the faintest clue where to begin, and I was starting to think that the best thing I could do was to call the police and let them know that my friend was missing.

No, Poppy, think about this for a moment. You don't know she's missing, and besides, is Svetlana even here legally? You could be getting here into a load of trouble for nothing.

I know! But instinct tells me something is wrong. Svetlana could be in trouble. I have to help her.

Then think, Poppy, think!

I looked around the room. Her wardrobe had been emptied, a heavy, old, wooden piece of furniture which looked out of place in this minimalist room. I crawled over to it, reaching into the small gap between it and the wall, feeling for something... anything, when my fingers brushed against a small pointed corner.

I reached in, pulling out what happened to be a small notebook. I flicked through the pages. There were some names and phone numbers, some of them circled, and pages of website URLs, physical addresses and notes. Svetlana used a mixture of Czech and English to write. I guess she found it good practice.

I didn't know what exactly I was looking for, some vital piece of information which would give me a lead to pursue. But, just as I was about to give up hope entirely, I found, at the back of the notebook, a list which Svetlana had written recently. It was a to-do list.

-Transfer money

-Find out where Poppy is

And finally:

-Meeting Andrei at 3.30pm, Leonardo Hotel Second Floor, Thursday.

-Personal security – mace? Alarm. **Security camera for flat.**

It was all the information I needed to know that Svetlana was in trouble. Desperate trouble, maybe. Who was Andrei? Whoever he was, Svet felt endangered enough to think about carrying something for her own safety. And I did wonder whether 'transfer money' and 'find out where Poppy is' were her last attempts to mitigate some problem which had reared its terribly, ugly head.

Had I let Svetlana down in her most desperate moment?

What I did have was a location: the Leonardo Hotel. It wasn't much, but it was a lead . But what chance did I have of finding Svet before anything terrible happened to her, if I wasn't too late already?

Well I wasn't giving up on her yet. And I had found, in the past, that when backed into a corner I was an incredibly resourceful woman. When motivated, I could get to the bottom of anything.

After all, wasn't that what I had done when I had begun to suspect that after two years of being in a relationship with Elliot Gardner that he was having an affair right under my very nose?

19

The past few weeks had seen Elliot transform into a completely different person with me. It was flowers and champagne, time spent with me whenever he could, compliments and attention all given to me in a way that reminded me of the Elliot I'd first dated.

All of it was pleasant, including the posh spa weekend at an upmarket Cheshire retreat, but when Elliot was asleep I would lie awake, thinking of that sudden flash of anger and the numb, stinging feeling in my face, along with the humiliation and sickness in the pit of my stomach, and I would question things with him, although I never acted on the fears and doubts that were tearing me apart.

To my optimistic self, things did appear as though they were changing for the better. In a work capacity, Elliot was nicer and more patient than he had ever been. He didn't admonish me for forgetting his appointments or for booking him in two places at the same time (although my mistakes were few and far between, for fear of his reactions), and he now made a much clearer attempt to distinguish between work time and our time. Soon enough, I started to feel better about the way things were heading.

One evening, he took me out on the balcony and we watched the sunset together.

'It's beautiful, isn't it?' he said, his hand on my shoulder, as we clinked glasses together. The way the light caught his neat hair and his 5 o'clock stubble, he looked fantastic, and I felt like the luckiest girl in the world.

'Yes, it is. Things have been really nice recently. Thank you.'

'You don't have to thank me. I want you to be happy. And I hope that I've been able to prove to you recently that I can be the man you deserve.'

'Of course.' The champagne and the complexity of the truth made me eager not to delve into my own feelings any further.

'Actually, there's another reason I planned tonight with you, Poppy. I hope you don't mind,' Elliot said. His eyes showed a sudden flash of joy, and I felt myself clam up in fright of what might be about to come next.

'What is it?'

'It's just a little something I wanted to spring on you.'

'You know I don't like surprises.'

'The thing is,' he said, 'that I've been feeling really close to you recently, more than I had expected. Our relationship has really progressed. Things are getting... serious.'

He wasn't going to, was he? *Ohgodohgodohgod, was he??*

'...and so, I thought a bit of down time was needed, for us both. I wanted to ask you if you'd go with me on holiday next month.'

'Oh,' I paused. Was I relieved? Why, then, did I feel a sudden sense of disappointment at Elliot's very normal request? I didn't want to marry Elliot yet, did I? Of course not.

'I'd like that very much.'

'Are you sure? You don't have to.'

'Yes, of course I'm sure!' I wrapped my arms around him. 'But where do you want to go?'

'One of my friends owns a holiday home in South Africa. It's right next to the Atlantic. We'll have a pool, a hillside view and all of the privacy we want. Does that sound okay to you?'

'It sounds fantastic,' I said, truthfully. 'But, South Africa?' The only things I knew about South Africa were bad. Little did I know that, alongside slums in Johannesburg, South Africa was home to some of the most luxurious properties in the world.

'You'll love it,' Elliot said. 'Trust me.'

And I did.

The next few weeks I spent buying clothes, getting my hair done and preparing for our time away. Elliot was busy making all sorts of plans for the holiday. We were going on a safari, scuba-diving and horse-riding, and much more. The whole thing sounded like a privilege only the aristocracy could afford.

'Will there be other people where we'll be staying?' I asked.

'I imagine so,' Elliot said. 'The entire area has been bought up by wealthy Brits and Americans wanting somewhere to unwind in the sun. You'll find there are a bunch of Italian restaurants, fancy hotels and wine shops. I know a few people there already, business contacts, and such.'

'That's great. I've been looking at our schedule, and there's one other thing I wanted to ask. I notice that we've got activities scheduled for two of the three weeks, but what about the third? You've left that completely empty.'

'You never miss a trick,' Elliot said. 'Actually, I have to do some work while we're away. Only for a couple of days. Seen as I was going to be in the area anyway, I thought it would be worthwhile to network and help promote some of the local businesses.'

'Right.' I had, in my naivety, thought that this was going to be a chance for us to unwind.

'You don't mind, do you?'

'Well, no, of course not. I just didn't think we'd be spending our time going around taking pictures, and hanging around with people we pretend to like.'

'*We* won't be.'

'What do you mean?'

'I knew you'd probably be fed up to death with my work, so I've arranged for you to have a spa week at The Table Bay. It's a luxurious hotel, with beautiful views of the ocean, fantastic breakfasts. I thought it would give you some much-needed relaxation time.'

'That's very nice of you,' I said, 'and I don't mean to sound ungrateful, but I wouldn't know what to do with myself. I mean, a spa *week*?'

'You'll be fine!' Elliot said, cheerfully.

'But I don't know anybody in South Africa. I'd much rather spend the time with you. Even if it does mean doing work.'

'You won't be on your own. There are a few friends of mine staying nearby. Do you remember Courtney and Eric? Besides, I've already booked everything. I couldn't really ask for my money back on the booking.'

'Well, then, that doesn't really leave me much choice,' I said.

'What? What have I done wrong now?'

'It's not… wrong. I just wish you'd have asked me for my opinion. A spa is really not my thing. I'd rather just stay at the house and watch TV, read a book, you know.'

'Nonsense. It's a holiday! It was supposed to be a surprise. I thought you'd like it.'

'Never mind. I really appreciate the sentiment. Honestly.'

Elliot grumbled. 'I don't know why I try sometimes.'

'That's not fair! I just…'

'I'm going for a walk.'

'Wait, Elliot!'

Elliot left the flat, and I held my head in my hands, sick to death of all of the tension and arguing. Elliot and I communicated very badly, him with his frustration, and his sudden ability to snap into a terrible mood with me, me with my inability to explain that all he needed to understand was that he and I were sometimes different. I didn't always want to do things the Elliot way.

I wished I had been able to convey how happy I was that Elliot had even thought of inviting me on holiday, but instead it had all come out horribly, horribly wrong.

There was a sudden buzzing sound emanating from the bedroom. I got up, went in and looked around. Lying on the bed was Elliot's grey jacket. He must have gone out without it. Searching through the pockets, I found Elliot's phone, vibrating relentlessly. I wondered for a moment whether I should leave it well alone.

Flashing up on the screen was an incoming call from a private number.

I decided to pick up.

'Hello?' came a voice through the phone. A female voice. I was silent for longer than I'd wanted to be, unsure of what to say.

'Hello. Who is this?'

The line went silent for a moment, and then the caller hung up. Elliot's phone was locked, and I didn't know his six-digit pin.

I didn't mention the call, and Elliot never asked me anything about it. He mustn't have kept a good track of his incoming or outgoing calls, because if he had, he would have bitten my head off for picking up his phone uninvited.

I placed the phone carefully back in the jacket pocket, lay it back exactly how it had been on the bed, and waited for him to come back home.

Although at times I barely noticed it, Elliot's status and sphere of influence was undoubtedly growing. When I first started going out with him, Elliot was already pretty well-off, but back then his follower counts were in the hundreds of thousands. Now he had a couple of million, thanks in part to the successful campaigns I had helped orchestrate.

With all of the extra 'social capital' flowing in from the internet, Elliot's revenue streams were booming, both from the fashion business (which had received great attention and now had a life of its own) and from the lucrative deals he was making through the advertising of the various companies he worked with, ranging from food to fashion, cars and gadgets and even, holidays.

The next big thing Elliot wanted to get into was TV. He'd become obsessed with the idea after seeing several of his peers – the online crowd, as I called them – appear on popular reality TV shows which broadened their appeal beyond their only fans. YouTubers, professional gamers, and Instagram models were all making their mark by featuring on reality shows like *The Real Housewives of Cheshire* and *Married at First Sight*.

To Elliot, getting onto TV was like hitting the Euromillions jackpot.

'Look at this,' he said, while watching an episode of *Made in Chelsea* one evening. Why he had started watching this stuff had been a mystery to me up until that point. 'Do you see that guy on the left? I know him. He used to play Fortnite in his underwear, now he's clinking champagne flutes and wearing fur coats.'

'I hardly think doing *Made in Chelsea* is an achievement, to be honest,' I said.

'Are you kidding? He'll be made for life now. Once you get on TV, that's when people really start to notice you,' Elliot said. His eyes were glued to the screen, and he looked as though he had just discovered the lost city of Atlantis, right in front of his eyes. 'TV is a massive, global, hell even international, audience. And it gives you a legitimacy which most online influencers lack. Do you know how much money Philip Schofield is on?'

I shook my head.

'A lot, I guarantee it. And once you're on TV, you can write a book. They practically give you the publishing contract straight away, you don't even have to write half of it yourself. Then, the sky's the limit. You can become a presenter, or do a documentary where all you do is travel around fancy places, eating and drinking.'

'I hate to burst your bubble, but they only make television shows about certain types of people,' I said to him. 'You need a sense of showmanship, or a tendency to be dramatic. They look for the types of people who will gladly kick off and risk their reputations for a chance at the limelight.'

'Nonsense. It's all totally scripted. They come up with the storylines in a writers' studio. Wait a minute.' Elliot pulled up a re-recording of the last episode of a programme we both enjoyed about selling luxury homes in the States.

'What am I looking at exactly?'

'Here she is, holding a champagne flute. And now, look,' he said, fast-forwarding a couple of seconds, and pausing the screen, 'now it's a wine glass. Same conversation, different drink. Isn't that amazing?'

'Fascinating. What's your point?'

'It's all made up. Staged. Scripted. None of them are real people. In fact, most of them are actors.'

'I'm not sure. A lot of the stuff, you couldn't even make up.'

'Of course you can. Google some of the people involved in these shows. You'll find a lot of them, a suspiciously large amount, went to drama schools in London or California. The rest are guests who apply for shows all of the time. Just recently, I saw a girl on one show who had appeared, two years ago, on a completely different one.'

'You're not an actor, Elliot.'

'No, but I am adaptable. I would, of course, have to be careful about what I wanted to appear on, and how. There's no point going on TV to make a fool of myself. But I've a good mind to look for a television agent, and see what they can come up with.'

'I don't want you appearing on *Naked Attraction*, Elliot,' I laughed. 'Even if it does 'boost your appeal' to a very wide audience.

'Wide-eyed, probably,' he said, laughing.

'Have you thought about that thing yet?' Elliot asked. He'd had his mind set on one other thing for the past few months. It was about me signing up to do some social media promotions of my own.

'What? Oh, no. I haven't gotten around to it yet.'

'Well, when are you going to?'

'Going to what?'

'Think about it,' Elliot said.

'Please don't pressure me about it, Elliot. Putting myself out there, on social media, is a big step. I told you that I had my reservations about it.'

'And I told you that nearly all of the other girlfriends are signed up. Courtney, Sophie, Alana, they're all on Instagram. I'm not saying you have to take your kit off or anything.'

'I know that,' I said. The thought of me doing something similar to Elliot, flaunting a fake lifestyle online for so-called 'fans' who didn't care if you lived or died, was sickening to me. I had just been putting off this conversation, because I knew how irritated Elliot was about it. 'It shouldn't be about what other people are doing, though.'

'Oh, come on! You know everything in this world we inhabit is about what other people are doing. Do you think I enjoy what I do? Sometimes I hate this work. But when people have certain expectations of you, you have to deliver on them.'

'...which is precisely why I don't want to create such expectations to begin with.'

'I just think you're wasting a lot of talent. I want to see you succeed. Sometimes, you have such an ambitious streak in you, but at other times...'

'What are you trying to say?'

'Never mind.'

'No. What was it you were going to say?'

Elliot's frustration was reaching a breaking point; his face showed the disappointment he felt in me clearer than his words could get across. 'Sometimes, Poppy, you don't appear to have any ambitions at all. You're content with what you have.'

'Are you saying I shouldn't be happy?'

'Of course not!' Elliot said. 'But don't you want to strive for more? I've given you connections, and experience, and insider knowledge. Don't you want to use that to expand your portfolio, gain new skills, develop new business ventures, improve yourself?'

'I don't need to *improve myself,* thank you very much,' I snapped. 'I'm not like you, Elliot. It's not all about carving myself out the biggest empire I can, and idolizing myself like some sort of Greek God.'

'Of course you'd go and turn it into something it isn't,' Elliot said. 'Of course you'd do that. Because whenever I try to have a mature conversation about something, you decide to get easily offended and change the subject. All I'm saying is you should think about doing it for me. It would really help me, if we were a team on this sort of thing.'

'In what way are we not a team?'

'Go on your phone, and look up Elliot Gardner. Do you see anything, anywhere, about Poppy Taylor? My fans want to see what I'm up to. They want to know who-'

'For God's sakes. To hell with your fans, Elliot!' I said. 'I don't care about them. I really don't.'

'Well, maybe you should. Because those fans are what's paying for all of this stuff, the house, the clothes you're wearing!' Elliot shouted. He had closed some of the distance between us, probably without even realizing. 'Where do you think it all comes from? Father Christmas?'

'That isn't fair. I never asked for any of this stuff.'

'No, of course not. But you accept it when it's there, just fine and dandy. And, you know, there are times, just times, mind you, when you come across like a real ungrateful *bitch*, Poppy. Do you realise that? Do you?'

I looked up at him. Elliot had squared his shoulders up, and his face was red and angry, and I noticed that one of his hands, hanging innocently by his side, was now clenched into a fist. Elliot must have followed my eyes, and then he must have realised, too.

He huffed loudly in frustration, turned around, and stormed out of the room, slamming the door shut behind him.

The previous thirty seconds had felt like an eternity. I had kept my mouth shut the entire time, and it was only after I was sure Elliot was gone that I realised my hands were shaking, and that was the moment I started to cry.

20

Up and down the busy streets of Amsterdam, I searched for Svetlana.

The city was crowded as usual; crowds of people bustled through the main streets, near the Rembrandt Museum and the house where Anne Frank had lived, outside the Royal Palaces and all of that tourist claptrap, but I didn't have time to take in any of the sights today.

I had to find her, and I had to do it quickly.

Yes, I could have wasted my time lodging a missing person's file at the police station – a move which, if I had even been believed or taken seriously, would have started a painfully slow process of searching. It was time I had a feeling she didn't have, and after Elliot's trial, the fear that I had of not being listened to or taken seriously by the police was stronger than ever. So, I had decided to go it alone.

All I had to give me an idea of Svetlana's next move was the note scribbled in her diary; a meeting with a man named Andrei at the Leonardo Hotel. Svetlana never talked about her past, but I strongly suspected she had some troubled memories locked away. Could that trouble have followed her here, to Amsterdam?

I had nothing concrete to go on, but I knew the hotel, and that was something. It was in the west of the city, along one of the main canals which led out in the direction of the airport.

I took a bus in the right direction as soon as I could, and made for the hotel. Svetlana's passport was missing from her room, which was concerning. If whoever had tipped the apartment upside down had both Svetlana and her passport, and was heading in the direction of the airport, I might not have had long before she was dragged onto a flight going back to the Czech Republic, or God only knew where else.

Before long I found the building, a towering block with dozens of floors and many more rooms, the car park filled with various cars and people coming in and out of the lobby. Composing myself, I walked in through the revolving door and made my way to the reception desk.

'Hi, I'm wondering if you can help me please,' I said. 'I'm looking for a woman, about 170 centimetres tall, dark hair. She goes by the name of Svetlana. I was told that she was meeting somebody here?'

The concierge looked up from his computer, raised his eyebrows at me, and shrugged. 'Sorry,' he said, 'We can't give out information about people staying at the hotel.'

'Please, it's important. She's my friend. I really have to find her. I was told she was meeting a man named Andrei at this hotel. Do you have anybody staying here by that name?'

Breaking into an amused grin, the man looked at me. 'I'm afraid I cannot help you. If you have business like this, you need to take it up with your husband somewhere else, okay?'

I slammed my bag down on the desk. A couple of people turned around to see what was going on. 'It's nothing like that, do you understand? It's not like that all. I think my friend is in danger. I think somebody is trying to kidnap her.'

'Have you spoken to the police?'

'The police won't help. If you know anything, anything at all...'

'My hands are tied, lady. I'm afraid if you aren't staying here at the hotel, I will need to ask you to leave.'

'Ugh!' I stormed back out, looking up at the exterior of the building for a moment. Even if I did manage to find a way inside, there were still hundreds of rooms to check, and I had no guarantee that Svetlana was even here. I thought for a moment about calling Neil, the detective on Elliot's case, then decided against it. I was too tired to think clearly. I took a bottle of anxiety medication out of my handbag and swallowed a couple, thinking of my next steps.

If somebody had come to get Svetlana, then chances were in my favour that they'd be heading for the airport. Driving across Europe was too fraught with danger, and besides, the Leonardo Hotel was one of the closest places to stay near the airport, and Svet had agreed to meet somebody here – a man called Andrei.

It was hedging my bets, but I didn't have the time or resources to investigate every possibility.

'Taxi!' I shouted, running back towards the entrance of the hotel where several cars were waiting. I jumped in the back of the nearest one.

'To the airport?' the driver asked.

'Yes. And make it quick, please!' I said, feeling that my only friend in the world was disappearing before my very eyes.

Schiphol Airport. I'd been here more than a few times, of course, with my trips to and from England, but I'd also passed through here at least once with Elliot. In my daydreaming I saw him, suited and clean-shaven, bringing me back a drink from the airport lounge, or some expensive perfume from the Duty Free shops. Then he was gone, and I was lost in a crowd of moving passengers, suitcases and pushchairs, walking onto escalators and filtering this way and that towards the various departure lounges and exits.

Where are you, Svetlana? Just give me a bloody sign!

I strode through the crowds, looking this way and that for a glimpse of her face, or a flash of her tell-tale green coat. My eyes would leap up, sure that it was her, and then I would realise I was looking at some stranger instead, and the feeling of urgency would shoot over me all over again.

By the time I got to the departure area, I was tired and my heart sank. She was nowhere to be seen. Even worse, I couldn't get through security to check any of the departure gates without a ticket of my own.

The board in front of the gate showed the flights which were leaving in the next couple of hours. I scanned the lists: Reykjavik, Breslau, Abu Dhabi...and *there* was a flight leaving for Prague – due to leave in forty minutes.

'Excuse me,' I said to a security guard standing nearby, who was watching over the entrance to the bag-scanning area. 'Is there any way I can look for my friend at one of the departure gates?'

'Tickets only,' he said, beckoning me to step back with a stern look on his face.

Suddenly, I had one last desperate idea.

'Excuse me, are you going to Prague?' I asked a couple who were passing by. They shook their heads, but undeterred, I carried on. 'Excuse me? Prague? Are you going to Prague?'

The security guard looked over again, and just as I thought I was going to be ushered out of the building, a couple of young people stopped to talk.

'Yes, we are going to Prague,' one of them said. 'Can I help you?'

I scrambled for my phone and took it out quickly. I looked for an old picture of Svetlana. She wasn't one for taking pictures, but there was one of the two of us near the docks, taken over a year ago. 'I'm looking for my friend,' I said, 'who might be getting on the next flight to Prague. This is what she looks like. Do you think you can remember to look for her, when you get to the gate?'

'Yes. I think I can remember her.'

'Great. Now, this is important please. If you see her, don't speak to her. I don't have time to explain, but you need to send me a message, okay? Here's my number. Would you do that for me, please?'

I handed her the number. She looked at her friend with an air of caution, and then nodded. 'Sure. I can do that. I will send you a message if I see her.

'Thank you so, so much.'

The girl and her friends took off, showing their tickets to the scanner, and then they were gone. I made my way down the escalators to the ground floor and found a place to sit down, feeling a little dejected. What were the chances? And if not, what else could I do except go home and wait for Svetlana to return?

'You've done everything you could,' I said to myself.

And I waited.

Just as I was about to call it a day and head for home, a message came up on my phone.

Is this her?

I waited a second for the picture to load up. It was taken from an awkward angle, so I had to tilt my head to really make sense of what I was seeing: the green coat, the dark hair. And Svetlana's face.

She was sitting on one of those silver metal benches they have in airport departure lounges, next to a man in a dark leather jacket. She was looking at the floor, and I noticed that her bag was on the seat next to her. With minutes rather than hours to do something, I desperately scrambled my brain, thinking of what to do next.

Think, Poppy, think!

It was no use trying to talk to the authorities. By the time I had explained everything, Svetlana would probably have flown, and there was no guaranteeing that, given the duress she was probably under, she would even admit that anything was wrong. On the wrong side of security, I was completely powerless, but if I could somehow reach her...

I wheeled around and ran for the nearest open gate where I could purchase a ticket.

'A ticket please,' I said. 'Hurry. Any ticket. The cheapest one you have, the next flight, anything.'

Wide-eyed and alarmed, the girl behind the desk tried to help me out as quickly as she could. She scoured the computer for flights which were leaving in the next couple of hours. I told her I didn't care which flight she picked, as long as she did it quickly. She wavered for a moment, then punched something through anyway.

Panicking, I glanced at the boards. I still had seventeen minutes to get through security and make my way to the gate before Svetlana and Andrei disappeared off into the great unknown.

'It will be one hundred and twenty Euros?' she said.

'Yes, yes!' I said, thrusting my card over the desk to pay.

Within a minute, the ticket was printing. The girl, bewildered, handed it over as I snatched it from the desk and started running. When I got to security my heart raced for a moment, but the previous security guard had gone, replaced by somebody completely new. I showed him my passport quickly and rushed through the gate.

'Hey, slow down, lady!'

'I'm sorry!' I shouted, flying through the people. There was a small queue at the metal detectors. I got into line, tapping my foot impatiently, wondering what on earth I was going to do when I arrived at the gate.

Hurry up, for God's sakes!

And then I was through, throwing my bag over my shoulder and looking for the gate number, as I ran along large, open corridors full of travellers with their luggage, trying not to bump into any of them as best as I could. Exhausted, I slowed to a brisk walk as I turned the last corner. It was up ahead: Gate 46, the flight to Prague, due to depart imminently.

Up ahead were the group of waiting passengers. As I made my way towards them, I made out the figure of Svetlana, sitting where she'd been the whole time.

I walked toward her without staring, glancing at the man sitting next to her. He wore a rough stubble, and with the gold chain around his neck and that awful leather jacket, I could only assume the type of character he must have been. All of it made complete sense: Svetlana was wanted by gangsters, and they had come to Amsterdam to take her away; away from me, and to do God-only-knew what to her in the safety of some foreign country.

Svetlana saw me first. I saw her eyes widen, and then she tried to signal to me by moving her eyes sideways to her companion. I nodded and stopped, pretending to rearrange my things for a second.

'The 2.45 flight to Prague will shortly be boarding. Le vol 2.45 pour Prague va bientôt embarquer…'

'Excuse me?' I said. The man who was sitting with Svetlana turned to look at me. 'Excuse me, I believe you are on the wrong flight?'

'Eh?' the man replied. Svetlana fidgeted uncomfortably, clearly not feeling secure about the situation. 'No English,' he said, shaking his head and going back to looking at his watch.

'Andrei,' I said. He looked straight up. 'We are going to have a very serious problem, you and I. Come on Svetlana, we're going.'

Svetlana started to speak, and then hesitated. I took her by the arm, while Andrei got off his chair and stared me in the face. We had attracted the looks of several other passengers, but I was in no mood to stand aside.

'I don't know you,' Andrei said, and he took Svetlana by the other arm for a moment. He looked around uncomfortably at the attention of the small crowd, and even the gate attendants had turned to look at what was going on.

I held onto Svetlana's other arm and threw my things down to one side.

'The police are already on their way. We're going, *now*. Give me her passport,' I said, defiantly staring him down. By now, one of the gate attendants had come over to the three of us.

'Excuse me. Is there a problem here?'

There was silence for a moment, Svet caught in the middle of us, still not saying a word.

Andrei paused for a moment – I could see him weighing up his options internally. 'No,' he said, shrugging casually, and letting go of Svetlana's arm. 'No problem.'

'Her passport,' I said again. Andrei shrugged again, but although his demeanour gave little away, I could see small beads of sweat forming on his forehead. Reluctantly, he reached into his inner jacket pocket and took out Svetlana's passport. I snatched it from his hand quickly, pulling her away from him and slowly backing away.

The man who was called Andrei stood still, watching us both, but especially Svetlana. I started walking fast, half-dragging her along beside me, looking over my shoulder.

Quickly we made our way out of the lobby and back in the direction of the main airport building, and the taxis waiting below. Svetlana was breathing fast. I held her hand tightly all the way outside and into the first taxi I could find.

'Are you alright?' I said.

'H-how did you find me?' she asked. And then for the first time since I'd known her, Svetlana burst into floods of tears.

21

Andrei, it emerged, was working for one of the largest sex-trafficking organisations in Europe; a cabal of men who controlled hundreds of women across multiple countries and made them sleep with other men in exchange for somewhere to live, a little food, and very little else.

Svetlana had been one of those girls once, she told me, flown from the Czech Republic to France, and then to Germany, and finally to Belgium, where she'd decided to run away. Although the men had confiscated her passport, she had managed to get it back – she never told me how – and fled to Amsterdam, which is where I had met her and where she'd started doing sex-work of her own to pay the bills. Now, Andrei had come to collect his money-maker.

Svetlana had unknowingly opened the door to him a couple of days ago, and he'd given her a choice: come willingly, or risk the chance of something extremely bad likely happening to her.

'He knows where I live now. They know where I live. That's the problem. I have no choice but to move; to run away again,' she said to me.

I poured a glass of water and handed it to her. As we talked, I helped her tidy the chaos in her bedroom, folding and putting away each item of clothing which had been strewn on the floor in a hurry.

'Have you thought about going to the police?' I asked. 'They could offer you protection, and go after the men who did this to you.'

'Oh, don't be so naïve. The police never have any pity for girls like me. Protection? No way. I'm as likely to be arrested.'

'Things are different nowadays. There are schemes, organisations which deal with this sort of thing,' I said. 'These men are criminals, Svetlana. Believe me, the police want them off the streets and in prison, where they belong.'

'Oh, really? And who do you suppose will sleep with the old men who sit in the government when they are bored of their wives? Do you think that I haven't seen my fair share of policemen over the years? I've seen plenty of them,' she said, still half in tears. I held her hand as we sat next to each other on the bed.

'You can't just keep on running, Svetlana.' As I spoke, I couldn't help but notice the irony of my advice to her. 'It's not easy, I know. But you need to try. Because men like... men like Andrei thrive on fear. They want you to doubt yourself, to doubt everything.'

Svetlana dried her eyes, holding in her hands a chequered scarf. I recognised it for a Christmas gift I'd picked up last year, and I felt that in that moment I was the closest thing to a friend she had ever had.

'Maybe you're right,' she said. 'I still haven't thanked you. For coming to find me. You didn't have to do that.'

'You would have done the same for me.'

'Still. Thank you. When they came... Wait. Where have you been?'

'I've... been in England. I'm sorry. There was something I had to do.'

'Something to do with Elliot Gardner?'

'Well, yes,' I said. I remembered that, unlike other people's ex-boyfriends, Elliot was all over the news. 'He was there, Svet. I saw him. In the courtroom. He spent four days convincing that incompetent jury that he was a good, honest, hard-working, law-abiding citizen. And he was found not guilty, Svet.'

'I'm very sorry to hear that. Did they let you speak?'

'No. The court case was too far along. They wouldn't let me testify. I just had to watch the whole thing from the side-lines.'

'So what will you do now?' she asked.

'I don't suppose there is much I can do,' I said. 'That's the end of it. Elliot gets away with murder, and I have to start watching my back all over again. And all because of a lousy FitBit.'

'A FitBit?'

'Yeah. You know, one of those heart tracker things? Apparently it showed that Elliot was asleep right up until the moment that girl, Rebecca, fell from the apartment balcony.'

'Do you think that's possible?'

'I don't know. Possibly. But it's also possible that Elliot found a way to get out of this. He's a smart man, especially when backed into a corner.'

'Maybe you should go to the police.'

'And say what? That I think Elliot did it, without any evidence whatsoever? I'd be laughed out of the station.' I let out a deep sigh. 'Besides, the trial has already gone to court. They can't just reopen it based on what could be, for all they know, just a jealous ex-girlfriend looking to cause some trouble.'

Svetlana was quiet for a moment.

'Still,' she said, 'maybe you should do it anyway. At least then, you can say that you've tried. I think you're right, Poppy. Right about men like Elliot, and Andrei. These men want us to be quiet, to leave things alone. That's how they function.'

'So will you go to the police then? About what's happened?'

Svetlana breathed in, and her eyes wavered for a moment again, but then she held the tears back. 'I have no choice. It's either that, or keep on running forever. I'll go tomorrow, once I've gathered my senses together.'

I squeezed her hand tightly. 'I'll come with you, if you want.'

'Yes, I think I would like that. Thank you, Poppy.'

'Don't mention it. Honestly,' I said. 'That's what friends are for.'

That evening, Svetlana and I had dinner together at a Chinese restaurant down the road. Neither of us particularly felt like home was a safe place to be, and the less time we spent there, the better. Svet had perked up considerably from the moment I had picked up at the airport. She'd brought a notepad and a pen along, and after our second course she presented to me a plan she'd been working on.

'A timeline. That's what the police like to go on. A record of every event in the order in which it happened. That's what you need to do.'

'Me?'

'Yes, you. Who did you think I meant?'

'Never mind,' I said. 'I just thought that...'

'I'm going to help you out any way that I can,' Svetlana said. 'And I know you don't want to give up on this. On ensuring that Elliot pays for his crimes.'

I didn't know what to say.

'I've been thinking about it all night,' she continued, 'and I think what you need to do first is to write a timeline. Also, you need to recall everything you can from the trial. Something, any little detail may be important. Can you do that?'

'I don't know, Svet. Every day it's Elliot this, Elliot that. I'm sick to death of it. Maybe it's better to leave this alone. Get on with my life.'

'Is that why you went to England? To leave it alone?'

'Well... no,' I said, slightly unsure why it was that I had gone in the first case. Was it to testify against him? Did I want justice to be served, or was it simply a case of morbid curiosity, my inability to move on from the profound influence Elliot had made on my entire life?

'So why did you go?'

'I guess I wanted to see whether I could make a difference. But I couldn't. One person can't make a difference against people like that.'

Svetlana crossed her arms and frowned at me. 'That's not true,' she said. 'You haven't tried. I don't know what it is you're afraid of, but that fear has let Elliot get away with everything he has done so far. You need to let it go. *Stand up to him*, Poppy.'

'I'm afraid I wouldn't know where to start.'

'At the beginning. You write down all of the key

events which happened between you and Elliot, right up to now. You start with meeting him, your first date, your time together. Any details that you can remember, no matter how small. Like this...' she said, dividing the page into two columns. 'You put the date here on the left, and on the right you summarise whatever happened; any witnesses to it, what Elliot said, and so on. Like a diary.'

'Yes, I think I could do that. But most of it is just my word against his. When Elliot and I broke up...' I trailed off.

'What? What is it?'

'This is the problem. Whenever I think back to it I get so hurt. So angry. I don't know if I *can't* remember everything, or if I don't want to...'

'You've run from your memories for so long, but all you did was suppress them. It's time for you to face up to them, internally, as well as externally.'

'So I'll start with the diary,' I said.

'Exactly. Don't worry about trying to fix the world in one go. Just focus on one step at a time.'

'One step at a time. This means a lot, Svetlana.'

'In the meantime, I am going to speak to the police about my situation. This way, we'll both help each other. And with our fingers crossed, maybe both of us will find some closure in order to move on with our lives.'

'Yes,' I said, 'maybe we will.'

But in my heart, I didn't think that was ever truly going to be possible.

So, I started right back at the beginning, and although the memories were cracked and sepia-toned, I found that once I had started the ball rolling, the events of the past few years started becoming clearer and clearer in my mind. It began with my eighteenth birthday, getting that awful job at the clothes store and then running into flashy Elliot Gardner one boring Sunday; a day that would change and shape my entire life to come. And on my little diary carried, and grew, and grew.

If nothing else, writing it all down seemed therapeutic, and although in my core I felt as though there was absolutely nothing more to be done about Elliot, the writing down of it was something, at least. It meant that there was a record of what happened, a record which was the truth, even though almost nobody else in the world believed me.

By the time I was writing about our relationship starting to break down, I was already into a second notebook. I was forming, on paper, a fairly clear definition of Elliot the businessman, Elliot the new-money socialite, and Elliot the partner and employer. I recorded the holidays we'd been on together, the money we had spent on cars and clothes and everything else; from Peloton exercise equipment to Egyptian cotton towels and luxury scent diffusers. But there was still a large gap missing in my accounts of everything which had happened.

Who was Elliot the abuser, Elliot the angry man who was prone to bouts of violence? Elliot the potential killer?

So far, I hadn't begun to flesh out that person, which was supposed to be the main point of the diary which Svetlana had urged me to complete. And if I was ever going to go to the police with my story, I knew that this aspect of Elliot's character was the one I would need to focus on the most, to lay out in the greatest detail.

It was a task which I felt was unavoidable, and yet it was by far the one which I wanted the least to do. Still, the thought of the crystal clear truth of what I was writing gave me some grounding. And so I began the second notepad with the first time Elliot had raised his hand to me, and the planned holiday to South Africa which was right around the corner.

I remembered that a feeling of dread had come over me in the couple of days leading up to that holiday. It was partly the fact that Elliot was saying all of the right things about our future at a time when, in practice, things between us were tense and uncomfortable. It was partly because of the week which Elliot had arranged for me without asking, a week during which we would be apart, and Elliot would be once again working on his precious fashion empire.

But mainly it was because for a second, on Elliot's balcony prior to us going away, I had thought that he was about to get on one knee and ask me to be his wife.

What would my answer have been if Elliot did pop the question? To say no would be to drive an irremovable wedge between us; to accept would be to cement myself into a relationship which I was still trying to work out, a relationship which made me feel increasingly unnerved instead of loved. But of course, the pressure of wanting to please my parents and to make things work with Elliot hung heavily over my head.

I mulled over the question again and again, searching inside myself for the right answer. I contemplated it as Elliot drove us both to the airport, and as we sat and waited in the VIP lounge with a couple of drinks and a sandwich, and then as the plane lifted off from the runway and took us high up into the clouds, and in the several hours that followed, until finally...

...the plane was descending through the clouds again, and there were green hills below, and beyond them lay the glittering Southern Atlantic, an awesome coastline lined with pearly white towers of rock, while further inland, staggering mountains rose up from the flat land.

Elliot was asleep. I nudged him awake and pointed out of the window.

'Look at that! It looks so beautiful from up here,' I said, forgetting that he had seen all of this several times before.

'Yep. Can you believe these headrests? I've a good mind to put in a complaint.'

'You haven't flown economy in a while, have you?'

'No. And I don't plan to again, either. Hey, look over there, on your right. Do you see those houses up on the hills?'

I looked out below. The foothills were full of green grass, and had winding roads snaking up them with lush houses on either side. They were separated by gardens filled with palm trees, shrubs and swimming pools. The houses were square, white, multi-layered homes with large glass windows on every face, and they wouldn't have looked out of place in the foothills of California.

'It looks incredible.'

'The area is called Camp's Bay. That's where we'll be staying. Isn't it stunning?'

I nodded. Elliot had, once again, pulled out all the stops.

'Is everything okay today? You seem quiet.'

'Yes, of course,' I smiled. 'I was just wondering if I'd packed enough things.'

'Ah. Well, rest assured, there'll be plenty of opportunity to pick things up here. If you want anything, anything at all, all you need do is just say the word.'

We got to the house as the sun was falling towards the horizon, casting its amber glow across the sea and over the mountains in front of us. As we turned up the final stretch of road, we were welcomed by the gates and the gardens of the properties all lit up, with spotlights illuminating the palms and fountains in the front gardens, though the houses themselves were obscured from view by the trees and the natural geography. The car drew up to an electric gate which opened up for us to pass through, and then right around the corner I saw the place where Elliot and I were going to stay.

'Oh, wow,' I gasped out loud.

The driveway led up to the back of a three-storey, spectacular modern building, inset with large, glass windows and a garage which could have housed at least a handful of cars. There were trees obscuring most of the living space from view, but as we pulled up I could make out a bit of the open-plan interior, and at the rear a set of deckchairs, and an infinity pool which looked out onto the sea below.

'I know I shouldn't ask, but how much is this place worth?'

'Oh, a good few million,' Elliot said, taking my hand and showing me inside, as our taxi-driver followed several feet behind with all of our suitcases.

22

The next few days were beyond a dream; calamari at one of the top restaurants in the world, according to the 2016 *Mercedes-Benz Restaurant Awards*, cocktails and tanning by the pool, shopping and sampling the nightlife in Cape Town, and a trip to a private game reserve. All of it was so adventurous, so mesmerizing that any issues I'd had with Elliot or about our future together had completely vanished from my mind.

And yet, as he and I had tea for two in a lodge at the dry and yet picturesque Karoo Highlands, the illusion that we were on a peaceful, trouble-free couple's holiday was about to be shattered.

'How do you like the sandwiches?' Elliot asked. In truth, poached salmon wasn't my cup of tea, and I'd much rather have had corned beef or cheese and pickle, but I smiled politely and told him that the dinner was excellent, as usual.

'They're lovely, thank you.'

'You know, on Tuesday I have to do that work I told you about.'

'I know.'

'Hopefully, it should only be four days, or five at the most. I've tried to pack everything in, so that the rest of our holiday can be spent together.' Elliot looked at me, searching for something, but the truth was that I didn't have anything to say in response.

He continued. 'And you'll be staying at...'

'At the Turtle Bay. Yes. I know.'

'You'll be alright, won't you?' Elliot asked. 'I've arranged for Courtney to come down and spend some time with you. You remember Courtney, right?'

'Yes. I'll be fine,' I said, screaming internally for this pointless conversation to come to an end. 'Is she staying there too?'

'She'll be staying for the week. You two can spend some time catching up, go out to eat, enjoy yourselves. Have some girly time. You won't have to put up with me for a change.'

'Mhm,' I said, as I sipped my glass of prosecco and looked away. For a second, I remembered that right about now, if things had gone differently, I'd have been studying for a psychology degree, living off tins of beans in some trashy, student accommodation. Elliot, by contrast, had given me a credit card, which he paid off every month. It was mine to do with, essentially as I wished, and I was determined to make him regret the next week by charging as much as was humanly possible to it in the time available.

'Great. That's sorted then. You know, I really appreciate you supporting my work, Poppy.'

'Of course,' I said, finishing my drink. Well, it wasn't as though I had much of a choice in the matter.

So, on Tuesday morning, Elliot helped me pack my things into a taxi and shipped me off to the *Table Bay*, a large and elegant hotel which looked straight out across the bay from its ornate columned exterior and sat beneath the imposing plate-like Table Mountain.

Although he must have been slightly guilt-stricken, I was determined not to let him off the emotional hook. I gave him the smallest of kisses on the cheek as we said our goodbyes, and when the taxi drove off I didn't look back.

Having access to Elliot's diary, I knew that the next few days of his were indeed packed. He was having numerous meetings to explore developing new parts of his company; South Africa brought opportunities to the table for expansion and promotion of Elliot's fashion brand. He would also be promoting a number of businesses based in Cape Town and Johannesburg. Being on holiday as an influencer meant showing the fans and followers a taste of the lifestyle.

I was glad that Elliot had kept our private life away from the public eye, at least, but it meant that he now had to have *two* holidays. The first was the real holiday, but the second was a photogenic, filtered, fake holiday, condensed into a couple of thirty-second videos and a dozen photographs. Elliot having dinner at a top restaurant, Elliot riding a hot-air balloon over vineyards, Elliot relaxing in a hot-tub, while still somehow managing to flaunt off his watch and keep it bone-dry.

Everything was fake, and the people at home ate it all up like suckers. They thought they were seeing the real lives of the rich and famous, but all they were really seeing were fake set-pieces. Elliot was good at it; all of the showing off came naturally to him, even if he didn't like to admit it.

I met Courtney not long after. Her and Eric had come

down for the summer of the Southern Hemisphere. She looked glad to be rid of him for a few days. I noticed she'd dyed her hair blonde, and she was wearing fake eyelashes as well; a definite contrast from the Courtney I'd met back in Miami.

'Well, isn't this just peachy,' she said, eyeing up the place as we greeted each other. 'Aaaand there we go! I spy a bar. Come on, hun; I'm well overdue for a drink.'

'A drink? It's not even 11 o'clock!'

'And your point is? Big fancy place like this, it's practically mandatory to have consumed several drinks before lunch-time. It would be rude not to,' she smirked, and took me over to sit at an empty booth in the corner of the deserted bar. On the far side of the room, a few people were having continental breakfasts and waiting for taxis to arrive.

'It's great to see you,' I said, when we'd bought our drinks. 'I have to admit, I was a little nervous about coming on holiday to South Africa. Especially when Elliot mentioned that he needed to work for a couple of days.'

'I can imagine. Still, I'll bet you're glad to be away from him for a while. Swimming pool, scotch on the rocks, and we can shop till we drop from sunrise to sundown. What more could a person possibly need?'

I smiled, realizing that Courtney valued time away from Eric in a way that I couldn't really understand. In contrast, I hated being away from Elliot. 'How's Eric? Is he working too?'

'Working? Eric? P-lease,' Courtney laughed, as she traced a circle around the edge of her glass with her finger. 'He's playing in a goddamned video game tournament all week. Blowing stuff up. Pew, pew. He tries telling me all about it, but the less I hear about it the better. Anyway, how are you and Elliot? I believe you two have had quite the romantic week together.'

Puzzled, I nodded. 'How do you...?'

'Oh, you should know by now that nothing is a secret around here. Has he, you know, yet?' she waved her ring finger around while grinning hysterically.

'What? God, no. I don't think that's on the cards just yet. But things are moving in the right direction. He's just always busy with work. It's never-ending, meetings and promotions. Elliot absorbs himself in it.'

'Mhmm. Elliot has always been obsessed with his business. Sometimes, you need to pull the reins back in a little. Tell him if he doesn't pay you enough attention, you're going to go and find someone who will.'

'I wouldn't ever say anything like that,' I said. 'Do you think I'm ambitious, Courtney?'

'I dunno. Sure, I guess. What makes you ask that?'

'Oh, it's not really important. It's just something Elliot said a while ago, when we were having an argument. He said I wasn't ambitious enough.'

'That's ridiculous.'

'Well, that's what I thought. I've been helping Elliot with the business, and so on. But he wants me to set up my own online profiles, and start doing what he does. But just because I don't want a multi-million-dollar business doesn't mean I don't want to do anything with my life.'

'Yeah, but it's a ridiculous thing to say, regardless. Listen, hun, nobody admits it, but people like us – all we need to do is stay young and look pretty. We're the equivalent of footballers' wives, *WAGs*, I think you call them in Britain.'

'Elliot and I...we're not like that.' *Were we?*

'I mean, why do you even *need* to be ambitious? Elliot

earns...a ludicrous amount. You've already got everything you could possibly want. If you want my advice, enjoy it while you can. Another drink?'

'Yes, I think I'll definitely have one,' I said.

What did she mean, *while you can?!*

'And in...and...out,' came a gentle voice from over my shoulder. Courtney's eyes were closed, her mouth murmuring pleasant *oohs* and *aahs*, as the professional hands of our masseuse ran their way up her back and across her shoulders. I'd been surprised when she had come out of the changing room without anything to cover her bare chest; girls back in Manchester definitely weren't *that* revealing to one another.

Far off in the distance were the calming sound of waves lapping into the coast. It was stiflingly hot outside, and I wasn't accustomed to the climate. In fact, the only thing which made me feel worse was the dreary, half-dead malaise that set in being on a holiday like this.

'This is the life,' giggled Courtney. 'Oo, do that again. My boyfriend could learn a thing or two from you, mister.'

'Are you still doing your veterinarian course?' I asked.

'Kinda. I decided to put off my finals for a while.'

'Why?'

'I'm not in a rush. I'm thinking to go back next year. Once I graduate, I'm going to work out here in SA, I think. My dream is to get in at one of the private reserves.'

'That would be incredible,' I said. 'I'm thinking of studying next year, too. I've been mulling it over. Although I don't know what Elliot will have to say about it.'

'What do you mean?'

'Well, it'd mean me packing in working for his business, and we wouldn't be able to spend as much time together. Elliot can be...difficult, sometimes. I don't know how he'd react.'

'Oh,' she said. I wasn't sure if she was really listening, until after a pause, she said, 'You know, the key is letting Elliot think that it was his idea. Ask him what universities he'd recommend, or something.'

'Courtney?'

'Yes?'

'How do you know so much about Elliot?'

'I've known him for a while. I told you, Elliot used to come to Miami every year when he was younger.'

'Did you two ever...?'

'What? No. Don't be ridiculous.'

'Don't be offended. I just wondered. It's just the way you talk about him sometimes.'

Courtney lifted her head up. 'I'm not saying I never considered it. Back when Elliot used to fly over to Miami, back when he was just starting out, we were close. But he was more like a brother to me. Elliot was...different, then. He was a lot less mature. He was going out with a different girl every week.'

'I thought you said I was his first relationship?'

'Relationship, yeah. Elliot was a bit of a heartbreaker during his early twenties. Didn't you know? He's changed a lot. He's thrown all of his energy into his business. Elliot is so much calmer now. He used to have quite the temper, you know.'

'Oh?' I suddenly felt goosebumps forming on my bare arms. 'In what way?'

'Like in the way that, if he carried on acting the way

he did all of the time, he was going to end up in trouble. What's wrong? Are you alright?'

'Yes, I'm fine. It's just the heat. I don't think it agrees with me.'

'I'm telling you, Poppy. The way I see Elliot now, it's like you've completely changed him for the better.'

'I guess so.'

'Shall we go to eat? I'm fucking hungry,' Courtney said, standing up in all of her undressed glory. I wrapped my towel around me and followed her to get changed. 'Look at you,' she said. 'Still as shy as a rabbit. We'll have to do something about that, one day, you know.'

I didn't have a clue what she meant by *that*.

Elliot had been quiet for the last couple of days. He and I had exchanged a couple of text messages throughout the day, but our conversations were to the point, and seemed like a formality. He said that he was busy, but that he missed me and that he couldn't wait to see me, and I said the same and said that things were lovely here at the Table Bay, and that Courtney had been very friendly and was looking after me well.

On Elliot's social media feeds, I could see that he had posed for a fashion shoot, helped to promote a restaurant in Pretoria, and had shared a couple of videos of the African wildlife, and a view of the South African mountains from a small aircraft. Sure enough, the website of the business, *Serengeti Air Tours*, was linked to in the posts.

It was all a show, I knew, but still the pang of jealousy, as I sat and waited in a lifeless resort for him to return, tugged at my chest whenever I thought about it.

As a distraction, Courtney and I hit the town

shopping. We spent an absolute fortune, and between all of the cafes and bars we frequented, had probably put on a couple of pounds as well.

'You know, I could almost get used to this,' I said, as we sat down after a hard day's work on the high street.

'See? I told you you'd be fine. Elliot wanted you to be ambitious, didn't he? Wait until he sees the credit card bill.'

'Don't! He's going to kill me.'

'I doubt that. He's probably just glad that you've had a good time and kept yourself occupied,' Courtney said. '*Some* girls wouldn't let a guy like Elliot out of their sight. They'd be following him around all week in the back of a cab, to make sure he doesn't get up to no good.'

I laughed. 'That's psychotic. I trust Elliot. And I can't wait to see him again. It'll be nice to have some time to ourselves for a while.'

'I'd say I knew what you meant, but...' Courtney burst into laughter. 'Oh, yes. Me, Eric, and the computer. I can't wait. I'm kidding. Or am I? Anyway, I've had a really nice time with you this week, Poppy.'

'Yeah, me too! You're a good friend,' I said.

Courtney looked thoughtfully into her glass of wine and then up at me.

'You too.'

As part of my work as Elliot's agent, I remained logged into most of his social media accounts on my smartphone. Elliot barely had any involvement with the accounts, except to post content or, on very rare occasions, to respond directly to advertisers or businesses who had contacted him directly with a proposal.

In the couple of years we'd been together, I had never

known Elliot to have a casual social life. In fact, he had very few of what you'd actually call friends. Most of Elliot's socializing took place at fancy events or organized parties, and most of his correspondence took place via e-mail. I suppose that he was so afraid of exposing any weaknesses that he avoided becoming intimate with people over text, or WhatsApp, or even over the phone. All it would take is one little scandal to put everything he had worked so hard for over the years into jeopardy.

So, for the most part, Elliot's accounts were quiet, and I wasn't really surprised to notice a notification on my phone relating to one of his most popular accounts:

1 MESSAGE RECEIVED

The message was from one of those accounts with a long string of numbers and letters, one which, had it been any other occasion, I would have simply ignored. But it was the content of that message which caught me most unawares, so much so that, although Courtney was talking to me in the background, I didn't hear a word she was saying.

R u at home tonight?

'What's wrong?' Courtney said. 'Is everything alright?'
'Yes,' I said. 'It's nothing.'

23

While Courtney wanted to stay up and drink ourselves into oblivion until the early hours of the morning, I told her I had a headache, and went back to my room early. Determined not to get into an emotional panic, I ran a hot bath to get my thoughts in order.

'Are you at home tonight?' Well, there was certainly some ambiguity in that. First of all, was the 'you' correctly aimed at Elliot Gardner, secondly, where on earth was 'home', and thirdly – who the hell was the owner of this random account? Well, it certainly was strange. Almost strange enough to cast aside as a random, unexplained phenomenon; people were getting odd, spammy messages from strangers all of the time.

And yet, stuck in my mind too were the things Courtney and I had been talking about recently – things about Elliot which I wasn't entirely sure I wanted to know. She'd said that Elliot had been different when he was younger; more brazen, it sounded like, and a boy who, although he'd never settled down, had been a hit with the ladies. Well, I thought, who hasn't had a past which they wouldn't like to admit? Elliot had changed, and people were entitled to a fresh start.

He used to have quite the temper, you know.

So? Who hadn't lost their temper at the wrong moment? And just because Elliot had shown... a lack of *restraint* on a particular occasion, it didn't mean that a whole pattern of behaviour of his had re-emerged.

How well had Courtney known Elliot?

He was going out with a different girl every week.

Well, that made me uncomfortable, but it didn't give me a reason not to trust Elliot. After all, he had shown nothing but commitment to me since we'd been together. He'd given me access to all of his...well, *nearly* all of his online accounts and methods of communication. He had only ever been away for work and had never gone out partying or anything like that without me, except for the Infinity London thing. And-

You need to ask yourself some difficult questions, Poppy.

Like what?

Is it possible — not likely, just possible — that Elliot isn't the person you think you know?

Well, yes, anything was possible. People discovered after twenty years of marriage that their partners were gay. You had to be cautious, but you also had to trust people. As Courtney had said, some women would be chasing their boyfriends all around town, or cat-fishing them via fake accounts. I didn't want to be one of those types.

R u at home tonight?

Well, was he? Elliot was supposed to be staying over in Johannesburg. He had an early morning appointment with a promoter in the city – a 9am start. Home could mean Elliot's apartment in London. Or it could mean Elliot's other

home, here, the villa up in the hilltops, just half an hour's drive away.

Why was I going insane over a single, random message which had happened to be received by Elliot's account?

I sat in the quiet of the hotel room for what must have been an hour, and I was no closer to resolving anything. Above all else, I felt guilty for feeling the things I was feeling about Elliot. He didn't deserve any of my mistrust, I was sure.

Maybe it was the holiday, or spending too much time with Courtney (who had done nothing but make me feel uncomfortable with her recollections of Elliot's past), or maybe it was the fear of marrying the wrong person which had made me so anxious, but there was one thing I could do to put things to rest in my mind. I could, at least, give Elliot a call. That would surely make me feel better, and after tomorrow we would soon be seeing each other again.

Taking in a deep breath, I picked up my phone and dialled his number. The phone rang for a couple of seconds. I paced back and forth across the room, cursing myself inwardly for having wound myself up to this point. Heart in my chest, I waited and waited for him to answer.

'Hello, you've reached Elliot Gardner. Please leave a message, and I will be sure to get back to you as soo-'

I hung up, sighed and sat down on the bed, with my head in my hands.

What was wrong with me?

Minutes went by. My phone, idly sitting on the bed where I had thrown it, screamed at me in silence. Left alone with the weight of all of my thoughts, I lay back and stared at the ceiling for a while. All I needed was some sign – just something to make me feel even slightly better.

In the end, I could take it no longer.

I grabbed my coat and, making sure that Courtney was nowhere to be seen, slipped out of my room, down the hotel corridor, towards the main entrance. It was dark outside, and I hated the idea of being out in Cape Town in the middle of the night, but thankfully there was a taxi driver whom I recognised waiting outside.

I hopped in, quickly and quietly. If this did all indeed become a symptom of my anxiety, nobody had to know that I'd ever left the hotel that night.

The suburbs were scarcely lit and intimidating at night, and I felt stupid for even being out here in the first place, but Pieter, my faithful taxi driver, kept me safe and comfortable as we headed out to Camp's Bay.

'It's late. Are you okay, miss?' he asked.

'Yes, of course,' I smiled back. 'I just forgot something important at home.'

What was I expecting? Elliot was in Johannesburg. And, even if he was up to something, he would be smarter than to do it here, just a few miles from where I was staying. I cursed Courtney for getting into my head so effectively, and the thought crossed my mind that for some nefarious motive, she actively wanted me to feel this way about Elliot.

We drove up the hill, towards the hilltop street where his villa lay. It was dark, but most of the properties had a light or two on for security. The street held an eerie quiet. Some of the palm trees were lit up in stale white or yellow lights, and with the curtains and blinds closed, the houses looked sealed up like fortresses.

I peered out of the window as we drew up to the house. I wasn't sure what I was expecting to see. A light on, perhaps, Elliot sitting in the hot-tub surrounded by a group of scantily-clad women, some sort of romantic dinner for two? Either way, the house was sitting exactly as I'd left it, dark and quiet. We pulled up outside, and I fumbled for the key Elliot had given me in my handbag.

'Please wait here?' I said to Pieter. 'I'll only be five minutes.'

'Of course, take your time.'

'Thanks.'

I closed the car door quietly, input the code to open the electric gate, and made my way to the front door. I felt ridiculous. Of course nobody was here; nobody had been here since last week, and the most ridiculous thing was that although, once again, my fears had been unfounded, I still couldn't prove beyond all doubt that the message I'd received had been purely innocent.

Quietly, I unlocked the door and stepped into the hallway. Though Pieter, the taxi driver, wouldn't say a word to anyone, I still felt obliged to go through the charade of retrieving something from the house.

The place was silent. I walked along the hall, passing a couple of spare rooms, and switched on the light in the living room. The blinds were closed. I sat down on the settee and waited for a couple of minutes, thinking about how ludicrous being here was, when I heard the sounds of muffled voices coming from the direction of the master bedroom.

I froze, the hairs on the back of my neck standing up at the sound, which for a second, I believed might have been coming from the house next door. It was quiet for a moment again. I craned my neck, seeing in horror that there was a crack of light shining from beneath the bedroom door.

I stood up, quietly, and moved, with careful poise,

towards the bedroom.

The door flung open, blinding me for a split second. There was a shout, and a figure rushed at me with one arm raised, some sort of crude implement held in it, and I lifted my arms up to protect myself in a second of pure unadulterated terror. But there was no blow, no blinding crack of pain or life flashing before my eyes, and then I looked up to find that my attacker was Elliot, who was breathing heavily, with his fists clenched ready to fight.

'Poppy?! What on Earth are you doing?'

It was an empty wine bottle. That's what he had come flying out of the room to beat me over the head with. I couldn't speak for a moment.

'Elliot,' I started. He still hadn't let the bottle go, and I held my hand out to him, trying to catch my breath for an explanation.

'Jesus Christ. I could have killed you!' he said, running his hand through his hair. He was fully dressed, wearing a dark shirt and trousers, though his feet were only in socks.

'Who is it, Elliot?' came another voice from the bedroom. *A female voice.* Elliot glanced at me, his confident exterior breaking for a moment. I stared back.

'It's... Poppy,' he said.

'Oh.'

'What's going on!?' I said, finally finding my voice. The girl came to the doorway and looked at me. She couldn't have been any older than twenty-four at the time. She was wearing a short, formal dress, but her hair was all over the place.

'Poppy, this is one of my agents,' he said. Both of them looked at me as though I was the one that had done something completely out of order. 'You remember, I said I had an agent who-'

'You said you were in Johannesburg!' I interrupted.

'It's not what it looks like,' he said. 'I know you're angry right now, but let me explain the situation.' He was still trying to remain cool, although I could see lines of uncertainty creeping into his expression.

'I do NOT need an explanation. It's perfectly clear what's going on here.' I paused, and turned away. 'You got rid of me for a week to see her, didn't you? After all this time, I can't believe...'

'*She* was here in South Africa on business,' Elliot said. 'She asked me if I had a bit of time to go over some potential business ideas...'

'Oh, come on, Elliot! How naïve do you think I actually am?!' Overwhelmed, I felt tears start to flood down my face.

'Poppy...'

'No. I am so done here. So, so done.'

'Poppy, wait. I swear to you,' Elliot said, 'that nothing has gone on here. Has it?' He turned to the girl, who was dumbly staring at the floor. 'Now I understand that I should have...communicated with you, about what I was doing back here, but...'

'She doesn't even work for you! You said you fired her! Did you?'

'Well, the thing is that...'

'Of course not. You're full of shit, Elliot. Everything you do, it's all one big lie. Well I am not having any part of it anymore,' I said. 'You might be able to lie to all of your followers, or to her, or anyone else dumb enough to sleep with you, but you're not doing it to me. Do you understand?'

'I....'

For a minute, I thought that Elliot might stop me, but he and the young girl just stood there, bathed in their own shame.

I slammed the door shut, stormed outside, and got in the back of the taxi, incandescent with rage. After a minute, Pieter did a U-turn and took us back onto the main road.

'Back to the hotel, miss?' he asked, after a long, awkward silence. I could see his concerned glances in the rear-view mirror, although he knew better than to say anything.

'Yes, please. Thank you, Pieter,' I said, drying my eyes as best as I could. My hands were still trembling, and I didn't know what on Earth to do with myself, or my life, or what I would say to anyone about all of this when the truth came out that Elliot and I were finished for good.

I was woken by Courtney knocking at the door, and try as I might, she wasn't going to leave me alone. Reluctantly, I opened up and tried to look as ordinary as I could. Apparently, it must have been a spectacular failure.

'Oh my God, are you okay? You look like you've been crying all night. Can I come in? What's happened?'

Courtney came in and sat on the bed. I wasn't sure really where to begin.

'I...found out that Elliot was seeing somebody else last night.'

'What? I mean, are you sure?'

'Pretty damn sure. I saw it with my own eyes, Courtney. I went back to the villa last night. It was his old agent, the one who he said he'd gotten rid of.'

And so I told her the whole story, from when I'd decided to head back to my room last night, to the message on Elliot's phone, and my horrifying discovery.

'I'm so, so sorry, Poppy,' she said. 'That's absolutely awful. What are you going to do?'

'The only thing I can do. I'm going to go home. I guess I finally got to see the real Elliot after all.'

'You know what? You're right. Elliot doesn't deserve you, Poppy. You can do so much better. I'm glad you're finally standing up to him.'

'I feel so...stupid,' I said. 'All of this time, I thought he and I were going somewhere. He told me a lot of things, things which I now know to be completely false. Why didn't I see this before, Courtney?'

'It's not your fault. His type are good at doing what they do.'

'I suppose you're right. Fuck! I'm sorry,' I said, wiping away more tears. 'What am I going to do now? I can't even envision a life without Elliot. I don't even know how to get home. I'm a mess.'

'Hey, calm down. It's going to be okay. I'm here for you. Now, you're going to use Elliot's card until you get home. It's the least he can do, and he won't make a fuss because if news like this got out, he'd have a lot of explaining to do. But first, I'm going to go and grab us both a coffee. So stay right here, okay?'

'Thank you. I realise now that all you were ever trying to do was to be a good friend for me,' I said.

'Of course. Now, there's one other thing. Lock the door, and don't open it for anyone except me. Okay?'

'Okay,' I said, and although I thought it was a strange request, I did exactly as Courtney said.

24

Elliot was lying in wait when I came to leave the hotel later that day.

It had been a tumultuous couple of hours, but I have to give full credit to Courtney for all of the help she gave me in finding a flight back to the UK. She helped me pack what I had (the rest could stay at Elliot's, for all that I cared), comforted me and told me that everything was going to be okay. And honestly, I wish I could have believed her. But in reality, it felt like my whole world was crashing down all at once.

'Poppy, please wait a moment,' he said, as he saw me approaching with all of my suitcases as I stepped out of the lift. Courtney came and stood in front of me, although she didn't say a word to Elliot.

'No. Go away. I don't want anything more to do with you.'

'I've been stupid. I understand that. You deserve a proper explanation before you go. *If* you go. I don't want you to.'

'Well, what is it?'

'I don't know where to start.'

'You have ten seconds.'

'Okay I... didn't fire my agent. The truth was, that I didn't know if you'd be able to handle the job. So I told her to let go of most of my work and just to focus on a few big clients.'

'Is that what you think I'm bothered about? I couldn't give a damn about your stupid business. I'm bothered about you fucking other women, Elliot.' The three of us were starting to draw the attention of people walking past.

'I swear to you, she and I never slept together. You have to believe me. I want us to have a future together.'

'Oh, come on. I don't believe that for one second.'

'It's true, I swear! Look, I admit, we did have dinner together. But the truth is, things between you and I haven't been going very well lately...'

'You don't say!'

'But I am so, so sorry. I just don't think it's worth throwing this away over...' Elliot said, 'a minor indiscretion.'

'Let her go, Elliot.'

It was the first time Courtney had spoken.

'You don't get it, do you?' I said. 'I don't trust you anymore. Not after what you've done. Every time you go somewhere, every time you say you're securing some contract, or meeting some business client. For all I know, it might as well all be bullshit. You even sent me away to this place so that you could have your fun. Well, I don't want to be here anymore. I'm going home, Elliot.'

'Can't we talk about this?'

'I don't see what there is to talk about.'

'There are things I can do to change. I want to be with

you,' Elliot said, trying to take my hand. I pulled it away.

'I just don't see any way forward after this.'

'So that's it? One mistake and you're gone for good?'

'It's not just about that. There are other issues. I'm not sure we're good for each other. I've been thinking about it for a while.'

'What do you mean?'

'I'm not ambitious enough? Just because I don't like flaunting my tits all over Instagram doesn't mean I have a problem, you know. And there's…other things as well.'

'I understand,' he said, quietly. 'I can see that you've made up your mind, and, well, I won't be getting in the way. Just, do me a favour, will you?'

'What?'

'When you get back home, think about it for a couple of days. And if you're still sure, well, I'm sure that we can part ways amicably.'

'I'll be sure to do that. Goodbye, Elliot,' I said, marching past him with my suitcases in the direction of the taxi.

He stood there and watched me leave, his face locked in a pose of silent contemplation. I didn't know what he was thinking, but I am absolutely without doubt that Elliot's thoughts weren't focused on the remorse which he should have been feeling, or about the feelings of the poor girl whose heart he had just broken.

'Make sure you drop me a message when you get home,' Courtney said, kissing me on the cheek and saying her goodbyes. 'Call me, text me any time. And don't worry. You'll be back on your feet in no time after this, I promise.'

'I'll call. See you.'

Courtney turned and walked back into the hotel. As

the car was departing, I saw her walk past Elliot in the direction of the stairs. He grabbed her arm (not too forcefully, but with a sense of urgency), and turned her around, as if to confront her about something. I could only guess what was said between them. I could see the two of them talking gravely, obscured through the glass windows of the hotel, as we pulled away.

And that was that.

'Sweetheart?' Mum answered the door to me standing there with all of my suitcases, my hands hanging loosely by my sides. 'I thought you weren't supposed to be back until next week?'

I started to reply, but instead broke out in floods of inconsolable tears. 'I'm sorry... the holiday was ruined...and Elliot and I aren't together...and I don't have anywhere to go... ' I sobbed in between gasps of air, my chest heaving as all of the pressure of the past few months came bursting out, all at once.

'You poor thing! Come in, come in, let me help you with those,' she said, fetching my suitcases inside and leading me to sit down in the living room. 'Do you need a glass of water? Give yourself a minute to calm down.'

I shook my head, took a couple of deep breaths, and tried to focus. Mum closed the door and came and sat down with me.

'Now, why don't you try and tell me what's happened?'

I started to recall what had happened in South Africa, starting with Elliot's reveal that he had to work for a week of our holiday. But when I got to the part with Courtney and my trip back to Elliot's villa, the story was broken up by me breaking into tears again.

Still, I think she got the picture.

'Oh no. I'm so sorry, Poppy,' she said as I told her about finding Elliot with the blonde girl at his villa. 'So what did you do after that?'

'I went back to the hotel and packed my things. After that, Courtney helped me with everything. I told Elliot I didn't want anything more to do with him, after what he'd done.'

'I see. And did he have anything to say for himself?'

'Elliot has a way of…twisting the facts,' I said. 'He said he didn't sleep with anyone else, that she and him were meeting to discuss work stuff. And he said that he hoped I would think about things and give him another chance.'

'And what do you think?'

'There's absolutely no way I can trust Elliot after this. He's treated me like a fool.'

'Can I ask,' Mum said, 'and I'm not trying to question you or anything. It's just that, I wasn't there, after all, so I don't really know what happened. But, well, are you sure that Elliot was doing what you say he was?'

'Mum!'

'I'm sorry for asking! It's just that… in the heat of the moment…'

'I'm *sure*. She was in his *bedroom*. He was sneaking around behind my back.'

'Of course. Well, you're welcome to stay, of course, for as long as you need to.'

The thought of staying at home for any lengthy period of time, after I'd so confidently left home to go and build something with Elliot, filled me full of dread. 'If you and Dad don't mind, I just need a bit of time to sort myself out. All of this has…been really, really tough.'

'Yes, yes! You know, you're still our little girl at the end of the day. If there's anything we can do to help, we'll always be here for you.'

'Thanks, Mum,' I said. 'What about Skylar? How is she?'

'Skylar's... doing okay. She's decided to, well, sort out a place of her own for her and the...baby.'

'So she's really going through with it then?'

'Yes. It's a topic of some friction between her and your father, especially. We discussed Skylar staying here, with us, but we felt...*she* felt, that it was better for her to have some space of her own. You should go and visit, as soon as you feel able to. I'm sure she'd appreciate it.'

'Of course. Now you have two failed daughters. I bet that feels like such an achievement.'

'Now, now! Don't say things like that.'

'That's how it feels.'

'Do you think that everything I did in life worked out great first time?' Mum asked. 'Do you think I haven't had my fair share of failed relationships? Or that your Dad didn't?'

'I suppose. But this is different. Men like Elliot... well, they don't come around every day,' I said.

'No, they don't. But you've got your whole life ahead of you. And some day, you're going to realise that finding somebody you love is more important than finding somebody with a private jet, or somebody who looks like a *Calvin Klein* model. It's about finding somebody who makes you feel like a superstar.'

'But I really felt as though Elliot was the one. I can't believe that things would ever end up ending this way.'

'I know, I know,' Mum said, hugging me tightly and

wiping my cheeks, which had turned bright red from all of the tears. I felt like a complete and colossal failure. I should have been grateful for my family, grateful for my Mum's kind and listening words, but I wasn't. All I could think about was that I had blown my one and only opportunity to be with somebody like Elliot.

A lifetime of mediocrity and sad loneliness lay ahead of me. I would never again know what it was like to live a life which mattered. And so, I thought that having a caring Mum and Dad was little consolation, when the rest of my life lay in ruins.

Mum's reaction may have given me a false sense of security, because Dad wasn't pulling any punches.

'You did what?!' he said, uncrossing his legs and staring at me in his own, patronizing way. 'Well, surely there must be a way for you two to work things out. You don't just give up after one setback, Poppy.'

'You can't be possibly be serious,' I said. 'Elliot was having an affair.'

'Now, you don't have much proof of that, from what your mother's told me,' Dad said. 'If it's true, of course, then Elliot has a lot to answer for. But you haven't even spoken about this with him, have you?'

'Dad! This is ridiculous.'

'I'm just saying, Poppy, that if there's something I've noticed recently, it's that you have a tendency lately to...well... walk away from things. Your university degree. And now your relationship with Elliot. Life is about persistence, you know. Your mum and I haven't been without our ups and downs.'

'Yes, I know. But...'

'You know that we've brought you up to have values. And an innocent person should be innocent until proven guilty. Shouldn't they?'

'Elliot *is* guilty, and quite frankly, I didn't ask for your point of view. I've made my decision, and that's that. I really don't find it helpful for you to be telling me I've made the wrong one.'

'Now, nobody's saying that at all. All we're doing is trying to look out for your best interests. I...don't want you to regret something which you might do in haste...'

'If you really don't mind, I've had enough of listening to this for one day.'

'What's happened to you, Poppy? First Skylar, and now you. All we ever tried to do was make sure you have a proper future. But it seems like no matter what I do, both of you are determined to give me a hard time about it.'

'Maybe you should try to listen then,' I snapped, 'instead of preaching all of the time. And maybe you should respect Skylar's decision to have a child. She's big enough to make her own decisions-'

'-her own mistakes.'

'That's your problem! You think that you always know best. All you really care about is the fact that Elliot had a lot of money.'

'That's not true. I'm worried about your future!'

'If you're really so worried about the future, then you should try and support me to move forward. Instead of lingering in the past. Because the sooner you accept that my future isn't going to be with Elliot Gardner, the better. For all of us. I'll see you later. I'm going out.'

'Poppy, wait...'

I turned and slammed the door shut, walking off

down the street in anger. Ironically, it was Elliot who had helped me to escape from the pressure-cooker of life at home, and now without him I had been thrust back into it. No wonder Skylar had been stressed lately. I wondered how on Earth she had mustered the strength to stick by her decision, given the way that Dad must have completely flipped about it.

The people who I should've relied on were siding with Elliot, without even having a clue what was going on. The injustice of it made me sick.

With nothing to do with myself, I walked to the park for a while and bought myself a cup of coffee. Mum and Dad had given me a small amount of money; somehow, I had to figure out how to get Elliot's credit cards back to him, but I wasn't going to give him any more ammunition by carrying on using them. A little while later, the phone rang. It was Elliot's number. I watched it ring five, six, seven times, and then he hung up.

Several minutes later, he sent through a message. It read:

Hello Poppy. I understand that you are angry, but I would very much like to talk with you. Our time together was too special to let go of it like this. Please please consider giving me a call. I miss you loads and loads. Elliot x

So now, he'd decided to go on a full-on charm offensive. I will freely admit, that all of the comments my parents had made, plus Elliot's annoying ability to appear polite and reasonable, had called some of my recent actions into question. Was I being overly harsh, or somehow unreasonable? Was it the case that Elliot had actually loved me during our time together, and was he now filled with regret at losing me?

But who knew how long Elliot had been seeing his agent, or however many others, how many lies he had told me since we'd been together?

I was still very, very angry. But the trouble with anger is that it quickly subsides. Soon, I would feel less bruised and furious, and then even I didn't know whether my own stubbornness would hold out against an onslaught of Elliot's nicest efforts.

I thought about visiting Skylar. But in the end, I decided that she had enough problems of her own to worry about, without adding my own to it, and therefore I decided against speaking to her until I had sorted my own situation out – a task which turned out to be much harder than I anticipated at the time.

25

'You look busy,' Svetlana said, poking her head in from the hallway. 'Can I come in?'

'Yes, of course,' I said, putting down my pen and notepad, which I'd been furiously scribbling away in. Svetlana handed me a glass of water. She looked a hundred times better than she had a few days earlier. The police were now investigating her case, and had given her an alarm which patched directly through to the station in case of any trouble.

'Is that...'

'The diary. Yes,' I said. 'I've been writing so much down lately. It's really helping me make sense of it, although I don't think it will do much to prove that Elliot is guilty of murder.'

Svetlana flicked through the pages. I had another full notebook on the bedside table, and I handed it to her. 'I can't believe it. You practically have a novel on your hands here.'

'I had a lot to get off my chest,' I laughed. 'But what about you? Are they any closer to getting hold of Andrei, or the other traffickers?'

She shook her head. 'It's complicated. So much paperwork. If they have any sense, they will be far gone by now. But that's something, at least.'

'Good. You look well. I'm glad you're starting to put this behind you.'

'Anyway, there *was* something I wanted to discuss with you. Something which might help you with your...project,' Svetlana smiled.

'Oh?'

'Well, don't get too excited just yet. It could turn out to be nothing. But it's something I thought you should know,' she said.

'What is it?'

'It's about something you mentioned regarding Elliot Gardner's trial,' she said. 'You said that one of the pieces of evidence Elliot's lawyer used was Elliot's FitBit watch, correct?'

'Yes, that's right. What of it?'

'Well, I was feeling bored the other day, so I sent an e-mail to the company asking them about their machines. And, to my surprise, they picked my query up, and sent through a full reply to my e-mail address this morning.'

'Saying what?' I admired Svetlana's perseverance, and her willingness to help out, but I could've cringed at the hopelessness of her attempt to get Elliot put behind bars via an e-mail to customer support.

'Well, firstly they said that their devices have a very large degree of accuracy. It would be almost impossible for somebody to hack into their servers and manipulate the data. But, they did also say it would be, in their opinion, unwise to rely upon data provided by FitBit in a court of law. In fact, they go as far as to suggest that unless the data was audited, it could be inadmissible, for a number of reasons.'

'Well, that is something. It's a start, at least. Did they mention anything else which might be useful to know?'

'The e-mail goes on to state a number of possibilities. Now, these are purely hypothetical, of course,' Svetlana warned me. 'One, a FitBit is usually linked to an online user account. Unless an audit of the data is conducted, it's not possible to say for certain that the data you saw in court was the data from Elliot's wrist.'

'He could have set up an account for somebody else,' I said. 'An account in his name. But wait a minute? Wouldn't that mean that the somebody, in this case, would have to wake up at the same exact time and...'

'It seems unlikely,' she admitted. 'However, the second point the company raises is that it is extremely difficult to prove *who* was wearing a FitBit device at any given time.'

'I have a thought forming.'

'Go on?'

'Well, there's nothing to suggest the data isn't correct. All we have to go off is a quick increase in heart-rate, just around the time of, Rebecca falling from his hotel balcony. But what if, for some reason, Elliot wasn't wearing the FitBit at the time of Rebecca's death? What if the data we're seeing isn't Elliot's, it's...'

'Rebecca's?'

Svetlana and I both gasped out loud.

'Do you mean to suggest that he took it off her, before she fell?'

'I'm not sure. Maybe there was a conflict. A fight,' I said. 'Maybe Elliot managed to incapacitate her somehow.

He knew that the fall would hide some of her injuries. And, he prised the watch off her as an alibi, knowing that only an extremely competent lawyer would call into question data linked to Elliot's accounts.'

'It's a theory. But it still sounds very implausible. Who would think to stop and remove a FitBit while they're in the process of killing someone?'

'You don't know Elliot,' I insisted. 'All I know is, that man always manages to find a way out of trouble. He's quick, he's clever, and good at planning ahead. This is a great lead, Svetlana. I don't know if it will be enough to achieve anything. But it's really, really good work.'

'Maybe we could open our own detective agency. We both seem to have a certain knack for it.'

I smiled. 'Thank you. For making me feel better. I don't think that anything will come of this, if I'm being honest. Elliot is just too damned good at what he does. But maybe, you know, what this is *actually* about is me moving on. I admit, I've felt far less afraid of Elliot in the past few weeks than I ever did before.'

'That is good news. Oh, there is one other thing I did think of. It's a long shot, but you may come up with something. I don't know.'

'What's that?'

'Well, I thought you could ask any of Elliot's other girlfriends if anything happened to them. Before you. Maybe, if a few of you came forward…'

'That would be impossible. Elliot didn't have any other girlfriends before me.'

'Nothing? Are you sure?'

'As far as I know. Elliot said he didn't have any long relationships before me. And Courtney, one of his friends, confirmed it.'

'Who is Courtney?'

'Just somebody who I met through Elliot. She... helped me out when things were a little rough. She said Elliot used to go over and visit her and her friends in the States when Elliot was a teenager.'

'Well, maybe she knows something?'

'I doubt there's anything she knows about Elliot that I don't know already. But...she did say he had a bit of a temper growing up. I don't really know what she meant by that, but it wouldn't hurt to ask,' I said.

'There you go!' Svetlana gave me a thumbs up. 'Why don't you give her a quick call and ask her what she knows?'

The thought of delving back into Elliot's life, given the fact that he had left me alone now for several years, felt like crossing a diplomatic boundary. I had no interest in setting off the personal equivalent of World War Three.

'Maybe.'

'I think you should,' Svet said. 'If this Courtney helped you out, maybe she'll help you again. You never know, there might be more to this story yet.'

'Yes,' I said, putting my two notebooks away. I had done enough trawling through the past for one day, and my head had started to feel dizzy from it. I was nearing the end of it, I could tell, of how it had all ended, with me living in Amsterdam on my own. But being this close to the edge was like walking a tight-rope.

Maybe, I thought, things would be better if I just left it all the hell alone.

'Hello?'

'Hi, Courtney.' In the end, boredom had gotten the

better of me. I hadn't spoken with anyone from Elliot's circle for almost three years. 'It's Poppy. Poppy Taylor.'

'Poppy! What an incredible surprise to hear from you,' she said. 'It's been a while. How are you keeping?'

'I'm okay. How are things?'

'They're great! I'm just... wait a minute. Let me FaceTime you back, okay? One second. Bye.'

The line hung up, and Courtney called me back on FaceTime. If I thought Courtney had changed the last time we'd met, then boy, was I in for a treat *this* time. She was wearing a tiny white dress adorned with gold jewellery, and her lips were bigger, I noticed, as well as some other surgery work which had clearly been done, although I couldn't tell what exactly. She was standing in a lobby with a marble floor and white columns ascending to the ceiling. I could see a white grand piano behind her, and behind her was a full-length mirror with a decorative gold frame.

'Well, what do you think?' she said. 'Eric and I just bought this place. You will *never* guess where we live now. I mean, I can basically see Will Smith showering from my garden.'

'California?' I said. 'That's incredible. Well done you! So you and Eric are still together, then?'

'Yes. Six or seven years now, I know. So much for marrying a doctor, eh? But yeah, Eric's doing great. He's over in Abu Dhabi at the moment, at some gaming convention or another. Same old Eric, right?'

'I'm just a little surprised,' I admitted. 'But you look good! You look...happy.'

'I look like a walking cliché,' Courtney corrected me, 'but what the hell, right? You only live once and all. It's great to hear from you, Poppy. I was worried when you dropped off the radar.'

'Thank you. I just needed to get away from everything.'

'I understand.'

'Which... brings me to why I called.'

'Elliot,' Courtney said. I could see her face tighten up at the mention of those old skeletons coming out of the closet again.

'Yes, Elliot.'

'I haven't spoken to him for a while. A couple of years, actually,' Courtney said. 'People drift apart, you know. I don't even keep his number. It's an unfortunate business, what's happened. I assume you know about the trial?'

'Yes, I heard about it. Which is part of the reason I'm calling. You said you were pretty close to Elliot, when he was growing up? I'd like to know a bit more about that.'

'Look, I told you – we were friends, but that's all. And I like you, Poppy, so I'm choosing my words carefully. If this is about some vendetta between you and Elliot, I'm not getting involved.'

'It's not that. Did you know that Sophie Romana was at Elliot's trial?'

'Yes, so I heard. Have you thought about the cost of what you're doing? I'm saying this because I care about you.'

'What cost? What do you mean?'

'There's a saying, Poppy, that if you go off on a journey of revenge, you should dig two graves.'

'It's not that. I'm not on some mission of revenge. This is important, Courtney. People could die.'

'Oh, don't give me that. People are always motivated

by self-interest, at the end of the day. So if you think you're involving yourself in Elliot's affairs out of some sense of ...moral altruism, you're not.'

'You're right,' I said. 'The truth, Courtney, is that whether Elliot killed someone or not has nothing to do with me. But lately, I've been doing some soul-searching, and trying to make sense of things. I just wondered if I could ask you a couple of questions, because I need to know if there is anything different I should have done. You knew Elliot better than anybody.'

'I've already told you everything I know. I don't see what else I could possibly add.'

'When we spoke about Elliot, you said he had a temper, that he used to get into trouble, fights and stuff.'

'So? Elliot was like any other testosterone-fuelled teenager. That doesn't mean he's a murderer.'

'You said he never had any serious relationships? Just one-night-stands, that sort of thing.'

'I'm sorry, Poppy, but I don't exactly have all day here,' Courtney said. Her face was tight and uncomfortable; I betted that she must have regretted choosing FaceTime as her medium of choice.

'I won't take long. So no girlfriends to speak of? Nobody who might have been in my situation, so to speak.'

'That's right. Just like I told you.'

'Well, here's where I have a problem putting things together,' I said. 'Because yesterday, I was curious about something, and I started having a look through something called the Internet Archive. It's a really useful resource, actually. Did you know that even if you delete old webpages, they can still be accessed through the archive?'

'No. So? What of it?'

'Well, there I was going through some stuff, and I found a mention of Elliot in an old blog about teenage entrepreneurs. And here's the interesting thing. It mentions that he juggles his time between business, family and his girlfriend. Shall I read it out to you?'

Courtney paused on the other end of the line. I carried on:

'Gardner may only be eighteen years old, but he is always on the look-out for business opportunities. He even manages to allocate time on vacation to chase prospective clients. Elliot says, 'Whenever I'm awake, a part of my brain is always focused on work. That might be a problem for some girlfriends, but not for Courtney. She's been really supportive and amazing when it comes to my need to focus on work, even when we are sometimes on holiday...'

'I...'

'You lied to me, Courtney. You and Elliot were more than just friends. You were his girlfriend.'

Courtney stayed silent for a long moment.

'Yes, I was,' she sighed.

'You didn't tell me.'

'I didn't, yes, but not for the reasons you think. When you and Elliot started dating, we were already ancient history. I didn't want the fact that I was still acquaintances with him to get in the way of your new relationship.'

'Right,' I said, 'which would make a little bit of sense, except for the fact that you continually misled me as to Elliot's nature. You said that he had a history of being violent. You should have looked out for me, at the very least.'

'And ruin your relationship with my ex-boyfriend? You do realise how vindictive that would've been, don't you? Even if I thought I had so-called noble intentions, if you'd found out… our friendship would've been ruined. Besides, for all I knew…'

'For all you knew, what?'

'People change, you know. Just because I knew Elliot as a teenager, that doesn't mean I have the right to write him off for the rest of his life.'

'That's bullshit. You should have warned me.'

'Warned you? About what?'

'That Elliot was a psychopath. You knew, didn't you? That's why you kept saying I could come and talk to you, if ever I needed a shoulder to cry on.'

'He's not a murderer, Poppy.'

'No, somehow I think even you can't be sure of that, can you?' I said. 'That's why you're telling me to stay out of this. You *know* what Elliot's capable of.'

'What do I know? I dated Elliot for a short while some years ago. He and I… didn't get along. We decided to separate. It was for the best,' Courtney said. 'But that isn't good enough for you, is it? You need to hear that Elliot's a homicidal maniac, because that's what you want to hear. You need me to tell you that Elliot beat me black and blue every weekend, and that I sure am glad I got away from him because if I didn't, I'd be the next Rebecca Doherty, that's what you want to hear, isn't it?'

'Well, did he?' I asked. 'Hit you, I mean.'

'I… don't know what to say.'

'You don't need to be frightened anymore.'

'I'm not afraid of Elliot,' Courtney said. Her lips twisted in a cruel smile, and she continued. 'At the end of the day, *I* don't have anything to worry about. It's you who seems so determined to see what lengths Elliot might go to to protect his name and reputation. I'm telling you this for your own good, Poppy. *Leave him alone.'*

'I mean it. You don't need to be frightened,' I said, 'people like Elliot, that's what they feed off. All of their power is based on the fact that people like you and I will do nothing, because we're too scared to challenge them. Because they have money, and powerful friends, and they're excellent liars, and brilliant at contorting the truth. Believe me – I know how intimidating that can be.'

Courtney was glancing down at the floor, avoiding eye contact, though somehow too paralysed to hang up.

'But there is one thing that Elliot Gardner is scared of, Courtney. The truth. He's terrified that one day, the mask will slip, and everybody will see him for what he really is. You and I, we're the chinks in Elliot's armour, because we know the truth. And all I'm asking for is your help.'

'The truth. You talk about that so easily. But do you really want to know the truth? It was my fault,' Courtney said.

'Your fault? What do you mean? What was your fault?'

'All of it. I killed her, Poppy,' Courtney said. 'It was all because of me. I... I killed Rebecca Doherty.'

26

You...you did what?' I asked, still unable to comprehend what Courtney Simmons, Elliot's secret ex-girlfriend, was telling me.

'I'm responsible,' she said. 'You don't realise at the time, when you're dating someone, but the truth is that if I had done something about Elliot's behaviour earlier, Rebecca might well still be alive.'

'So, you think you're somehow responsible for Rebecca's death?'

'I do. If I had done something earlier, told somebody...'

'Maybe there's more you could have done to challenge Elliot, but he was the one who threw her from his balcony. Don't you ever forget that,' I said.

'It just... well, it starts off so slowly. At first, it's just the odd jibe or disagreement, or an object thrown in anger. People like Elliot test the waters...'

'...to see just how far they can go before getting into trouble.'

'Exactly. I can't help but feel as though I'm partly

complicit, in that respect,' Courtney said. 'Elliot... lashed out at me a couple of times. I told him I didn't want to be with him anymore. That made him very, very angry. He said that I had absolutely no right to be breaking up with him; it was unthinkable to him. Finally, he told me that if I did go through with it, Elliot would make sure that a lot of very bad things would happen to me. I was terrified, Poppy.'

'So what did you do?' I asked.

'I did the only thing I could, and that was to back down for a while. In the end, I convinced Elliot that breaking up with me was his idea. I managed to set him up with somebody else, without him knowing. Can you believe that? I put another young, innocent girl right in the path of him, knowing full well what might happen to her. Just to save my own skin.'

'You were young, and frightened. You didn't know for sure what type of person Elliot was.'

'Oh, believe me, hun, I knew *all* about Elliot. That's why I made sure that, by the time things had fizzled out between Elliot and his new fling, I was already with somebody else. Then I met you, and I still didn't say anything. I'm a terrible person, Poppy.'

'No, you're not. And there's still time to do something about this,' I said. 'To do the right thing.'

'Which is?'

'To tell the world what type of person Elliot is.'

'I'm afraid it's not that simple. Elliot has lawyers, fans, media-savvy people working for him. We wouldn't stand a chance. I'm sorry. I just can't bring myself to get involved in this.'

'You have to. *We* have to. Not just for Rebecca, but because sooner or later, there'll be another poor woman in

Elliot's line of fire. And you know, now that he believes he can get away with murder, I don't believe any woman would ever be truly safe with him.'

'I wouldn't know where to start.'

'With the truth,' I said, and I told her all about the diary I had been writing for the past couple of weeks since Elliot's trial.

Unbeknownst to Courtney, and for the purposes of gathering evidence for Elliot's trial, I had decided to record the audio of our call with another phone, which was sitting on the table, out of view. Her confession was all I needed, and with it I decided to make my next move.

It took some phone calls and a lot of persistence to track down Detective Inspector Neil Braithwaite. Apparently, he had moved away from murder investigations, following the disaster of the Gardner case, and had instead taken up a position investigating sexual harassment cases; a role which, as I understood it, was considered a low-priority and lousy job for a detective. I eventually got hold of him, and following a brief conversation where I told him as little as I could; he reluctantly agreed to meet me to go over some details from the trial.

'Thank you so much for agreeing to meet me, Neil,' I said, shaking his hand firmly. 'I know this isn't your job anymore, but I did want to speak to someone who knew the ins and outs of Elliot's case.'

'That's not a problem. Meeting you here is a hell of a lot easier than flying to Amsterdam, that's for sure. Have you moved back over, now?'

'No, I'm just visiting some people,' I said. The truth, that I had only flown over to meet with Neil, and was once again staying in a hotel, would have only complicated things.

'I see. I suppose you must have a lot of complicated feelings right now.'

If he was going to ask such leading questions, then I was determined not to make things easy. 'Complicated? Like what?'

'Frustration? Hurt? Anger? You made it no secret that you believed in Elliot's guilt.'

'I did, and I still do,' I said, 'but at the end of the day, you have to respect the judicial process.'

'Now, I know you don't believe that, and you do too. So why don't you get to the point of why you wanted to speak to me? You said you had some information about Elliot's case?'

'Yes, I do. But before that, can I ask you a question?'

'Look, if you want to ask me what *I* think, then I'll spare you the trouble. It's entirely possible that Elliot killed that girl, but we have to conduct the case as according to the evidence, at the end of the day. Even if I knew, absolutely, without a shadow of doubt, that he was guilty, that's not how our justice system works. You saw the trial.'

'Yes, I did,' I said. 'And I saw how effective it was, too. A performance in front of a jury, a flawed piece of evidence, and a known abuser gets off entirely scot-free.'

'I want to say this, Poppy, just so you know,' Neil said. 'I did an entirely professional and thorough job of the Gardner case, just like I do of any other. The evidence simply wasn't there. On the contrary, there was evidence directly matching Elliot's testimony of what happened on the night in question.'

'Right, his heart tracker. Which showed that whoever

256

was wearing it was asleep right until the point of Rebecca's death.'

'I can see where you're going with this. So your theory is that Elliot woke Rebecca up in the middle of the night, stopped to take off her watch, and then threw her over his balcony? You...know how that sounds, don't you?'

'I'm not saying that's precisely what happened. The truth is, nobody will ever know exactly what happened in that room. But no one can prove that the heart rate we saw was Elliot's.'

Neil mulled this over for a moment. 'It's circumstantial, at best. What we needed was good, solid evidence, of which I remind you, there was none.'

'The evidence is that Rebecca Doherty died. Elliot was the only one there. Nobody can prove that she committed suicide, either, right? So what this comes down to is which scenario is more likely.'

'I'll humour you. So why is murder more likely than suicide, in this case?'

'Well, for one, Rebecca Doherty was on top of the world,' I said. 'She was going out with one of the richest, most handsome young men in England, and she had her whole life ahead of her.'

'All sorts of people take their own lives.'

'Two, may I remind you that neighbours heard Elliot and Rebecca arguing an hour or two before she was killed.'

'An argument which could have also led her to, for whatever reason, end her own life.'

'Thirdly, Rebecca had no history of mental illness. None, whatsoever. Whereas, on the other hand, Elliot Gardner had a history of repeatedly being violent towards women. Now, wouldn't you say that that changes things a little?'

'It could,' Neil said, 'if you had any evidence to support it.'

'I do. I have eye testimonies from two witnesses saying that Elliot was abusive and threatening on numerous occasions. Myself, and a girl called Courtney Simmons.'

'Courtney Simmons? Who's that?'

'One of Elliot's ex-girlfriends. I spoke to her a few days ago, and she told me that Elliot not only hit her on more than one occasion, but that he threatened her with violence if she ever did anything to ruin his reputation.'

'And he was violent to you, too?'

'Yes. That's what I was trying to tell you during the first trial. Even when I tried to leave Elliot, things were... difficult.'

'Okay, but let me play devil's advocate for a second. Now, I'm just assuming the role of Elliot's defence. Elliot is a successful, wealthy person. I'm sure he has his fair share of enemies. So who's to say that a couple of bitter ex-girlfriends aren't just... trying to get back at him for breaking their hearts?'

'There will be other witnesses. All you have to do is follow them up.'

'That's a lengthy and costly process. In order to re-open a trial, you need tangible evidence. It's not good enough to just say you're sure that somebody killed somebody else, Poppy.'

'What about death threats?' I asked.

'What about them?'

'I have text messages from Elliot saying that I had better think about what might happen if I split up with him. Saying that my reputation, and me, would go down in flames.'

'That isn't really evidence on its own. So, do you have anything else? Or is this just a case of you holding onto something you can't let go?'

'No,' I said, 'I do have something else. I don't know where to start with it, though. Until now, I've been too frightened to even think about it.'

'What is it, Poppy?' Neil asked.

'It's something that happened not long after we broke up. I don't know why I haven't thought to bring it up earlier. But I've been having headaches recently, black-outs...'

'In the nicest possible way, have you thought about seeing a psychiatrist? It's not uncommon for people to suffer symptoms as a result of deep-rooted trauma.'

'Perhaps,' I said. 'But right now, what's important are the facts pertinent to Elliot's case. And I think that this might be important. Just...give me a minute, to compose myself.'

'Of course,' he said. I drew in a deep breath, thinking about how to tell the next part.

Of course, I had broken things off with Elliot. I was living with Mum and Dad, unsure of what to do next. And one morning...

...as I was about to head downstairs to head into town and look for work, there was a knock at the door. I heard Mum answering the door and talking with somebody in quiet, muffled voices, and then she quietly came upstairs and said that somebody wanted to speak with me.

'Who is it?'

Mum was whispering and pointing downstairs with an intrepid, almost unbearable look on her face.

'It's for you. It's...you know.'

259

'No…NO. Tell him to go away. I'm not interested.'

'Can't you tell him? I don't feel that I should get involved in this.'

'What is he even doing here?!'

'I suppose he wants to talk.'

'For God's sake!' I exclaimed, looking myself in the mirror before heading downstairs, slowly, one step at a time.

Elliot was standing a couple of steps back from the doorway. At first, I could only see his shoes and the bottoms of his trousers, but then the hairs on my neck stood up a little as the rest of him came into view. He was well-dressed, as usual, and well-slept too; nothing to suggest that he'd been emotionally affected by whatever had gone on between us.

And yet, at the same time, on his face was a genuine expression of grief and heartfelt sorrow.

I reached the bottom of the stairs and looked at him, my arms folded angrily.

'You can't just turn up at my house,' I said.

'I'm very sorry,' Elliot said, glancing at me before staring out again at the middle distance. 'I didn't know what else to do. Can we talk?'

'About what?'

'Not here. I thought that, perhaps, we could go somewhere for a coffee.'

'No. Anything you have to say, you can say right here.'

'Okay, well the thing is…'

'The thing is what, Elliot?'

'I made a mistake. I know that. And I understand why you would have the right to be very, very hurt, and let down.'

'Okay.'

'But the thing is, the truth is,' he continued, 'that I can't imagine carrying on without you. All of the...business deals, and the fancy things, they don't matter at all without what we had.'

'Is that what you told her, too?'

'No. With due respect, I'm here. Because I want to be with you. And I was hoping that we could find a way to put this behind us and move on.'

'What way would that be?'

'What do you mean?'

'I mean, what are you asking for? Are you asking me to forget all about it? And then it's what, oh, by the way Poppy, I just need to go on a quick business trip for a couple of days? There's absolutely no way I can go back to that. You've broken my trust, Elliot.'

'I know, I know,' he said. 'There's not really much I can do right now except to try to earn it back. Step by step. I'm not saying it would be easy, mind you.'

'You don't say.' I looked Elliot up and down. He was a sorry sight right now, looking like a kid with his tail tucked between his legs. And I felt like the coldest-hearted bitch in the world for the way I was speaking to him. 'There are other issues, anyway. Don't act coy. You *know* what I'm referring to.'

'I...I can change!' Elliot said. 'I've already been thinking a lot; about what I want from my life. About the kind of person I want to be. I don't want to be a bad boyfriend, a bad husband. Do you think I wake up in the morning and think, oh, how can I treat Poppy badly today? Of course not.'

'You just do it accidentally, then.'

'I swear to you, that if you give me another chance, things will be different. Will you at least think about it?'

I stood silently for a moment, reflecting on the relationship Elliot and I had. Would he get a grip of his temper? Would the business and Elliot's public image take a back seat?

Or would he continue on the same as he'd always been, always chasing the next opportunity, always living life as though he had two heads, always putting on the correct face before he stepped outside into the public eye?

'I'm sorry,' I said, finally. 'But I can't. You don't understand. I just...don't want to be with you anymore.' Elliot took it like a direct slap across the cheek. I could see the muscles in his face tighten as he thought about it for a moment.

'Right,' he said. 'Well, I hope you're happy with your decision, then.'

'Goodbye, Elliot.'

He turned away and strode away down the path, before stopping at the end of the garden.

'You know what?' he said. 'I think you're going to regret this very much. Because you've never had to work a proper day in your life, Poppy.'

'Excuse me?'

'That's right. Everything you have, you got from me. I don't even know why I'm here. Because frankly, I can do way, way better. I hope you think about that. I hope it eats you up at night. You're *pathetic*, Poppy. You know what? It was a mistake ever thinking you were going somewhere that day when we met at the clothes shop.'

Elliot turned and put his hands in his pockets, then calmly walked away.

'Are you alright?' said Mum, as she came out of the kitchen. I tried to keep things together, but my hands were still shaking.

'Yes. If he comes back, tell him I'm not in,' I said.

'Are you sure, then? Is there no way of you two getting back together?'

'I really don't think so.'

'These things happen,' she said.

Though she tried to hide it, Mum looked disappointed. The truth was, that while there was absolutely no way I would contemplate getting back with Elliot, his impression was still very much in my life. And even if I thought I had heard the last from him, there was still much, much more to come.

27

'Poppy, it's Skylar.' The phone call had been unexpected, but I was glad to hear from a friendly voice after everything that had happened with Elliot recently. 'Where are you?'

'I'm just in town, signing up with a few job agencies,' I said. 'Is everything okay?'

'Yes, yes I'm fine. It's about you, actually. I thought I'd better let you know straight away.'

'Let me know what?'

'You don't check your phone much, do you?'

'No. Why?'

'It's…Elliot. You need to see what he's been saying on the Internet. About you and him.'

'What?' I was so confused. 'I need to have a look. I'll call you back.' What would he have to say about me, and why? It didn't make sense; Elliot had been at my house this morning, saying how much he wanted to be with me. Had he posted some declaration of his love online?

Quickly, I scrolled through to Elliot's Instagram account. There was a short video he had posted, with the title: *A quick update.* Elliot was wearing the same clothes he'd been wearing that morning, but I couldn't say for sure where he had taken the video.

'Hello, everyone,' he sighed, looking directly into the camera. 'This is just a quick personal update for you all. I know a lot of you have been asking about my absence for the past few days, and I just want to let you know that I have, regrettably, decided to separate from my former girlfriend, Poppy...'

'Oh, no...' I breathed, as the video went on.

'Things have been difficult lately,' he went on, 'and unfortunately, during a recent business trip to South Africa, I was unjustifiably accused of not being faithful. And, despite my attempts to make reparations, I have been subject to hurtful slander from numerous sources as a result of these recent events.'

What was he talking about!? Hurtful slander? I had barely stepped foot outside of my room for the past week.

'I can't really say more at the moment, I'm afraid. I am in contact with a solicitor, for the reason that I recently discovered one of my credit cards was missing, with several thousand pounds of charges attached to it. The important thing is that I am staying positive. Rest assured, I'll be back on my feet soon. Thank you so, so much for all of your support and best wishes. Elliot.'

I called Skylar back straight away.

'It's all lies,' I said, my voice trembling. 'All of it. I don't know what he's trying to do, but I...I can't believe it.'

'Did you really run up a load of charges on his credit cards?'

'It's not like that,' I tried to explain. 'Elliot had let me use them. And I just needed to get home...What am I going to do?'

'I guess you just need to ignore it for now. Maybe go to the police. I don't know. I've never encountered something like this before.'

'Me neither.' I genuinely had no idea that someone could behave in this way.

In hindsight, I should have steered well clear of Elliot, and headed straight for legal representation. But my fury drove me to call him directly.

There was no answer. I tried again, impatiently listening to the empty line ring out. A minute later, I gave up and messaged him instead:

Elliot, what you are doing is NOT okay. You need to stop this immediately. Am I making myself clear? Poppy.

Moments later, Elliot replied:

Hi. Please stop contacting me. I do not wish to communicate with you any further. Please direct any correspondence to my solicitor. Elliot.

ELLIOT, YOU NEED TO STOP LYING ABOUT ME NOW!

If you continue to contact me, I will have no choice but to ensure that you stop harassing me legally. Elliot.

'God damn it!' I shouted, not caring about the looks I received from the people on the street. I felt violated, like half of my soul had been ripped out. The most hurtful part was that it was Elliot, the man who, until recently, I had thought to be in love with me. Getting trampled upon by the person I'd been so close with – well, that was far worse than getting attacked on an internet page.

Elliot's post already had forty thousand views. He hadn't said anything particularly outright venomous or threatening in his original post. But he didn't need to. The commenters all came crawling out of the woodwork to support him, and what they wrote was what Elliot would have written in a world without rules, a choir of hateful voices in unison, a mob pursuing me down the street, yelling:

You are so much better off without bloodsucking parasites like her, Elliot. Stay strong and I know you'll put this behind you soon and move onto better things.

OMG. The cheek of some people boggles the mind. You need to call the POLICE, because she is probably wrecking your credit rating as we speak!

Forget that SLUT and start living your best life. You be you!!

It went on and on.

I didn't tell my parents about the online abuse, but fuelled by Elliot's vague condemnations, it continued. All of the vitriol coming at me was coming from a place of genuine concern from Elliot's fans. He was well and truly playing the victim.

Very soon, I had instant messages coming through to my Facebook account, e-mail and LinkedIn profile, telling me what a bad person I was, and how I should kill myself, and so on. In between periods of crying, I locked all of my accounts and hid in the refuge of my room, the only place where I felt safe from Elliot's grasp.

One morning, when I decided to go for a walk to clear my thoughts for a while, I was horrified to find that somebody had taped a photo of me to a nearby lamppost.

Attached to the photo was a small note. It read: 'Dear Pops. Why don't you just leave Elliot alone. He is smarter, better looking, and an altogether more decent person than you will EVER be. He's better off without you and you know it. Leave Elliot alone or else.'

I tore it down and ripped it up, stuffing the pieces into my pocket, and I sobbed my way down the road looking for any others. The note wasn't in Elliot's handwriting, and I genuinely didn't believe he had any involvement in it being placed there. But this was surely the work of his army of followers.

Sooner or later, my parents were bound to find out.

There weren't any more notes. But I double-checked that the front door was locked before I went to sleep, and I stopped walking on my own from then on. Somebody, after all, knew where I lived, and I couldn't be sure that they weren't watching my every movement, looking for a moment to strike.

'Is that all?' Neil asked. 'I don't mean to be rude, and from what you've told me, Elliot is a nasty piece of work. A narcissist, sure. But a murderer?'

'Wait,' I said. 'There *is* something else. I was just trying to give you an impression of what impact Elliot's attacks of me on social media had on my life first.'

'I can imagine how difficult that must have been.'

'The worst part of all was that the person doing this to me was somebody I deeply cared about,' I said. 'But from the moment I ended things with Elliot, he seemed to switch completely. It was like I'd become a threat to him, one of his many enemies who was on a mission to destroy his character.'

'Men like Elliot portray an image of themselves, often against reality,' Neil said. 'But you were in an intimate relationship with him. You must have known things about Elliot. Secrets; things he wouldn't want other people to find out about. He would've seen you as a chink in his armour. He was probably trying to scare you, to make sure that you never tried to jeopardise everything he had built.'

'I'm still afraid, you know. Since he saw me in the courtroom. I've been waiting for something to happen,' I said.

'I very much doubt that Elliot would be stupid enough to come after you, if that's what you mean.'

'You don't know him like I do. You don't know what he's capable of. I suppose I didn't, either, not until...'

'Until what?'

'Not until the thing which I need to tell you about. The reason why I left home and moved to Amsterdam. I've been holding onto it for so long. But you *need* to know. The world needs to know. What he's capable of.'

'What do you mean?' Neil asked.

'It was only about a month or so after the note,' I said. 'There was... an incident. It happened out of the blue, in the middle of the night. There was no warning. I was fast asleep, and I...'

...awoke from the first deep and peaceful sleep I'd

had in weeks. My eyes opened slowly to my old room, which now felt unfamiliar. Coming to, I remembered that this was the place I used to call home, before all of the business with Elliot had started and ended so spectacularly.

I felt ill and woozy: a combination of worry, plus some medication I'd been taking recently for anxiety. Hoping for a glass of water, I clumsily reached out. The glass fell and smashed, spilling its contents onto the bedroom floor, although the sound of the breaking glass seemed muffled and far away.

I tried to stand up.

My legs nearly gave way, but at last, fighting off an overpowering drowsiness, I got up and looked around. The bedroom window was firmly shut. I walked slowly over to open it and get some fresh air, because the atmosphere inside the house was stifling. My eyes were actually starting to water because of it.

As I reached for the window handle, I realised that it was hurting me to breathe. The bedroom itself seemed thick, and hard to see through, as though a blanket of fog had somehow managed to creep in from the outside. Dragging the window up, I gulped in a fresh lungful of air. There were tiny tendrils of smoke letting themselves out of the crack in the window and into the clear night air.

Smoke?

Turning around, I noticed that the room was full of it, too. There was a thick stream coming from under the bedroom door, and a flickering, warm glow, and then I realised all at once what was happening.

'Mum! Dad!' I shouted. There was no answer. With the most ironic of timings, the smoke alarm downstairs started to ring: a shrill squawk. Coughing, I grabbed a t-shirt, and held it over my nose and mouth.

To this day, I can still taste the stench of that smoke. It had the sweet, choking smell of chemically-infused wood, with a metallic taste which lingered far back in your throat. I reached for the bedroom door handle, which was red hot, and as I touched it my hand pulled back, as if on an invisible string.

'Help! Fire!' I tried to shout through the smoke.

Nobody answered. I wracked my brain for a moment, vaguely remembering that Mum and Dad were *somewhere else* tonight, a concert, I seemed to remember. The timing of my being alone in the house seemed very convenient. Shit! The front door and back doors were probably locked, and I hadn't gotten around to getting a key. Well, that was if I could even get out of the bedroom.

As if to hurry me along, the smoke made my lungs cough up again. It was pooling up now in the upper quarter of the room, hugging the ceiling.

Wrapping my hand in as much material as I could, I reached for the door handle again. I could hear the fizzing of the cloth as it touched the red hot metal. I pulled, and the door flew open, and with it came the heat, and a scene which my brain couldn't properly comprehend. It was like looking into Hell. There were flames licking their way up the stairs, and so much black smoke in the air that my eyelids instinctively shut; I had to force them back open.

'Mum! Dad!!' I tried again. It was dark outside, but how many hours it would be until they got home, I had no idea. I was still drowsy from the meds, and thought once about charging through the fire, but I was beaten back by the thought of being trapped downstairs, and I fled back into the bedroom, shutting the door behind me.

'Poppy!?'

I ran to the open window. To my immense relief, Dad

was standing outside, looking up at my window with fright, and the neighbours were out too; all looking up at my little face, which was surrounded by the smoke.

'Dad!'

'Thank God you're alright. Now, don't panic. We're going to get you out of there in just a minute.'

'The window!' I cried. 'I won't fit through.'

'You're going to have to break it with something,' he said. 'Don't panic. Just look for something heavy.'

There was so much smoke accumulating in the room that I could barely see the door. *Look for something heavy.* But what? Frantically, I fumbled around on the bedside table, my fingers touching nothing but the wood.

It was no use, no use at all, and any minute now I would pass out from the smoke inhalation. I was too exhausted and frightened even to cry.

I counted the steps around the bed and reached my chest of drawers. On top was the object which had first popped into my head. It was a clothes iron. I picked it up and hurled it, with what remaining strength I had left, straight at the middle of the glass, but to my horror, it bounced off, coming to a stationary position on the floor.

'That's it, Poppy! Try again.' Dad's voice was on the verge of breaking, but he was still keeping me going. I picked up the iron again, and although I'd never believed in any higher power in all of my life, I prayed for something to save me from this situation I was in.

My mind recast itself to that evening a few years ago – the evening I had nearly choked to death in the restaurant in front of all those people. Back then, I had blindly accepted my fate, but the woman I was now wasn't the girl I'd been back then. I had within me an angry, impulsive need to survive, the need for this not to be the end, the need not to die after having been through so much. It was this need which I converted, almost effortlessly, into one final ounce of strength.

I launched the thing with all of my might.

It hurtled through the glass with a loud crash, and for a split second, I looked at my work with satisfaction. Snapping out of it, and using a thick jumper, I cleared the remaining pieces of glass from the window frame. I might have cut my hand once or twice – that I don't remember.

What I do recall is my Dad, having brought his stepladders from the garage, reaching out to me, my Mum steadying the ladders, and me leaping for Dad's arms as black billows of smoke came out of the window in waves.

'Jump!'

Dad caught me, and together we fell backwards onto the grass in the garden. His collarbone broke in the process, but that was something which neither of us realised until later. I coughed and spluttered my way up onto my knees. Mum was crying, dressed up in all of her night-out finery, and the fire crews had just arrived to put out the blaze, and all of the neighbours were staring – staring just like those people in the restaurant had stared – while somebody handed me a bottle of water to drink.

My parents both shook their heads in disbelief.

'How did this happen?' Mum said. 'Our home...our things... Poppy, I was so scared. I know I didn't leave anything on downstairs...did you? How on Earth did this happen?'

Later, the fire-fighters would say that the origin of the fire was likely due to an electrical fault in the hallway, but that they couldn't be sure. The wiring in the house was ancient, and there was some evidence of singed rubber behind the electric meter. There was no evidence of foul play, to their knowledge. But I knew differently; the problem was that nobody else would believe me.

'It was him, Dad,' I said, my face still wet with tears.

'Who? What are you talking about?'

'The fire. It was him. I know it was. It was Elliot. He must have...started it somehow.'

'You're not thinking straight, dear,' Mum said. 'I know things are hard for you right now, but Elliot simply wouldn't do something like that. It's just an accident, sweetheart.'

'Think about it. What are the chances that this would happen while you two were out? Please, you have to tell the police. You have to tell them that Elliot did this.'

'Poppy, I don't mean to...' Dad cut himself short. 'But, well, you heard the fire service. What you're saying, it's...'

'It's what?'

'It's just... not possible, Poppy.'

'You don't know him! He *wanted* it to look like an accident!'

'Here, have a drink of water. You're in sho-'

'No! Why is nobody listening to me?' I cried. 'Why does nobody believe a single word I say?'

28

Neil took his notes and left after our conversation, and all there was to do was wait. The next month or two were agonizing, and while I tried to get on with my life back in Amsterdam, all I was really doing was waiting for the phone to ring.

Eventually, after what seemed like an eternity during which I had given up all hope, I received a phone call from the Criminal Investigations Department. I couldn't believe what I was hearing; due to the evidence supplied by myself, Courtney, and several other witnesses (as well as a heap of political pressure from activists, I guessed), the Elliot Gardner case was going to be re-opened.

While I should have felt some joy in what was, by anyone's measure, a huge victory of persistence and evidence-gathering, all I felt instead was a pit of terror and apprehension in my stomach.

Going up against Elliot would mean speaking in front of the whole world. It would mean having my credibility questioned, my story critically examined by Elliot's team of highly-professional, well paid lawyers. In fact, the only consolation I had was that other key pieces of evidence against Elliot were starting to stack up; re-examination by a pathologist had revealed some further findings, to which I was unable to gain any more information, and yet another woman had come forward to say that Elliot had struck her on at least two separate occasions.

The newspapers were having a field day, and for the first time, I imagined that the pressure and scrutiny of the story was starting to make Elliot squirm.

'Is it time, Poppy?' Svetlana asked, as I stuffed the remainder of my things into my suitcase. At the bottom, I had neatly packed the diary I'd written, several snippings from online articles, e-mails back and forth with some of Elliot's old acquaintances, and so on. Elliot was sure to have done his homework; I only hoped that my efforts would match his in depth and tenacity.

'Yes, I'm going. This is it. Wish me luck, Svet.'

'You don't need luck,' Svetlana said. 'You've got this. Remember – you have the truth on your side. I'm sure that you will be absolutely fine.'

'Thank you. I'll be thinking of you. And I'm sure you'll be able to find out about the trial on TV. God knows, it's turning into the story of the decade online.'

'You stay focused on yourself, Poppy. Good luck!'

'Although I didn't know it at the time, that was the last time I ever spoke to Svetlana.

Life has a way of closing some chapters and opening new ones, and Amsterdam, for me, had served its purpose. It had been a safe and quiet refuge from all of the things I'd been frightened of, but now I was stepping back out into the light. There wouldn't be a need for me to hide away any more.

Elliot was waiting.

Everything seemed so familiar the second time round – the court-house, the crowds of people shouting and cheering outside, the TV journalists talking about what was supposed to be a 'landmark case' when it came to abusive relationships – but this time, I was being escorted into court as a key witness, instead of as a spectator. Neil was no longer handling the case, but as I walked down the corridor I saw him standing there in his shirt and trousers, smiling, with his hands in his pockets.

'Thank you for coming,' I told him. 'It's good to see a friendly face.'

'I have a particular aversion to loose ends, I'm afraid,' Neil said. 'I couldn't be anywhere else. You look well. How are you feeling?'

'A little nervous,' I admitted. 'Incredibly nervous, actually. But I haven't gone this far just to quit now.'

'You're an incredible inspiration, Poppy. Actually, there's a couple of people who have come to see you, too. I thought it might give you some joy to have their support.'

Behind him, dressed in all of their finest Sunday clothes, were Mum and Dad. I gave them both a hug, not quite knowing what to say next.

'I'm so proud of you, Poppy,' Dad said. 'Can we...have a talk? There's a bit of time before the trial starts.'

'Yes, of course. Let's find somewhere to sit.'

'I'll leave you to it,' Neil said.

'Look at you,' Mum said, as Dad went to get us a couple of drinks. 'All dressed up. You're so brave for going through all this. We read all about it on the news.'

'Thank you. How are things?'

'They're fine, I suppose. Things haven't been the same without you. We are so, so sorry, both of us, for the way we handled things. It was inexcusable.'

'Well, I suppose running off to Amsterdam wasn't exactly fair, either. It's been… a difficult time for me.'

'Yes, I can imagine,' Mum said. Dad brought us the drinks, and sat down. 'It takes a mature person to admit when they've made a mistake. But your Dad and I made the biggest one when we chose not to believe you about that awful man. We're sorry, both of us. And we really hope you'll be able to forgive us in time.'

'I do forgive you. Honestly,' I said. 'Going through this process has made me understand… how difficult it is to believe in what's happening in front of you sometimes. Sometimes, things are so outside of our comprehension that even if somebody tells you about it, you still can't cross over that threshold, and believe them.'

'But we should have, regardless.'

'Yes – you should have listened to me. But I can at least understand the reasons why you couldn't process what I was saying; why you thought it was absolutely ludicrous that a man like Elliot Gardner would try to kill us all in our sleep.'

'You'd had an awful lot going on,' Dad said hesitantly. 'It wasn't inconceivable that your feelings could have been getting in the way of things…'

'But as your parents, we should have listened,' Mum interjected. 'The day you left was a day that broke my heart. I was so worried about you, worried that you weren't yourself. And then Skylar told us that you'd been in contact with her, but that you weren't ready to talk to us yet. And then we read about that poor girl, Rebecca, in the news. That was the moment when we started to think – maybe there was something untoward about Elliot. But then he was found not guilty, and we thought, everybody did, that maybe that girl did just take her own life.'

'That's what he wanted everybody to think,' I said.

Mum wiped a tear from her cheek. 'You poor thing,' she said. 'I can't bear to think that we could have lost you. That's what's been playing on my mind the most. The fact that it might not have been Rebecca Doherty who lost her life to that…monster; that it might have been you.'

'Come here,' I said, and I hugged her tightly for a minute. 'The important thing is that you're here, and I'm here. And as soon as this trial is over, we'll support each other as a family. I love you both so much, honestly.'

'We love you too,' Dad said. 'Now go out there and give him hell. Are you ready?'

'Yes,' I said. 'I'm ready.'

'Ladies and Gentlemen of the court, please rise for the case of Regina vs Gardner.'

I stood up, feeling the eyes of the judge and jury passing over me and the other witnesses as the barristers for the prosecution and defence prepared their cases. Courtney was sitting next to me. She looked far more terrified than I was, and I smiled at her discretely to reassure her that everything would be okay.

Finally, as the court session was brought into being, in walked Elliot.

He was escorted by a pair of policemen, and still wearing his usual suit and tie. At the first trial, Elliot had seemed unphased. But now I could make out the look of distinct uncertainty etched into his face. He didn't glance over in my direction at all, instead sitting down and looking straight ahead, his face scarcely moving.

'Elliot Gardner,' said the judge. 'This is a case of appeal; therefore, a plea is required once again. You are accused of the murder of Rebecca Jane Doherty. How do you plead?'

'My client,' interjected Elliot's lawyer, 'pleads not guilty, your Honour.'

'Very well. Let's proceed?'

The prosecution lawyer stood up, cleared his throat, and laid out the case against Elliot in plain and simple terms. In some respects, it was a re-hashing of the old case, simply put, that Elliot was responsible for Rebecca's death and that several new, key pieces of evidence had emerged to warrant the re-trial.

'This case was brought about,' the lawyer stated, 'because of the perseverance and bravery of certain young women, who are here to testify today in open court. It is thanks to the courage of these women that a further investigation was launched into the death of Rebecca Doherty, and their testimonies will reveal that Elliot repeatedly, throughout his adult life, has displayed a pattern of violent, controlling, and abusing behaviour with several partners. Thanks also, to renewed efforts, the investigation has found evidence that, prior to her death, Elliot Gardner plied Rebecca Doherty with benzodiazepines, or what are referred to within the public definition of tranquilisers...'

'Psst! Did you hear that?' Courtney whispered to me.

'Yes. I can't believe what I'm hearing.'

'...and did subsequently end her life by throwing her from the balcony of the fifteenth floor of his apartment building. During his trial, Elliot knowingly and deliberately misled the jury by presenting evidence designed to show that he was asleep at the time of the murder. But new understanding of this technical evidence has shown that it cannot be relied upon to prove that a) the data is reliable beyond all reasonable doubt, and b) that the data even shows the heart-rate of Elliot Gardner himself.'

'Look at his face,' Courtney said. 'He's in trouble this time, and he knows it.' I glanced at Elliot's face, and I saw that Courtney was right. The mood in the courtroom felt different this time around – like a reckoning.

Still, I knew that the hardest part was yet to come.

'Rebecca cannot be here today, but these young women,' he said, pointing towards our place on the witness stand, and drawing up to his final conclusion, 'have attended in her place. They knew the real Elliot Gardner, just as, no doubt, she did. And they will tell you, in their own words, just what kind of person Elliot Gardner is, and the lengths he would be willing to go to defend his sense of honour. I commend these women for being here today, and I hope you will give them the admiration they deserve for taking to the stand. Thank you.'

I breathed in a deep breath, wondering what was going to come next.

'Will the prosecution call forward their first witness?'

'Of course. Poppy Taylor, will you please take to the stand.'

Shaking a little, I stood up and made my way to the witness stand. In the gallery, looking down upon the case from afar, I made out the faces of Mum and Dad, and of Neil. They were all watching me intently, as I raised my hand to be sworn in.

'Do you swear to tell the truth, the whole truth, and nothing but the truth, so help you God?'

'Yes. I do.'

'Will you please begin by telling us how you met Elliot Gardner?' asked the prosecution lawyer.

And so I started, with all of the eyes of the world upon me, to tell my story.

In as much detail as I could, I told the court everything, from being swept off my feet by Elliot's charms, to the blossoming of our relationship, to the way I found out he was cheating, and the fallout of that separation; the online abuse, and finally, to the fire which nearly took my life, and which left my parents homeless.

I hesitated once or twice, and on occasion I would be interrupted by the prosecuting lawyer to clarify such-and-such a point, like 'how hard did he hit you, exactly?' or 'what were Elliot's exact words to you that evening?' and so on, but I regained my momentum swiftly, and moved on. Courtney watched on from the witness stand, and so did the viewing public; my parents, the judge, everyone, in fact, except for Elliot.

He kept his head down the entire time I was speaking, and I supposed that was a part of his strategy to extract some pity from the audience.

'Miss Taylor, do you have anything further to add?'

'No,' I said, at long last, 'nothing further.'

'I would like to ask you a few questions,' started Elliot's defence lawyer, a corporate man, with absolutely no scruples and a head full of money. 'You stated that the fire brigade ruled that the cause of the fire was accidental, did you not?'

'Yes,' I replied. 'That was the impression of the fire brigade.'

'But you believe that Elliot Gardner started the fire? Why?'

'Well, for one thing, the timing was convenient. I think that Elliot believed that he could get away with anything. And I think he felt hurt, emasculated, somehow, by my rejection of him.'

'Elliot was a success with women, is it fair to say? In a casual, dating sense.'

'I suppose so.'

'So, why would a separation affect him so deeply, when he could, presumably, find somebody else without relative difficulty?'

'That's the thing with people like Elliot,' I said. 'They want everything. They don't understand the word 'no'. And when they hear it, they explode, because people like Elliot are used to flashing their money and getting whatever they want, across all walks of life.'

'You've talked about the emotions you felt when separating from Elliot. Did the separation affect you in any other ways? Your living situation must have changed?'

'Yes, of course. Elliot was giving me thousands of pounds to spend every month. We lived in a luxurious apartment and went on big, fancy holidays,' I said.

'So, is it fair to say that your financial situation was considerably altered, as a result?'

'Yes.'

'Some people would see that as a potential motive for revenge, Miss Taylor.'

'They would. But some people would also see it a different way.'

'And which way would that be?'

'They would think to themselves, 'here is a girl who

has a good-looking, entrepreneurial, wealthy and successful boyfriend, who gives her everything she could possibly want,' I said. 'So what could possibly be so important, so off-putting, that she would throw it all away?''

The courtroom atmosphere was stifling, and I could hear the sounds of people shuffling in their seats. 'Miss Taylor, you stated before that your mother and father were concerned about you following the fire. You said that they made comments about your mental state. Is that correct?'

'Yes, they did.' I wanted to add a correction – that they had since apologized and made amends for doing so – but he had already moved on.

'How has your mental state been since, Miss Taylor?'

'I was affected by everything that's happened, of course. Who wouldn't be, after all that I've been through?'

'Of course. But if, and I stress the word, *if* what you're saying is true about Mister Gardner, that sounds like it might be enough to quality as Post-Traumatic Stress Disorder, or PTSD. Can I ask, please, whether you have spoken with a mental health professional since the separation?'

'No.'

So, here was Elliot's last line of defence – to call my sanity into question. I felt assaulted by the endless list of questions, as demeaning as they were pointlessly distracting from the case.

'You haven't sought any treatment whatsoever?'

'I felt as though bringing Elliot to justice would be the best treatment money could buy,' I said.

'I see,' the lawyer frowned, putting his hands in his pockets. 'One more question, if I may. Are you taking any medication at the moment? Anything which might affect or alter your mental state?'

I paused. They had clearly done their homework.

'Yes.'

'What are they for?'

'For anxiety. I get anxious sometimes, because of everything that's happened, like you said.'

'Are you anxious currently, Miss Taylor?'

'No.'

'Are you sure? A courtroom can be a pretty stressful environment.'

'No, I'm not currently anxious.'

'And everything you've told us today is your honest account of what has happened?'

'Yes,' I said.

'Thank you. I have no further questions,' said the defence lawyer, and I was escorted, shaky legs and all, out of the witness box and back towards my seat.

29

I could tell that Courtney was incredibly nervous throughout giving her testimony, but to her credit, she held her head high and conducted herself well on the stand. First, she was asked about the nature of her relationship with Elliot, and how it had transpired that Elliot and her had decided to separate. Then, she was asked some details about my communication with her after the first trial.

'Might I ask, Miss Simmons, how you happened to be here today? Were you approached by the police, or...?'

'Not originally,' Courtney said. 'Originally it was because Poppy, who was a friend of mine, gave me a call about Elliot.' I could see her glancing his way, thinking about what bonds of loyalty she was breaking by even being here today. Elliot stared back blankly.

'She wanted you to become involved in this investigation, did she not?'

'Yeah, I suppose so,' she said. 'She said that it was really important that I come forward and talk about what happened between me and Elliot.'

'Do you recall what you said to Miss Taylor,

following this?'

'Yes I do. I told Poppy she should leave well alone.'

'What do you mean?'

'I... I was concerned for her safety.'

'Did you ever question Miss Taylor's intentions during that conversation?'

'I don't know. No.'

'This is a transcript of your conversation over the phone on the 15th August, which was recorded on Poppy's phone. You said, and I quote, 'So if you think you're involving yourself in Elliot's affairs out of some sense of ...moral altruism, you're not.' Were those your words, Miss Simmons?'

'Y...yes.'

'Did you think it a possibility that Miss Taylor was out for revenge?'

'No! I mean, I thought it was a possibility, at first. That's why I said that, because I wanted to see what Poppy's intentions were. But everything I've said during my testimony, it's true. I haven't lied, not once...'

'Did Miss Taylor collude with you to misdirect this trial, Miss Simmons?'

'What? No.'

'Did Miss Taylor meet with you to discuss your testimony before the trial? Did she tell you what to say, perhaps, to ensure your stories matched?'

'No.'

'In fact, isn't it true that Mister Gardner never used violence against you?'

'No, it is... he did. Elliot hit me on at least two occasions that I've told you about, maybe more. When I left him, it was because I was afraid for my own safety.'

'Very well. Can I ask why, then, did you not come forward during the first trial? What circumstance changed, in order for you to feel that it was so important to testify here today?'

Courtney was not dealing well with the pressure. She was looking from side to side, looking for somebody to rescue her from this maze of traps that she was now in, but no help was forthcoming, and the steady voice of Elliot's lawyer rained down upon her like machine-gun fire.

'I was afraid,' she said finally, and quietly, and the lawyer left an area of silence around her words, waiting for the pressure to overwhelm her.

'I put it to you that what changed is that Poppy Taylor contacted you, asking you to invent evidence so that this innocent man would be convicted of a crime he didn't commit. Is that true, Courtney?'

'No,' she mumbled, and the lawyer asked her to repeat her answer so that everybody could hear it. 'No, that's not true at all. I swear. I was just afraid...' she said. Her makeup was starting to smear with the onset of teardrops running down her cheeks.

'Thank you, your Honour, I have no further questions,' said the defence lawyer, as he slinked back to his post, and Courtney was led away from the stand.

'Mister Gardner, what was your relation with Poppy Taylor?'

Elliot was facing the gallery where, beyond the teams of lawyers, sat my Mum and Dad. He looked straight ahead as he answered, briefly making eye contact with the prosecution lawyer, slowly and carefully taking his time to respond. Watching him speak was like watching a maestro at work; there was, in a way, still a part of me which admired his cunning, his ability to cast spells over people.

'We were in a relationship, which started in 2014. We were together for around three years. During that time, Miss Taylor also worked for me as a secretary and general assistant.'

'Did that complicate things? Having Poppy as both your significant other, and your employee?'

'A little. It was, admittedly, sometimes difficult to keep those two worlds apart.'

'Some would say that would lead to some friction, perhaps? Some tension, within the relationship,' suggested the prosecution lawyer. Elliot had regained some of his confidence; now it was his turn to speak.

'Yes, absolutely. It led to one or two arguments, for sure.'

'And those arguments could get fairly heated?'

'Yes, I'd say so.'

'During those arguments, did you ever use physical force against Poppy Taylor?'

'No.'

'Did you ever strike Poppy Taylor? With your open hand, perhaps? Did you ever use violence against her?'

'No, I didn't,' Elliot said.

'In that case, why do you think that she would accuse you of doing so?'

'I...' Elliot hesitated for a moment. 'I don't know. It's not really my place to speculate. What I do know is that I never, ever once hit Poppy, nor would I. I don't believe in violence, especially towards women.'

'Thank you. Mister Gardner, during the testimony of Poppy Taylor, which we heard earlier, it was suggested that you subjected Miss Taylor to a targeted campaign of harassment online. Did you?'

'I don't believe I did.'

'You posted several videos wherein you referred to the separation, did you not?'

'Yes, I did. In my line of work, it is an expectation that you share aspects of your private life. In hindsight… perhaps I should have worded things differently.'

'The content you posted directly led to Miss Taylor being harassed, didn't it, Mr Gardner?'

'Well…I suppose it did,' Elliot said. 'But that honestly wasn't my intention at all. If I had known that one or two misguided souls would take what I was saying, and use that to commit acts of harassment, then I never would have done what I did. I just wanted to get some feelings off my chest; that was all. I never meant for anyone to get hurt.'

'Did you ever, following your break-up with Poppy, and barring the single visit which we have already established, visit or enter the property of Mr and Mrs Taylor?'

'No, I did not.'

'Were you in any way responsible for the fire at that residence?'

'No, I wasn't.'

'Thank you. Your Honour, I have no further questions,' said the defence lawyer, who sat down quietly and waited for the cross-examination to begin.

Although my mind was struggling to keep track of events, it had been a long day of testimony in court, and Elliot was on the stand, being critically questioned by the prosecuting barrister. His confidence had waned, more and more, as the trial had gotten under way properly, and I thought he was already starting to show signs of cracking under the pressure. Still, Elliot was a force to be reckoned with. He wasn't taking any prisoners with his responses.

'On the night in question, you and Rebecca had been out drinking, is that correct?'

'Yes,' Elliot answered.

'Do you recall how much you'd had to drink?'

'A fair few, I'd say.'

'Do you know how much Miss Doherty had to drink that night?'

'I would say, maybe five or six glasses of wine?' Elliot said. 'Enough to be somewhat drunk, but not completely senseless. Rebecca was good at handling her alcohol.'

'Was she able to stand, to have a conversation, when you arrived home?'

'Yes. Rebecca very much didn't want the night to end, but I had a business meeting the following morning. We had a drink when we got back to the apartment, but then that descended into an argument, following which Rebecca left to sleep in the bedroom.'

'And you slept on the sofa, is that correct?'

'Yes.'

'And your story is that you were asleep right up until the point of Rebecca's fall?'

'Yes.'

'Was Rebecca a light sleeper?'

'Pretty normal, I would say.'

'When you and Rebecca got back to your apartment, you said that you had another drink?'

'Yes. I had another beer. Rebecca had a glass of wine.'

'Did you pour her the wine?'

'I... I think so. Why?'

'Can you be sure?' the prosecuting lawyer gave Elliot a long, hard stare, and Courtney nudged me in the ribs. I nodded, looking on.

'Yes. I'm sure I poured her the wine.'

'I refer you to the toxicology report produced by the pathologist, Mister Gardner. It says that among the alcohol in her system, Rebecca Doherty was also found to have ingested diazepam – valium, in other words – on the night in question. Did you witness Rebecca taking this?'

'Not at all.'

'Was Rebecca, to your knowledge, in possession of any such medication?'

'No. I would've known about that,' Elliot said, moving uncomfortably in his seat.

'I refer to page three of the toxicology report, showing traces of diazepam equivalent to 35mg in the remnants of Rebecca Doherty's wine glass. I posit to you, Mister Gardner, that on the night in question, you spiked Rebecca Doherty's wine in order to sedate her.'

'No.'

'You knew that Rebecca was going to split up with you, just the way Poppy Taylor and Courtney Simmons had done. You knew that your reputation was on the line, that sooner or later, these young women were going to go public about the way you'd been treating them. Isn't that true, Mister Gardner?'

'No. I...'

'You're an abuser, aren't you? You're an abuser of women, and a liar. So you did the only thing you could think of, which was to make Rebecca's death look like suicide.'

'But it *was* suicide,' Elliot said. 'I admit, that there

may have been one or two occasions where I lost my temper. But I don't remember ever hitting any of those women. I'm a good, hard-working person who...'

'You were afraid of being exposed, weren't you? Afraid that your social media empire was going to come crumbling down at the first mention of domestic abuse.'

'I've never abused anybody,' Elliot protested.

'And you came up with a perfect alibi - your FitBit watch - which would show the court that you were asleep right until the point of Rebecca's death.'

'I *was* asleep. If you want to ignore the evidence, then that's up to you,' Elliot said irritably.

At this, the prosecution lawyer suddenly stopped asking questions. He put his hands in his pockets, walked quietly over to the bench, and drew out a small yellow folder. He reached in, and pulled out an A4 size piece of paper, which I soon recognised to be a photograph. Elliot watched intently, as the lawyer walked over to the court projector, switched it on, and slid the photograph into view.

'Do you recognize this photograph, Mister Gardner?' Sure enough, standing next to Elliot was the young, feminine frame of Rebecca. They were standing outside of the famous Harrods store in London, and Elliot had his arm around Rebecca's waist, and both of them were smiling.

'Yes. I do,' Elliot said.

'Please could you tell us who is in the photograph?'

'Myself, and Rebecca.' And what of it? It was just an innocent photograph, one which bore absolutely no relevance to the case, unless...

'Can you tell the court when this picture was taken?'

'Let me see, it was...around the middle of December. I remember because I had an important conference just after that,' Elliot said.

'So, approximately one week before the night in question? Is that correct?'

'Yes,' Elliot mouthed.

I looked the photo over again. What were they getting at? I must have seen it at about the same time as Elliot did, because his face changed abruptly.

My mouth suddenly dropped open.

'Will you please tell the court what Miss Doherty is wearing on her left wrist, Mister Gardner?'

Elliot paused before answering, and one by one, the people in the court realised what was going on, too, and murmurings spread through the viewing gallery of the court. Neil Braithwaite was nodding, and then Elliot did the strangest thing that anyone could have predicted.

He looked directly over at me.

Elliot looked at me for what must have been five, ten whole seconds. The hairs on the back of my neck stood up.

'It's my FitBit watch,' he said. 'Rebecca had borrowed it to keep a track of her exercise the week before.' He sank back in his chair and let out a deep breath.

'Was Rebecca wearing the watch on the night in question?'

'No... I swear she wasn't. She had given it me back.'

'I have no further questions,' said the prosecuting lawyer.

Already, the first couple of journalists were leaving the courtroom, desperate to break this quickly developing story. And Elliot never looked my way again, not the entire time while the rest of the trial drew up to its inevitable conclusion.

The next day, while the court deliberated, I found the nearest bathroom and threw up, my head spinning around in dizzy circles. It was still too early to tell, and yet, Elliot looked worried for the first time I could remember. He had seen the photograph, digested what it meant, and then he had stopped, paused, looked straight across the courtroom and stared me directly in the eye...

'Poppy, are you in there? Are you alright?' came a voice from the bathroom. It was Courtney. I gathered myself as best as I could and met her outside.

'I'm okay,' I said. 'Just a bit peaky, you know.'

'You did well, Poppy. You did so, so well. Did you see the look on Elliot's face towards the end?'

'Yes, I did. Thanks, Courtney. You did well, too.'

'You probably don't want to get your hopes up just yet. I understand that. But I think he may be found guilty, you know. What we've managed to do here today...we told the world the truth about Elliot.'

'I know.'

'Even if he wasn't found guilty, which is looking extremely unlikely, I should think that Elliot's reputation will have taken a hit from which he can't ever recover.'

'I hope you're right. Whatever happens, I'm glad it'll all soon be over. It will, won't it? Because that's what I'm really afraid of. What if...what if it never ends?'

'I promise you, Poppy, soon it'll be over.'

And it was.

'Ladies and Gentlemen of the court, please rise as the jury delivers their verdict.'

Courtney stood, as did the rest of the lawyers and witnesses, my Mum and Dad, Rebecca's family, Neil standing at the back of the courtroom, and everybody else. Elliot stood patiently, with his hands held behind his back, and all of us waited quietly, in nervous anticipation for what was to come next.

'Have you reached a verdict?' asked the judge to the lead juror, a woman wearing glasses and a grey suit, who had been chosen to represent the group. She nodded and acknowledged that yes, there had been an agreement reached.

I felt a gentle touch at my side. It was Courtney. I took her hand, and she held mine back, in that space which could have lasted for an eternity for us all.

'On the charge of murder, how do you find the defendant, Elliot Gardner?'

My hands were shaking.

'We find the defendant guilty.'

At once there was an uproar from the court; cheers and exuberant celebrations from some, including my parents; confusion for others, and shock from the journalists reporting the case. The people who had been loyal to Elliot slowly made their way out, their allegiances already starting to shift away from him, but I didn't really take notice of them, because my eyes were on him, the star of the show. I could barely believe what I was seeing.

Elliot was laughing.

He had broken into a huge roar of laughter, as though the trial had been the most hilarious thing on Earth, and the people who saw him laughing quietened up until that laugher was the only thing any of us could hear.

'Remove him from the courtroom at once!' yelled the judge, and the police came and took Elliot away, although he was still laughing as he exited the courtroom.

Mum and Dad met me outside. They were both smiling. The weight of it all had still barely managed to hit home; Elliot was guilty, and finally I could rest. And yet, I couldn't celebrate yet; I didn't know how to. It took weeks for the full truth to hit home for me, to truly realise that Elliot was behind bars, where he belonged, and that all of this was over.

Because of mine and Courtney's actions, Elliot would pay for what he had done. But to truly heal from my time with him; well, that was a thing that would take years. Like a stubborn wound that refused to stop bleeding, it would open up again from time to time, until eventually scar tissue grew over where Elliot had once been. But for now, that wound was something which needed tending to.

And that's what I did, every day, in the time which followed.

30

The American poet Emily Dickinson once wrote, 'fame is a fickle food upon a shifting plate'. If I had any worries that Elliot would somehow turn his incarceration into a form of public martyrdom, I needn't have worried. Things moved on pretty quickly: from the sponsors pulling out of any agreements they had with him, to the dissolution of his fashion company, and finally, the shutting down of his once-envied social media accounts.

Elliot was sentenced to life imprisonment. His attempts to deceive the court during the first trial were seen as an aggravating factor to his sentencing, as were the other assaults and lesser crimes to which he was guilty of. I must admit, even as I loathed Elliot, I also felt a little sorry for him. I, after all, knew what it was like to go from having everything to having absolutely nothing.

After a couple of weeks, Elliot the Internet superstar was no more.

Courtney flew back over to the States almost straight away. She and Eric got married a few months later. Although I wondered at first whether Courtney's betrayal of one of the 'elite' would somehow hinder her future success, well, the times they were a changin'. Stories of female empowerment were on the rise, and so, not long after, I was pleasantly surprised to see her appearing on one of America's top talk shows to talk about her first-hand experience of an abusive relationship. Later, Courtney went on to found a charity, launched several successful businesses, and successfully ran for local government – although she never married a doctor, or finished veterinary school.

As for me, well, I had experienced more than enough of the limelight for one lifetime. And so, I got an ordinary job as a junior editor at one of Manchester's bigger independent newspapers, and started to work on rebuilding my life.

Mum and Dad desperately wanted me to come back home and live with them, but it would've been like taking several steps backward, so I found a cheap flat to rent instead. It was a pretty basic place, but had the advantage of being just down the road from Skylar. I visited her and Harvey twice, sometimes three times a week.

'You're doing really well, Poppy,' she'd say when she saw me, but most of the time, I didn't feel it. Instead, I felt as though everybody else had left me behind; still the victim of some inescapable trauma, which no one else could understand.

Did I miss the high-life, the parties and holidays, the fancy houses and expensive food, the champagne, and the glitz and the glamour? I'd be lying, of course, if I said that I didn't. But that wasn't the issue. Every time I turned on the TV, and saw some girl done up from head to toe pretending to be the happiest and most successful person on the planet, I would remind myself that behind that smile was a world of loneliness and insecurity.

No, I think what bothered me was that Elliot had given me purpose. Bringing him to justice had been the sole reason for my existence for months and months, and now it was gone, leaving a void to be filled.

Weeks went by, and then months, until one day I received a knock at the door from somebody who had almost completely faded from my memory. It was Neil. He was dressed in casual clothes, and he was carrying a small red envelope by his side. He smiled at me, although I was too surprised for a moment to register who it was.

'Hello, Poppy. I hope you don't mind me dropping by. I heard you'd moved.'

'No, not at all,' I smiled back. 'It's been a while.'

'Yes, it has. How are things?'

'They're good. Would you like a cup of tea?'

'That'd be lovely,' he said, and he handed the envelope to me. 'A birthday card. It's a few days late, but, well...'

'Thanks! Come in,' I said, showing him into the living room. Neil sat down and looked around as I boiled the kettle and brought him a couple of biscuits. 'You'll have to excuse the mess. I'm still in the process of doing the place up.'

'It looks great! You have a real eye for colour, you know. I especially like the bookshelf.' It was one of those diagonal affairs with books zigzagging their way up, and on top of it were a couple of photos. 'I assume that's Skylar's son?'

'Yes,' I said, 'that's Harvey. He'll be turning five this year.'

'He's a cute kid.'

'Yeah, he is.'

'And how are you getting along?'

'Me? I'm doing okay,' I said, shrugging, 'just, you know, trying to get on with things as best as I can.'

'I imagine you must be relieved, now that Elliot is behind bars. You're a budding journalist now too, is that correct?'

'You've done your homework, I see.'

'Sorry. Force of habit,' Neil said. 'Actually, I was just curious how you were keeping. Sometimes, we have a tendency to treat witnesses as assets, rather than people. But I know that we wouldn't have managed a conviction without all of your hard work on the case.'

'That's very kind of you.'

'How are things with your parents now?'

'Things are...getting better. They're pleased with the fact that I'm back here, closer to home. They still have their moments,' I laughed. 'You know parents.'

'All too well,' Neil smiled.

'What about you? Are you still...?'

'Working cases? Hardly. I think the time has come for me to move onto something else. Something which involves less time sitting at a desk. The police work, well, let's just say I've lost too many nights sleep. Sometimes you just need a fresh start, you know?'

'Yes, of course.' I sipped my tea. Now that he came to mention it, Neil did look much more at ease now. He looked more relaxed than at any time I'd seen him before.

'I shouldn't ask, but what about...?'

'Elliot?' Neil shrugged. 'Oh, don't worry. He won't be out for a good few years, ten at least, even with good behaviour. I believe he's lost everything. Strange, really, to throw everything away over a short, meaningless relationship.'

'Well,' I said, 'I guess that's why they say pride comes before the fall.'

'And what a fall. Not that I sympathise with him, of course, but, well, with the record that he has, Elliot will be lucky to land a job stacking shelves. Did you know that his mother is in hospital right now with terminal cancer?'

'What? No, I didn't.'

'Apparently so. Life can come at you fast. One minute you're the cock of the walk, and the next you're a feather duster. Still, thanks to you, the family of Rebecca Doherty got justice for their daughter. I know they'll forever be thankful for that. And I know I will be, too.'

'I was only doing the right thing.'

'Of course. Listen, would you mind if I used your bathroom?'

'Not at all. It's up the stairs, first door on the left,' I said.

'Super. Thanks.'

I sat waiting for Neil to return, thinking about... well, what? About how unusual it was for a police detective to come to my door with a birthday card in his hand, about the unusual comments about Elliot and his poor, sick mother?

Or about something else?

'You know, I've been thinking a lot about the case,' Neil said, when he came back downstairs and sat opposite me. 'Can't help it, I suppose. Did you ever stop to think *why* Elliot murdered Rebecca?'

'What do you mean?'

'I mean, Elliot is a lot of things – a terrible person, no

doubt – but not a reckless one. He's thoughtful, meticulous. So why kill her? He could have just as easily broken things off with her and trashed her name, just like he did with you. Do you think she knew something about him? Some secret, perhaps?'

'I don't know,' I said, feeling a little uncomfortable from the conversation topic. 'Sometimes, people don't need a reason to do bad things, I guess. They may justify it to themselves afterwards. Invent some reason as to why killing someone was their only choice.'

'You might be right. Still, I find it strange,' Neil said. 'Elliot was a manipulator who sought to control people, to make them do whatever he wanted. Rebecca seemed, to me, perfectly pliable. She was young and stupid – not exactly a threat to the prodigious Mister Gardner, don't you think?'

'I really don't know what you're getting at, Detective Braithwaite,' I said. 'But if you're questioning whether Elliot did kill that poor, poor girl, after everything we've been through, then me and you may have a slight problem.'

'I've worked a lot of cases, Poppy,' Neil said, 'and I've put a lot of people behind bars. From my experience, killers usually crack. But Elliot never did. He was so damned devoid of remorse; it was as though he'd managed to convince himself that he was innocent. Don't you find that...unusual?'

'You and I both know that Rebecca's death didn't fit suicide. There's no other explanation.'

'Well, there is *one* other explanation, of course.'

'What's that?'

'Well, that somebody else murdered Rebecca. Somebody who wanted to make sure that Elliot took the blame.'

'An interesting theory. But nobody else could have had access to his apartment.'

'Yes. That is a difficult one to explain, isn't it?' Neil said. 'Still, if it were possible, it would almost be the perfect crime. A known abuser like Elliot, no possible alibis... A criminal investigation is sometimes a bit like solving a jigsaw puzzle, you know? You keep thinking to yourself, if only you had one more piece, one more bit of information...'

'You'd see the big picture.'

'Yes, exactly.'

'I think I'd best be getting on. It's been nice seeing you, Neil,' I said.

'Yes, you too,' Neil said, smiling at me, and then he started to laugh. 'I really have outstayed my welcome, haven't I? No matter. I only came to wish you a happy birthday. I like the place. You've done a really nice job.'

'Thanks.'

He stood up, straightened his collar and made for the door.

'Neil?'

'Yes?'

'Don't come here again.'

'Oh, don't worry,' he said. 'I very much doubt we'll see each other again. Well, I'll be going, then. By the way, I just had one more question. During the trial, you said that you discovered Elliot was having an affair while you were in South Africa?'

'Yes, that's right.'

'I'm curious. Not once, during your entire testimony, did you think to clarify that the girl that Elliot was sleeping with behind your back was Rebecca? You might think that would be an important detail, given your closeness to the case.'

'Goodbye, Neil,' I said.

'Bye Poppy,' he said, stepping out into the garden. He put his hands in his pockets, and as he strolled away he starting humming a quiet little tune. He didn't turn back around to look at me. I shivered. Going back inside, I closed the door and bolted it shut behind me.

I walked carefully upstairs and sat down on the bed, trying to piece things together, but there was a confused blur where my memories ought to have been.

How many nights hadn't I slept? How many times had I blacked out for minutes at a time before, during, and after Elliot's trial?

I went into my bedside drawer and took out the diaries I had written, the events of which I had recounted to the trial as well as I could remember. Flipping through the pages, I looked for the trip to South Africa, to Elliot's affair. Of course I had mentioned Rebecca during the case – Neil was mistaken. After all, why wouldn't I? Yes, here it was, I walked into Elliot's villa, and heard a noise, and out from the bedroom came Elliot with a young girl...

'This is my agent, Rebecca,' Elliot said, 'you remember, I said I had an agent who looked after my affairs in Britain.'

'You said you were in Johannesburg! I trusted you, Elliot.'

'It's not what it looks like. I know you're angry right now, but let me explain the situation. Rebecca was here in South Africa on business. She asked me if I had a bit of time to go over some potential business ideas...'

I checked the couple of pages again, looking to see if I

had made some kind of error. No. This didn't make sense. 'Elliot was having an affair with a young girl,' I'd written here, on the first page. And on the next page, the story was the same. But then on the third, the narrative had changed, now it was *Rebecca* this, *Rebecca* that...

'Elliot told me that Rebecca was only here on business. I was furious. I stormed out of the house and went back to the hotel...'

There was a feeling, tightening like a tight, twisting knot in the pit of my stomach, which I couldn't shake off. The fire had almost killed me, hadn't it? Yes, it had, and Elliot had made it his business to follow me, to get his army of trolls to ruin my name and call me a slut and a liar, to follow me around and then the fire had almost taken my life, and...

Of all the people who should have believed me, it should have been my parents. They should have listened, listened to the fact that it was Elliot who was ruining my life and was determined to put an end to it if he could...

I had screamed the place down; that much I could remember. And we'd stayed at a friend's house with some salvaged bedding, and we'd argued once again about the fire, and I had furiously announced to my parents that I was leaving.

What had happened after that?

I didn't know. There was a black hole where those memories should have been, and wasn't that what they called

Post-Traumatic Stress

and PTSD could do funny things to a person, couldn't

it? It could make you tremble at the sight of a balloon, or at a certain smell or sound which reminded you of the terrible things that had happened. It could make you afraid to go outside, afraid to speak to people or go anywhere where the trigger might come along and catch you unawares... and it could make you block things out, things too difficult to remember.

What had happened after that?

Mum and Dad had protested, sure, but I had taken my suitcase and stormed out of the house and down the road. And Mum had been crying, but Dad had turned around to her and said, let her go, she needs some time to process what she's been through, and reluctantly, Mum had agreed, and...

Where had I gone?

To Amsterdam, to live with Svetlana, and-

No, that was later.

To the police station?

No.

To a hotel.

Yes, to a hotel, where I'd sat alone and cried so much that I thought it wasn't possible to cry any more. My throat still hurt from the smoke, and my lungs could barely take in a solid breath, and so after I'd laid on the pillow a little while trying, in futility, to sleep, I had gotten up and headed to the pharmacy, and I'd taken as many of those useless over-the-counter things as I could, and then I'd bumped into Svetlana, and she was-

No! You didn't know Svetlana yet. You didn't know Svetlana for over six months...

I had only thought of Amsterdam later, I recalled. Because after the hotel I'd used the remainder of the money I

had to rent a place for six months, six months of sitting with the curtains shut, six months of popping pills, six months of watching the same things on television over and over again – six months of *Made in Chelsea*, and *The Only Way is Essex*, and *Selling Sunset*, and *The Real Housewives of Beverly Hills*...

Six months of waking up in a cold sweat in the middle of the night, to the sound of an incessantly beeping smoke alarm which existed only in my mind...

After watching all of those fake, pretentious people going around spending money like it was going out of fashion, living their nice, pretty little lives while I coughed up black tar from my lungs, suddenly, I knew what had to be done.

Elliot and his kind were a plague on the world. They needed be stopped, something needed to be done, but nobody else in the world would act. They just let them all get away with it, all of the lying and the cheating, and the private jets and fast cars, abusing us all – psychologically, sexually, financially – while the world collapsed and burned all around us.

We had all let them get away with it far too long. Somebody needed to do something once and for all. And after realising that horrible truth, one which I could see clearly now for the first time, I...

31

...found myself standing outside the building where Elliot and I used to live. It was a calm, quiet night. There were a few people, here and there, but as a young, well-dressed woman, I blended in unnoticed. Counting the floors, I looked up at Elliot's bedroom window. There was no light on, and the curtains were closed.

I didn't know what I was doing here. Elliot was living inside my head, like an animal clawing at me from the inside. When he and I were together, I hadn't grasped just how deeply rooted the 'Elliot problem' was. It wasn't just about the affair, or the fire, or the harassment. It was about a world which embraced and held up people like Elliot Gardner as heroes.

Elliot, and people like him, were all over the magazines, and the TV screens, and the notifications on billions of smartphones across the world. We were all hoping to get a taste of the lifestyles of the rich and famous, but only a tiny fraction of us would ever manage to do so.

And how did those people get there? It wasn't through hard work – don't make me laugh! – or entrepreneurial success. It was through the sociopathic manipulation of everybody else around them; all extracted through the lie that everyone would get a chance to share in their success.

In this game, Elliot Gardner was one of the best. He was a social parasite who had managed to convince everybody that he had gotten to where he was through determination, talent, and philanthropy, but the truth was that he was a vampire like everybody else. People like him sucked the life out of everyone around them, and used it to climb right up to the top.

Of course, Elliot having an ordinary girlfriend looked good for him. Not only did it make him look charitable, but my self-esteem was low enough to mean that I would never step out of line – so that when my back was turned, he was out having fun with other girls like Rebecca Doherty.

Rebecca! She might have been young, but people like her knew exactly what they were doing. I had seen it first-hand. They lied and flirted their way through life, spending the proceeds on designer handbags and expensive jewellery.

You see, the worst injustice was that standing up to Elliot had cost me everything. Most people stayed quiet, pretended to be the good wife, giving out fake smiles and compliments to everybody they met. They had personal trainers, and plastic surgery, and expensive make-up, and people thought they were beautiful because of it. They inherited money and profited from the proceeds, and people called them geniuses as a result. And if you didn't pledge your loyalty to them, they would make sure you ended up working long hours in a dead-end job, living in some mould-ridden flat which you could barely afford, exiled from ever setting foot in their world again.

Elliot's false sense of security had become his

weakness. Online, I had been keeping a track of various parts of his life – his accounts and e-mails, and his whereabouts. Elliot had given me too much power, early in our relationship. Now, any time he changed his passwords, I would receive a handy message letting me know.

Sitting in my rented room, I read all of his correspondence and kept a track of his daily movements. He and Rebecca were having quite the time, it seemed. After only a couple of months of going out, Rebecca was now working as his full-time agent and secretary.

He also, I was shocked to discover, was planning to wed her. He had proposed after only a few months, and already, Elliot's e-mails were full of wedding arrangements and invitations. I was a little irritated by this, having not made the guest's list.

Without missing a step, I walked up to the building and went inside, past the concierge and the reception desk without receiving even a glance in my direction. It had just gone quarter-past-eleven. It would still be a couple of hours until Elliot and Rebecca arrived home after their night out in a couple of prestigious London bars. This I knew, because Elliot had already told a few people that she and him were going to be there, and that he was looking forward to 'catching up' over a couple of drinks.

To my credit, I had put in a great deal of effort to do myself up. Weeks without sleep had taken its toll on my face, but tonight I was ready for the red carpet. I was wearing a small, sparkling dress underneath a woollen mulberry hat and scarf, which I used to hide my face as I entered the building. I matched it with an oak natural grain leather handbag and lambskin gloves. I was also doused in my favourite Chanel perfume.

I had become Cruella de Vil.

As I went up, a man entered the lift on the tenth floor and looked me up and down. He was clearly drunk. I smiled back at him as we made eye contact in the lift.

'Nice night, ishn't it?' he said.

'Yes, it's wonderful.'

'Do you live here?'

'Yes, I live here. Do you?' I said, in the best London accent I could possibly manage.

'Yes. Maybe I'll… maybe I'll shee you around.'

'Oh, I doubt that,' I said.

Several seconds passed, and then the lift came to a halt at the floor of my elevator-guest.

'You have a good night,' he said, smiling as he exited the lift and stumbled away. I breathed a quick sigh of relief. It was unlikely he would even remember such a brief encounter the following day, let alone attach any significance to it.

Ding!

I walked out and made my way up the corridor. It was quiet outside Elliot's room. Hopefully, the key card I still had possession of would get me inside. I pressed it up to the receiver for a second. The light flashed red – signalling *no entry*. I gave the door a quick, gentle shove, but it refused to open.

'Excuse me, Miss?'

One of the hotel cleaners was doing the rounds on this floor. I snapped quickly around and smiled, holding my key card down at an angle, so that he couldn't see it.

'Hello,' I said, 'I was just…'

'No problem. Key card not working, eh? Happens all of the time. Here, let me just open up the door for you.' He reached over and used his master key. The light turned a pleasant shade of green, and I opened up the door.

'Thank you,' I said.

'No worries. Have a good night!'

I stepped into Elliot's apartment and turned on the light. It was exactly as I remembered; clean and fresh, with not a single item out of place. I strolled around the living room for a moment, and then opened up the curtains and admired the view. I could make out the murky dark shape of the river below, and a pale glow of moonlight behind a thick patch of cloud in the sky above.

I decided to have a look around. The kitchen and bedroom were the same as I remembered. In the bathroom, I noticed some of Rebecca's things, her towel and hairbrush left inelegantly to one side. I went back through to the kitchen and opened up the fridge. Elliot barely had anything in the house, except for alcohol. I noticed some unopened bottles of wine, as well as one which was corked and almost full.

Taking care not to leave any evidence behind, I took out the corked bottle and opened it up, slipping in a good handful of the medications that I had been taking for my anxiety, before sealing it back up.

Then I closed the curtains, chose myself a good spot in one of the unused cupboards in a spare room where the bedding was kept, and I waited.

It was after midnight when they arrived home, steaming drunk and noisily making their way up the corridor to Elliot's apartment. I heard the sound of Rebecca laughing, then a pause as Elliot shut the door and hung up his coat.

In my hiding space, I was conscious of every intake of

air and the tiniest movement of my cramped limbs, half-imagining that Elliot or his new fiancé would burst in and find me at any moment.

They were talking in quiet voices. After a couple of minutes, I heard Elliot open the fridge and take out a couple of drinks. There was the satisfying clink of glasses, and then the conversation carried on, just out of earshot. Finally, it started to get a little louder. The drink, it seemed, had gotten to them both.

'So, you're telling me that I'm supposed to just get over it!?' Rebecca said. I heard her stand up and pace around the room a little. Elliot must have followed her.

'No. Will you listen to me?' Elliot said. 'I'm telling you, somebody is trying to set me up. Will you stop walking around and look at me for a second?'

'Oh, come on, Elliot. You must think I was born yesterday.'

'I swear to you! Look at me. I care about you. Why would I be interested in anybody else?'

'It's in black and white, for fucks sake!'

'I'm telling you the truth. I didn't send those e-mails. Will you stop and sit down for a second?'

'No. In fact, I'm taking my stuff and leaving right now,' said Rebecca. 'I should have known better than to think you'd changed. You're full of shit, Elliot. Always are. Always have been.'

'Don't be ridiculous. You're drunk. It's not safe.'

'I don't care!'

'You're not going anywhere,' Elliot said sharply. 'Sit the fuck down for a second.' He lowered his voice a couple of tones. 'Just… hear me out. You don't want to do anything rash.'

'What? Like this?' Rebecca cried, and then I heard a loud smash as something landed on the floor.

'You broke it! I swear to God...' Suddenly, I froze, as somebody – I wasn't sure which one of them it was - walked into the spare room where I was hiding, just a couple of feet away. A hand reached out and grabbed a couple of spare bed sheets, which were sitting just inches away from where I was hiding. I held my breath until once again the sound had faded back into the living room.

'What's that for?'

'It's for you. You can sleep on the sofa tonight.'

'Are you serious?'

'What?' Rebecca said. 'Are you going to make me have the sofa? That's very gentlemanly of you, Elliot.'

'Fine. You can have the bedroom, okay? There's no use going over this now. We'll sort it all out in the morning.'

'In the morning? I'll be leaving, first thing, back to Gloucester.'

'Okay, okay. Just...'

'Just what?'

'Nothing,' Elliot sighed. 'My head hurts.'

'Yeah, well, so does mine.'

'I'll speak to you in the morning, then.'

'Fine,' Rebecca replied.

Elliot must have stayed awake for a short while afterwards. He poured himself another glass of wine and drank it quickly, before getting up to switch off the light.

I must have only waited fifteen or twenty minutes, but in the silence of Elliot's apartment, it felt like an eternity.

After a while, I heard the quiet, rhythmic noise of Elliot's snoring coming from the living room. Gently, I opened up the door and waited for a second to listen, then stepped out into the room. It was blindingly dark, at first, but the flashing green light of one of Elliot's kitchen appliances gave me my bearings as my eyes adjusted.

I had removed my shoes earlier; my feet, wrapped in black tights, made the lightest of treads on Elliot's pristinely-polished wooden floors. I slipped through the house like a ghost, making sure to think about each careful step before I placed it, although I very, very much doubted that either Elliot or Rebecca could be disturbed.

After a while, I came to stand over him. He was lying uncomfortably on his side, with a pillow stuffed under his head and an improvised blanket on top of him. From here, he looked peaceful and angelic, and you'd never have thought of the things he was capable of, although I knew them well enough. He didn't stir; judging from the smell of alcohol coming off him, he would be out of action for a good few hours, at least.

I had a good mind to reach down, to put my gentle fingers right around his neck and squeeze the life out of him right then. But that would never do; I refused to let Elliot win anything, even in death. Instead, I moved away, and headed towards the bedroom.

The bedroom door slid open quietly, without a fuss, and I looked around. Rebecca was a quiet shape underneath the covers, her delicate little frame reeking of booze and sweat beneath the air-freshened tones of the apartment. On the far side of the room was the window to Elliot's balcony.

The view was still very nice, I had to admit. It was a nice, clear night.

In warfare, there is the principle of collateral damage, when innocent civilians get caught up in a conflict, but Rebecca was no innocent civilian in all of this. She was complicit, in fact, in all of Elliot's crimes. She would sail through life leeching off of people like him, saying whatever they wanted her to say, and propping up some of the worst behaviours humanity had to offer.

Looking at her cute little face, all wrapped up in messed up hair and bedding, I felt a sudden sense of profound admiration for her. Rebecca was an extremely lucky girl, indeed. She was to be sacrificed for a cause far greater than her own. In fact, if everything turned out the way I hoped she would be remembered as a poor, innocent victim of Elliot and his temper. *She* wouldn't have to deal with years and years of unending, painful trauma.

I brushed my fingers through her hair. She was in a deep sleep from the wine and the valium coursing through her body, and I became bolder as each second passed by. Moving her arm out of the way, I lifted the cover aside. Her naked body lay in front of me: perfectly shaped, with smooth, taut skin.

With a little difficulty, I picked her up. She was a little thing, and I may have banged her head a little, but Rebecca didn't resist. As I touched her, I couldn't help but observe how smooth and marble-like her legs were. Her skin had formed up in tiny goosebumps.

We shuffled our way over to the balcony together, and I opened up the door with one hand. The cold air rushed in, although Rebecca didn't seem to notice it. She made a small sound, like a sheep's grunt.

I pulled her head down, and noticed that one of her eyes had slid open a little.

'Wha?' Rebecca said. Her eyelids fought to open, and her lip, paralysed a little from the drugs, twisted upwards. 'Po...Pop...'

'Shhh,' I whispered. 'It's me, Poppy. Let me help you

up.'

Rebecca's head hung loosely by my shoulder, and her limbs were as limp as jelly. I propped her against the balcony railing and tried to lever her up. I wasn't the strongest person in the world, and Rebecca's limpness made her awfully heavy, but at last I managed to get half of her across. Her other leg was hanging loosely by her side.

'Lift your leg up,' I said to her, and under the influence of the drugs, Rebecca numbly tried to comply. Finally, she was close to the edge. It was a beautiful night, and I felt much better now.

Rebecca must have finally realised what was going on. She let out a pathetic, half-considered sound of protest.

'Ally up,' I said, and I shoved her over the edge.

For a second, there was a moment where Rebecca's weight was teetering over the edge, and then she was gone, gone into the dark depths below. I let out an excited little yelp, and rushed back through the apartment, grabbing my shoes and making a break for the front door.

As I strode towards the door, adrenaline rushing through every ounce of my body, Elliot was already beginning to stir. In spiking the wine, I thought I had dealt with the both of them, but lying next to him were two empty beer bottles; he must have had a change of habit recently, it seemed.

I froze for a second, sensing when the moment was right. Elliot shuffled a little. I used my gloves to open the apartment door and let myself out into the hallway, just as quietly and as unnoticed as a field mouse.

There was no time for standing about on ceremony.

I ran, just as quickly as I could manage, for the stairs

which led to a fire escape further down. As soon as I got outside, I walked swiftly a couple of blocks away and called an Uber to take me to the airport. There was barely a trace of me having been there, and a fantastic feeling of peace, and satisfaction, and fulfilment, suddenly came over me.

Elliot, I knew, was finished. Things looked bad for him. He would surely slip up under the intense pressure of being the only and main suspect. And if it looked as though things weren't going to plan, if he somehow, miraculously looked as though he was going to walk free, I would be there to make sure that he didn't. I would go to court, speak to the police, do whatever it took to make sure that the world saw him as a privileged, wealthy man who had finally snapped and taken his girlfriend's life. And everyone would believe it, hook, line and sinker.

Because everything, at the end of the day, was all about appearances.

Epilogue

I never heard from Neil Braithwaite again.

In fact, no matter how many times there was a knock at my door and I was sure, sure beyond doubt that my time had finally come, that I'd left some crucial piece of evidence behind at the scene of the crime, my great reckoning never came. I'm sure Neil knew, or at least had an idea of what I had done. But months turned into years, and the big outside world just carried on.

Elliot, it must be said, served his sentence with dignity. I thought about visiting him, once or twice, but that would have been too much, for the both of us.

He didn't take his case back to appeal, nor did he take to the media to protest his innocence. Part of the reason for that, I think, is because Elliot knew that he was right where he deserved to be.

It was fitting, of course, and only right to ensure that the publication of this book coincided with Elliot's release from prison. So, as you read this, know the scary and terrifying truth – Elliot is out there. I am sure he has cast off any sense of remorse for what he has done. I am sure he thinks himself unfairly treated. And even if he has changed, just know that there are hundreds – thousands even – of people still out there *just like him.*

I don't regret what I've done; not at all. And when the time comes, I will gladly hold my hands up to pay for what I've done. But how many people out there can say the same?

How many crooked politicians still walk the streets? How many gangsters and fraudsters, abusers and corrupt company CEOs sleep peacefully at night, and walk around proudly during the day? And how many of them would willingly confess to everything they've done, and pay for their crimes with dignity and with grace?

Do you honestly think Elliot would have, had I not forced his hand?

Well, would he?

Sometimes, when I close my eyes at night, I still see her cold, intoxicated face looking up at me through drugged, twitching eyelids. That, above all, is why I need so much medication to help me sleep; because every time I do, I'm terrified, above everything else, that I'll dream of her.

Gradually, the nightmares have become less and less. But every once in a while I'll still wake up in the middle of the night to the voice of Rebecca whispering in my ear, and my body becomes cold and rigid at the sound of it. She says to me, *I am waiting.* And I remember everything.

But then I rub my eyes and realise that it's only a dream, and I drop right back off to sleep.

ABOUT THE AUTHOR

Bryan Blears developed a passion for writing at an early age, inspired by the works of Ernest Hemingway, Stephen King, and Sylvia Plath. Raised in Salford, he writes about contemporary issues through the lens of fiction.

His first novel, *These Walls Were Never Really There*, set in the heart of Manchester's homeless community, was published in April 2022, and has been described by critics as 'a fantastic talent, and a potential prize-winner in the making.'

An NHS worker by day, he has a daughter, Dakota, and lives with his girlfriend Lauren. They would very much like to own a cat.

Printed in Great Britain
by Amazon